Rock Steady

Also in this series published by Protea Book House
Turtle Walk (2011)

Rock Steady

Joanne Macgregor

PROTEA BOOK HOUSE
Pretoria
2013

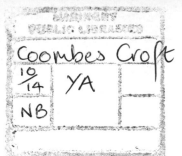
Rock Steady – Joanne Macgregor

First edition, first impression 2013 by Protea Book House

PO Box 35110, Menlo Park, 0102
1067 Burnett Street, Hatfield, Pretoria
8 Minni Street, Clydesdale, Pretoria
protea@intekom.co.za
www.proteaboekhuis.com

Editor: Danél Hanekom
Proofreader: Amelia de Vaal
Cover design: Hanli Deysel
Cover images: Thinkstockphotos and Joanne Macgregor
Typography: 11.5 on 14.5 Arrus by Ada Radford
Printed and bound by Creda, Cape Town

© 2013 Protea Book House
ISBN 978-1-86919-903-6 (printed book)
ISBN 978-1-86919-905-0 (e-book)

This is a work of fiction. All characters, institutions and events in this book are the product of the author's imagination and no resemblance to real people, or implication of events occurring in actual places, is intended.

For Nicola, who first read to me and now reads for me.

1
Newbies

"Is he a creep, or what?" whispered Jessie, pointing her chin in the direction of the stage.

It was the first assembly, on their first day of grade 9 and all the pupils of Clifford House Private School for Girls were sitting cross-legged on the hall floor. Outside, the fierce January sun beat down on the high Drakensberg mountains that surrounded the school, on the spacious grounds and green fields, and on the slate-roofed, sandstone buildings and paved quadrangles; inside the hall, it was already hot and stuffy. Samantha Steadman sat between her two best friends, Jessie Delaney and Nomusa Gule. Up on the stage, standing behind the podium, was Mrs Grieve, their headmistress; she had just introduced the man who was to be their new Maths and Science teacher.

"I don't know. I think he looks a little ..." said Samantha.

From where they sat among the grade 9's, she could not see much of the man except for a pale face with a thin, pointed nose, and a neatly pressed dark suit. She thought he looked a little like an undertaker.

"I know what I think," said Nomusa, on Samantha's right, "I think I preferred Mrs Naidoo."

"We shouldn't judge him before we've even had a class with him. He might be really good," said Samantha, but she sounded doubtful. Perhaps it was something about the way the man stared unsmilingly out at the assembly that made her feel uneasy.

Mrs Grieve was speaking into the microphone again. "We're *very* pleased that Mr Delmonico has joined our staff here at Clifford House. He will be teaching Maths and Science to classes in grades 9 and 10. Mr Delmonico is one of the examiners who set our South African national mathematics matriculation examination. He was head of the Maths department at Academy Girls High School in Johannesburg last year and I am sure we are all very fortunate that he has consented to step into Mrs Naidoo's shoes."

A titter of laughter rippled through the hall.

"I am speaking figuratively, of course," their head-mistress said. "And speaking of Mrs Naidoo, you will be delighted to hear that, just yesterday, we received a card from her. Her adopted baby is a little girl, whom she and her husband have named Sharissa. She is now three months old and Mrs Naidoo says that baby formulas are easier than algebraic formulas, although a lot more messy!"

There were a few exclamations of "Cute!" and "Ag, shame!" at this, but Samantha's troubled grey eyes continued to study Mr Delmonico. He sat very still on his chair up on the stage, gazing steadily out at the wriggling mass of girls seated in front of him. Samantha saw him move only once, leaning forward to remove a speck of something, perhaps lint, from the sharp crease of his trousers, before sitting back in his chair and staring expressionlessly out again at the sea of tartan.

"A few more notices before you go to your first classes of the year," said Mrs Grieve. "Swimming team try-outs will be on Friday afternoon – kindly meet our Physical Training teacher, Miss Gamion, at the pool at 2.30 p.m."

Miss Gamion half-rose from her seat on the stage, looked as if she wanted to add something, but then sat down and busied her hands with smoothing her halo of flyaway hair.

"Remind me to be there. Not," said Jessie softly, but she perked up at the next announcement.

"And Ms Zenobia has asked me to tell you about a new art appreciation club which she is starting. The club is open to those in grades 9 to 11, but I am afraid I have had to insist that our matric girls focus on their *real* work."

Ms Zenobia looked rather miffed at this, but she stood up and walked up to the podium. Brushing aside a length of her long, coarse black hair, which had draped over the microphone, she said in a deep, throaty voice, "Every year, we will be studying different forms of art, and going on field trips to see the actual works. We start at the beginning of the story of art, and so this year our focus will be on one of the oldest forms of indigenous South African art, namely San rock art."

"Bor–ring!" Samantha heard a familiar voice say loudly from the row behind them. "Like anyone thinks a bunch of scribbled stick-figures on a cave wall is *real* art! Any monkey could do that."

"Shut up, Cindy," snapped Jessie, who was trying to listen to the details of when and where Ms Zenobia would be holding the first meeting of the club. Samantha turned to look at Cindy Atkins, a very pretty girl with long blonde hair, now braided into an intricate plait, and a pair of ice-blue eyes, which were currently giving Jessie a filthy look.

"So sorry, Jessica Delaney," Cindy smirked. "I should have known you'd be interested – they say that simple things attract simple minds. I figure you'll fit right in with the Art Appreciation Society – A.A.S., for short. Yep, I think you'll make a fine AAS!"

Kitty Bennington, Cindy's dark-haired best friend, giggled. Samantha took a quick breath, ready to defend Jessie, but just then all the girls around them began standing up and Samantha realised that the assembly had been dismissed. With a last glance at the stage, where Mrs Grieve was talking animatedly to Mr Delmonico, Samantha followed Jessie and Nomusa out of the hall to their first class of the day. They were walking along the corridor that bordered the school quadrangle – complete with its grey stone columns, water feature, sundial and statue – when a little girl with high pigtails of bright red hair stopped in front of them and stammered, "Excuse me, b-but can you tell me where room 23 is? I've got History there and I don't know where it is."

"Of course," began Nomusa with a kind smile. "It's…"

"… on the fourth floor," interjected Jessie. "All classrooms starting with the number two are on the fourth floor – that way." Jessie pointed down the corridor which lead to the dining room and the little girl thanked her and trotted off.

"Uh, Jessie – there is no fourth floor," said Sam.

"Yeah," said Jessie with a satisfied grin. "Sucks to be a newbie!"

2

Big and small

They had arrived at Clifford House School the day before, less nervous than they had been the previous year when they started high school, but also less enthusiastic. Samantha thought the best thing about starting a new year of school was meeting up with old friends, especially her two best friends, Jessie Delaney and Nomusa Gule, and she had been relieved to find that they were all three in the same class again.

After registration, they had all headed to the Austen House dormitory. Nomusa, a slender girl with dark skin, shoulder-length braided hair and soft, brown eyes, carried a single large duffle bag which Samantha knew would contain few items of high fashion, but at least three pairs of running shoes. Jessie struggled along under the weight of several matching designer bags and suitcases, pushing her short, dark auburn curls out of her hazel eyes. Samantha knew from experience that Jessie's cases would be stuffed with a haphazard collection of clothes, handbags, art materials and at least a dozen pairs of shoes. The only takkies to see the inside of one of Jessie's bags would be a very fashionable pair of designer trainers. Cassandra, Jessie's younger sister, who was now in grade 6 in the primary school, tagged along behind her sister, long dark curls bouncing.

Sam was the tallest of the three. She had grey eyes and long, sun-streaked, sandy hair, which swung over her shoulder as she reached down to grab one of the bags that was slipping out of Jessie's hands. There was nothing expensive inside her one, slightly battered suitcase. She attended the school on a generous academic scholarship; there was no extra money for designer clothes.

Austen House dormitory was the last in the line of school buildings and sat closest to the fence which marked the boundary between the school grounds and the green veld that stretched over the foothills of the uKhahlamba Drakensberg to the distant high ridge of Devil's Peak. As they walked, Sam allowed her eyes to stretch over the mountains – smudges of purplish-blue in the heat-haze of summer.

"So how were your holidays?" Jessie asked. "Give me all the details."

"We went to the bungalow at St Lucia, as usual," said Sam. "James wasn't there, he went on matric vac with his friends to Umhlanga. He starts varsity in February." Sam looked sideways at Jessie to see her friend's reaction to this news about her older brother. Jessie said nothing.

Cassandra said, "Jessie lurvved James!" Jessie aimed a kick at her sister's left shin, while Nomusa asked, "Which varsity?"

"He's going to Wits, to study law – a BA LLB. At least, that's the plan."

"So, did you have a good holiday? Did you see any turtles? Was Dan with you and your father?" asked Jessie.

"Yes, Dan was there and no, we didn't see any more

turtles. Actually, I was a little turtled-out after last year, so I mostly lolled in the hammock and read."

"How many books?" asked Nomusa, with a knowing smile.

"Oh, a few," said Samantha, turning slightly pink.

"A few more than 50, if I know you!" said Nomusa, "Did you go away, Jessie?"

"We went to Nice. It's in the south of France! France: in Europe, in the northern hemisphere, on planet earth, in the solar system, in the universe!" chimed Cassandra.

"Cork it, short one!" snapped Jessie. "My father had some or other finance conference there, so we tagged along."

"The south of France – for a family holiday. Wow!" said Samantha, who had never been out of South Africa.

"It's OK, I s'pose. We've been there before. But it wasn't much of a family holiday. Dad was in the conference centre all day, and mom was on the 'Spouse Programme' – going to spas for massages and going on tours to olive oil mills and stuff. So Caz and I mostly hung about the hotel, watching TV and swimming. There was an indoor heated pool, which was pretty cool."

"Jessie tried to order a cocktail from the waiter at the pool!" said Cassandra, her eyes wide.

"You don't sound too enthusiastic about the holiday," said Nomusa, looking searchingly at Jessie.

"Well, when we *were* all together, the fossils were at each other's throats. I honestly don't know why they ever married."

"So they could have me!" piped up Cassandra.

"How was your holiday, Nomusa – hey, how was your birthday?" asked Jessie.

13

"Not bad at all. We went to Simon's Town and saw the penguins, and I only had to listen to one lecture on how important it is that I continue the work of the revolution by single-handedly transforming the entire nation and uplifting the masses. There were some party heavyweights there on Christmas, so lots of talk about the next elections over slices of dried-out turkey. But I got in some good long-distance runs, and my birthday was good – I got your cards and prezzies, thanks, they were great! My folks gave me a book, *Heroes of the Struggle.*"

Jessie pulled a face and groaned.

"And," added Nomusa, this time with a sparkle in her eyes, "this! Yay! – finally, I'm properly connected!"

From the pocket of her jeans, she whipped out a small object. Looking closer, Samantha saw that it was a tiny cellphone, sleek, metallic and with a sliding lid. It fit completely into the palm of Nomusa's small hand.

"Snaps!" said Jessie, rummaging through the four bags hanging over her shoulder before finally finding the phone in the pocket of her own jeans. "I also got an upgrade. It's the same make and model as yours – though mine's black."

"Don't you love it?" said Nomusa.

"It's great, I've already loaded my music on the player, and the camera is terrific."

"Five megapixels, sister! And an HD screen, and all the apps I can download. Though it chows the battery life something chronic."

"I got a cellphone, too," said Sam.

"You did?" said Jessie, surprised.

"Yup. It's not new – it's an old handset of my father's. He was due for an upgrade and he gave his old phone to Dan, and Dan gave his old phone to me. So this was dad's first cellphone."

Sam pulled the phone out of her bag. There was no way this handset would fit into a pocket of her jeans. It was old, heavy, and very big. The only small thing about it was the tiny screen, glowing with green numbers, which rested in the light grey plastic cover. Jessie and Nomusa stared at the phone in fascinated silence for a moment.

"What is that?" asked Cassandra, genuinely puzzled.

Nomusa said, kindly, "It's great you've got a phone, Sam, now we can text each other."

"It *can* send texts, can it?" asked Jessie, sounding a little dubious. She was staring at the clunky phone as if she had never seen anything quite like it. Which she probably hadn't, mused Samantha wryly.

"Well, it works," said Samantha, trying to sound enthusiastic, "and that's what matters. And, it has a very long battery life! Do either of you know what room we're in?"

"Apparently Matron McKensie has to allocate us to our dorm rooms. We'll still be on the third floor with the other grade 9's and the 8's, though," said Nomusa.

"I guess it's too much to expect that we'll have a four-bed room for the three of us again," said Jessie. "I just hope we don't get stuck with some dork of a roommate."

"As long as we aren't sharing with *her*, I don't really mind who it is," said Samantha, her grey eyes fixed on Cindy Atkins, who stood at the entrance to Austen House dormitory, talking on a small, pink cellphone, her sleek blonde hair shining in the sun. As they walked past her, Cindy flipped the glossy pink lid closed and said, "Still here, then, Steadman?"

15

"Still here," said Sam.

"And still the undefeated academic heavyweight champion of the grade. Still the current recipient of the Clifford House Full Scholarship Award!" jibed Jessie.

"Well, I guess the deserving poor need it more than I do. Besides, they probably gave it to you because of affirmative action."

"Oh yes? How do you figure that one out?" asked Samantha.

"Well, now that *her* lot," here Cindy tossed her head at Nomusa, "are running the country, the only truly disadvantaged are the poor. Like you!" Cindy laughed. Then, catching sight of the cellphone in Samantha's hand, she said, "What, in the name of all that's holy, is *that*?"

"What does it look like?" snapped Samantha, trying to shove the phone back into her bag.

"It looks like a walkie-talkie!"

"It's a cellphone – as any moron could see," said Nomusa.

"That's not a cellphone – it's a brick! OMG! It even has an aerial!" Cindy was talking very loudly and girls around them were turning their heads to look.

"Do you know what I think you should do, Steadman? Well, apart from sticking your head down the loo and flushing, I mean? I think you should donate that chunk of clunk to a museum. They could stick it in the display of *Ancient Methods of Communication*, alongside the Egyptian clay tablets and tribal drums. Kitty!" she called to her friend, who was walking towards the stairs of the dormitory, "Come see this! Steadman's brought a primitive artefact to school for show-and-tell!" She burst out laughing.

16

Face burning, Samantha brushed past her and walked angrily into Austen House, followed by Nomusa, Jessie and Cassandra.

"I can't stand her," said Nomusa, through gritted teeth.

"She is such a cow!" said Samantha.

"No, no," said Jessie, steering Sam and Nomusa over to where Matron McKensie stood, clipboard in hand. "I know that she *seems* all mean and spiteful, but honestly, underneath all that, she's really and truly … evil!"

"Ah, 'tis you three lasses, is it?" said Matron McKensie with a broad smile, peering over her enormous bosom to scan a bright eye over her lists. "Delaney, Gule, Steadman … Ah, here ye are! Room 317 it is, this year, follow me," she said and set off up the stairs. She was out of breath halfway up the first flight of stairs, and wheezing by the time they reached the third floor. "Och! Those stairs ne'er get any flatter!" she gasped, fanning her red cheeks with the clipboard. When she had caught her breath, she set off down the corridor, saying, "I may as well tell ye that there's good news and bad news about your room."

"What's the good news?" asked Nomusa, as they passed the grade 9 noticeboard, which was jammed with start-of-term notices. A single high-heeled red sandal was perched precariously on a top corner, together with what looked like a plaited extension of purple hair.

"I've been looking for that!" said Jessie, snatching the shoe off the board as she passed, and dropping a bag in the process.

"I got it," said Samantha, scooping up the bag.

"Weel, the good news is that the three of ye will be in a bedroom all to yourselves."

"Yes!" said Jessie, punching the air and causing another bag to slide off one shoulder.

"Oh, good!" said Nomusa, "Things are looking up."

"Aye, I thought ye'd like that, considering all the nonsense ye were up to last year so as not to get another girl in your dorm-room. Inventing a Russian lass and pretending she was the fourth girl in the room!"

"We didn't invent her," said Samantha. "We just didn't highlight the fact that she never pitched up."

"It's not like we're anti-social," added Nomusa.

"Yeah," said Jessie, who was now panting as she dragged the heaviest of her many bags behind her down the smooth floor of the corridor. "We just really needed the extra space. A girl's got to have a place to put her clothes. It's a right enshrined in the constitution."

"Aye, well that brings me to the bad news," said Matron, stopping outside a room at the end of the corridor with the number 317 on the door.

"Oh dear. What's the bad news?" asked Samantha.

In reply, Matron merely pushed open the door and stood aside for them to enter. Samantha walked in, and her heart sank. Behind her, Nomusa let out a sigh of disappointment and Jessie said, "This isn't a dorm-room – it's a cubbyhole!"

The room was very small, stuffy and cramped. Three beds, each with a footlocker at the end of it, were jammed alongside each other with scarcely enough room to manoeuvre between them. The ceiling slanted down from one end of the room to the other so that Samantha could not even stand up straight at the far end of the room. A series of exposed pipes lined the wall opposite the small window.

"It's a hobbit-hole!" said Jessie, disgusted, "a blimmin' broom cupboard."

"Aye, ye'r not far wrong there, lass. It was used as a storage room last year, but it was Mrs Grieve's express wish that you three lasses get assigned this as your bedroom for the year. She's a canny one, Mrs Grieve, she doesna' forget easily."

"It's not right. We did our punishment fair and square last year," said Samantha, remembering how, after Cindy Atkins had told on them for pretending that a fourth girl lived in their room so that they could enjoy the extra space, they had been made to scrub all the dormitory's bathroom floors with toothbrushes.

"The boot in my dad's car is roomier than this," Jessie chuntered on.

"What can't be got round must be got through. I'll leave ye to unpack and get settled," said Matron, squeezing past Nomusa to get out of the room.

"Unpack? Where am I supposed to put all my stuff? I've never seen anything this small. My mother's got handbags that are bigger than this room!"

"Look Jessie," said Nomusa, pulling open a small door at the low end of the room. "This looks like a storage cupboard, it's low, but deep – I reckon you could get all of your stuff in here."

Jessie peered inside the cupboard. There were a few shelves which stretched into the deep gap between the floor and sloping ceiling. Jessie asked, "Anyone mind if I stow my stuff in here?"

"Go ahead," said Samantha, "I'd rather not have that bed anyway – I'd always be banging my head on the roof. I'll trade you ceiling height for cupboard space."

"And I'll take the window and the view – what little there is of it," said Nomusa, flopping onto the middle bed and peering out of the small window. "I never

19

thought I'd miss the invisible Princess Anastasia so much!"

While Jessie heaved and pushed her bags into the low cupboard, muttering under her breath about "rabbit warrens" and "shoeboxes", Samantha began to unpack her own bag, glad, for perhaps the first time in her life, that she had fewer clothes and belongings than her friends.

3

Crimes

Now, as they filed out of the hall, after the first assembly on their first day of grade 9, Samantha, Jessie and Nomusa compared timetables.

"Looks like Languages first period," said Samantha. "Mr De Wet's taking us for Afrikaans again this year."

"And I've got Mr Dlamini for Zulu again," said Nomusa.

"And we still have ze divine Mademoiselle Abeille for French," said Jessie.

"Meet you in the quad at first break."

They peeled off in the different directions of their classrooms, Samantha heading for Mr De Wet's classroom on the second floor. Calliope Katakouzinous, a petite dark-haired girl who was one of the few pupils from Samantha's class that also took Afrikaans, was already waiting outside the classroom.

"Hi, Poppy."

"Hi Sam, how were your holidays?"

"Good, how about yours?"

"Oh, you know, the usual. But I heard all about how you and Nomusa and Jessie helped to catch the illegal long-liners and saved the turtles and got an award or something. It was in the papers – good job!"

"Thanks," said Samantha, pleased but also a little embarrassed. "So, are we joining another class for Afrikaans again, do you think?"

Poppy sighed and nodded. Looking over her shoulder and into the classroom, Samantha saw that six girls from 9A had already taken seats in the two back rows. Among them were Cindy Atkins and Kitty Bennington. It was Samantha's turn to sigh. It seemed that another year of listening to Cindy's jibes and snipes loomed.

"Perhaps it's not too late to change to Zulu?" said Poppy, but a loud voice called from inside the classroom, "*Kom julle.* Come inside, girls, the year is begun!"

Mr De Wet's classroom looked much as it had the year before. Poster-sized pictures of kudu, springbok, rhinos and leopards – which looked as if they had been torn from an old calendar – were stuck on the walls and a small carved, wooden elephant stopped an untidy pile of papers from slipping off the corner of his desk to the floor. Mr De Wet, tall and sturdy, rubbed a hand over his ginger beard and smoothed his bristly moustache.

"Welcome to your second year. Most of you did very well in the exams. I was proud and pleased with your marks, Samantha, proud and pleased. And Cindy, you did very well, also," he added with a smile. Cindy scowled. "I hope you will try for an A also this year, Poppie," said Mr De Wet, pronouncing the name *pawpie*.

"How were your holidays, sir? Did you go to your game farm in the Waterberg?" asked Uvani Moodley, a friendly girl with a very long plait of shiny dark hair, who was sitting in the seat next to Samantha.

"It was excellent. First class!" said Mr De Wet, smiling broadly and hitching up his khaki pants, "We had some good rains. Man, the veld is looking green and lovely! But I know you, grade 9's," he said, wagging a thick finger at them, "You are trying to distract me again! You want to get me telling stories about the farm and the veld and then you get out of doing your work, not so?"

Uvani just grinned.

"Well, you are not going to track me to the side, even though I have a great story to tell, though not a funny one, because at New Year I was hijacked in my bak-kie, and hit on the neck with a revolver, and it were no laughing matter, that I can tell you."

"What happened, sir? Were you hurt?" asked Samantha, concerned.

"Ag, not too bad, just had to take the anti-inflamma-tories, but I'm damn sad about that bakkie truck, man. It was a *kanniedood* – a car that cannot die. 150 000 k's on the clock and still going strong! They don't make pickup trucks like that anymore. I remember, I bought that car when I was just…" Here, Mr De Wet inter-rupted himself with a sheepish smile.

"There I go again, hey? But it's not totally off the point, that hijacking. Because afterwards I lied awake thinking, and I realised that we must maybe have crime as our first theme for the year."

"I'll tell you what's a crime – the way this guy teach-es, and butchers the English language," Sam heard Cin-dy whispering behind her.

"So, our work for today is to increase our vocabulary and here," Mr De Wet switched on the overhead pro-jector and slipped a transparency onto its screen, "are the new words. Once you have copied them down, we will do the correct pronunciation and you can memo-rise them for homework."

Samantha looked up at the screen, and read the words and their English translations.

woorde (words)

misdaad (crime)	misdadiger (criminal)
kaping/staking (hijacking)	kapers/stakers (hijackers)
gyselaar (hostage)	dief, diewe (thief, thieves)
polisie (police)	tronk (jail)

uitdrukkings (phrases)
gewapende roof (armed robbery)
roep die polisie (call the police)
stuur asseblief hulp (please send help)

The remainder of the lesson was spent copying down the vocabulary, learning the pronunciation and pairing off to discuss crime using the new words and phrases. Samantha was shocked to hear that Poppy and her family had been victims of an armed robbery at their house the year before, and they spent a very peculiar quarter of an hour laughing at each other's attempts to speak Afrikaans while talking about this most serious of subjects.

"We've got our first lesson with Mr Delmonico next – Science, in Lab A," said Samantha, consulting her timetable during first break.

"I still don't like the look of him," said Nomusa.

Jessie made a dismissive noise as she tilted her crisp packet to tap the last crumbs into her mouth. "He looks like a refugee from the Adams Family, but he'll probably be like all the others: boring but okay."

Half an hour later, Samantha knew that Jessie had been dead wrong in her prediction.

4

Understood?

When they filed into Lab Λ on the ground floor, Mr Delmonico was seated at his desk. On one corner of the clear expanse of wood there was a round, stainless steel pen-holder holding a single black clutch-pencil and a sharp-edged metal ruler. On another corner sat a small model of an atom. Mr Delmonico read something off the screen of the small grey laptop which rested in the precise centre of his desk, and then wrote on a piece of paper with a slim, silver fountain pen. He did not look up when the girls walked in, chatting amongst themselves and choosing their high stools behind the lab counters. Samantha, who would have liked to sit near the back of this classroom, saw with chagrin that the only remaining counter where there were three seats next to each other was in the second row. She, Jessie and Nomusa took the seats and unpacked their pencil bags and exam pads. Mr Delmonico still had not looked up.

Samantha glanced about the classroom; it looked different from when Mrs Naidoo had taught here. The only adornments on the walls now were a large periodic table, and black-bordered posters of mathematical and chemical formulas. The blackboard was completely clean, except for the name "Mr A. Delmonico", which had been written in narrow capital letters in the exact centre of the board. The bookshelves to the left of the board were filled with a dozen identical black files, each with a neatly typed label on its spine, while the shelves to the right of the board, near the door, had rows of books arranged in order of height, from tallest to shortest.

A hush settled gradually on the class as the girls stared curiously at Mr Delmonico. When the class was completely silent, he clicked the pen into its lid, and deposited it into the pen-holder, then he stood and walked to the front of the class, letting his eyes wander from girl to girl. They were small eyes, and Samantha noticed that the bottom of the brown irises did not quite touch the rim of the lower lids, so that they appeared to be floating in the whites of his eyes.

While he silently stared at each of them in turn, Samantha observed him. Mr Delmonico had a slight build, and was perhaps only as tall as she was. His black hair was thin and fine, cut short, and deep widow's peaks curved sharply back from his forehead. His skin was very pale, almost translucent – Samantha could see the thread of blue veins beneath the skin at his temples and on the backs of the small hands which were now holding a single sheet of paper. He had a sharp, narrow nose and, against the white of his skin, his thin lips seemed very red.

Mr Delmonico smiled. It was a smile which curved his mouth to reveal small, sharp teeth, but which did not warm his eyes.

"In future, when you enter my classroom, you will do so in silence," he said. He spoke in a quiet voice which reached all the way back to the corners of the lab. "Noise is chaos. And nothing can be achieved in chaos."

He looked down at the paper. "I have here a class list.

When I call your name, you will indicate, by raising a hand, who you are. Understood?"

Samantha nodded and snuck a look sideways. She could not see Nomusa's expression, but Jessie's lips were moving in a way that indicated she was trying to fight a smile. Samantha felt no urge to smile; there was nothing funny about this man. Just the way he stared at them made her feel uncomfortable.

"Mercy Tshabalala?" Mr Delmonico said.

"Yes, sir," called Mercy from the front row, raising her hand into the air.

"I have been briefed as to your difficulties with mathematics. You will attend extra Maths classes before school on Tuesdays until such time as I am satisfied that you have a sufficient grasp of the subject. The class starts at 7 a.m. sharp. Understood?"

"Yes, sir," said Mercy softly. She looked down at the desk in front of her and her soft, plump shoulders seemed to crumple a little.

"Charné Roos, Uvani Moodley, Poppy Katakouzinous, Skye MacAdam?" Several hands went into the air.

"Stand up."

The handful of girls stood up alongside their stools and looked apprehensively at Mr Delmonico.

"I have compared your performance in examinations and class tests with the aptitudes listed on your personal records, and have determined that you are performing below potential. Your will do what is necessary to improve your marks. You will find that I set a very high standard in my subjects, and unless you wish to fall further behind, you will need to work a great deal harder this year. Underachievers will not be tolerated in this class. Understood?"

The girls nodded glumly.

"Sit."

The girls sat back down, while Mr Delmonico consulted his list again.

"And where is Jessica Delaney?"

"Here, sir," said Jessie, raising her hand. There was no trace of a smile on her lips now.

"Watch yourself in my class, young lady."

"But I didn't do anyth-" began Jessie in an outraged voice.

"Quiet. Nomusa Gule?"

Nomusa put up her hand.

"Hmmm," said Mr Delmonico, narrowing his eyes but saying nothing more.

Mr Delmonico continued to work his way through the list, making some comment to each girl. He seemed to know something about each of them. Samantha could feel her stomach clenching. What would he say to her?

Finally, Mr Delmonico looked at Samantha, "And that leaves ... Samantha Steadman, am I right?"

"Yes, sir." Samantha's voice came out a little croakily.

"Ah," he said and continued to contemplate her with his small, dark eyes.

"I am told you were the top student in both Maths and Science last year. Indeed, the top student across the board."

Samantha, who was unsure how to respond to this, said nothing.

"We shall see ..." He took a quick breath through his nose; the thin nostrils pinched together. "Do not think that your prior achievements will earn you any favours in this class, Miss Steadman."

"Sir, I never–"

"I was not inviting conversation," he said, "I was merely cautioning you. The students who achieve the highest marks in school are not always those who achieve best in life." Pointing to a cupboard in the corner of the room, he instructed Mercy and Charné to collect and hand out textbooks to the class.

"Each of you will ensure that your textbook, plus one A4, 288-page hardcover exercise book, will be covered by your next class. Brown paper and plastic, I am told, are available for this purpose in the library.

"When you write your notes for Science, or for Mathematics, come to that, you will always write the heading on the top left-hand corner of the page, and the date in the top right. Both will be underlined, with a single line. You will use ballpoint pens with blue ink only. When you have finished the notes, or the assigned exercise or homework, you will skip one line and then rule a line across the page – *with a ruler*. You will begin the next exercise immediately beneath.

"You will discover that, in my class," Mr Delmonico said with that mirthless smile, "there is only one way of doing things – the correct way. Now, pay close attention while I explain our first exercise, as you will be completing it for homework."

It felt to Samantha that she held her breath all through the rest of the class, and only exhaled once the bell had rung and they were well clear of Delmonico's classroom.

"How horrible was he? So unkind to Mercy and Poppy and the others! And 'hmming' at me – what did that mean?" said Nomusa, as they walked down to the fields to their Physical Training class. Samantha was so eager to get away from Lab A that she found herself actually looking forward to the next hour of "Physical Torture", as she called their P.T. lessons.

"And picking on me – I haven't even done anything wrong yet! It's unfair. What's he got against me? He creeped me out. Totally," said Jessie.

"He *was* creepy," said Samantha. "He had actually researched us – read our personal files. He knew stuff about each of us. And the way he talks – *you will do this and you will do that – understood?*"

"Yes, and *sit!* – as if we were dogs!" said Nomusa. "I'm sure I've got a cousin in Jo'burg who went to Academy Girls High. Maybe I'll try and get her number from my mom and then call her for a heads-up."

"And I didn't understand what he was saying about vectors at all. Did you get it, Sam?" asked Jessie.

"I think so, though I was also a bit confused."

"What a way to start the year," said Jessie, peering at their timetable. "And we've got another two sessions with him before the weekend."

Their next lesson with their new, least-favourite teacher, which was after second break the next day, was even worse. Mr Delmonico instructed them to place their covered books on the desktops and walked around inspecting them. When he got to Jessie, he lifted up her exercise book between his thumb and forefinger and asked, "What is this?"

"It's my book, sir," said Jessie. She sounded puzzled but confident. Samantha had nagged her and Nomusa the evening before to cover all their books and textbooks for both Maths and Science, determined to give Mr Delmonico no cause to complain. But now, looking at the way Jessie had covered her book, Samantha knew that Mr Delmonico would do just that.

"I meant – what is this covering it?"

"It's paper and plastic, sir."

"What kind of paper, Miss Delaney?"

"Well," said Jessie, sounding a little less sure now, "It's a sketch I made, sir, of atoms. See, I arranged them as if they were planets in the solar system – to give it a scientific theme. To be a bit original and creative, sir, and to ..." Her voice petered out as she looked at his face.

"I do not remember instructing this class to be *original and creative*, Miss Delaney. Did I or did I not say that your exercise books and textbooks should be covered in brown paper and plastic?" he asked, addressing the question now to Samantha, whose own books were, in fact, covered in just this way. Samantha hesitated. He wanted, she realised, for her to confirm Jessie's fault.

"Well, actually, sir," she said, trying to make her voice sound respectful, "what I think you said was that brown paper and plastic were available in the library to cover our books, but, ... but you didn't say that we *had* to cover them in that only."

There was a flash of anger in Delmonico's eyes. "My meaning was clear," he said. Then he ripped the plastic and the beautiful sketch off Jessie's book, crumpled both and dropped them onto the desk in front of her.

"Into the wastepaper bin," he said.

"But sir, can't I keep–"

"I said, into the wastepaper bin, Miss Delaney. Are you hard of hearing?"

Jessie grabbed the crumpled sketch and the plastic, stalked over to the bin to throw them away, and returned to her seat. Her mouth was pulled tight and she looked as angry as Samantha felt. Samantha wanted to say something, to protest against the unfairness, but

31

she was afraid of pushing her luck any further. Nomusa, she saw, gave Jessie's arm a consoling squeeze under the desk.

"If anyone else has been *original and creative*, kindly remove and dispose of your covers now, and ensure that your books are covered, exactly as instructed, by tomorrow's lesson. Understood? Now, copy down these notes, and then complete exercise 2 on page 17 of your textbooks."

As he spoke, he pressed a button on the wall to the side of the board and then keyed in an instruction on the computer. A solid white screen descended in front of the board and soon a page of notes was displayed on it. Looking overhead, Samantha noticed for the first time that a hi-tech projector had been mounted on the ceiling of the classroom.

She turned over a page in her exercise book and took a deep breath before beginning to copy down the notes. They did not seem to make a great deal of sense to her, but perhaps that was because she was still seething with anger on Jessie's behalf. Jessie's cheeks were bright red and her pen was gouging deeply into the paper as she wrote.

When she had finished copying down the notes, Samantha began the exercise, but could not get further than the first three questions; obviously, she had not fully understood what she had written down. With any other of her teachers, she would simply have asked them to explain, but she could not bring herself to ask Mr Delmonico.

She glanced at Nomusa and Jessie's work. Nomusa seemed to be stuck on the second question. Jessie was not attempting the exercise at all. She was furiously

32

sketching something on another sheet of paper. Samantha looked closer and saw that it was a caricature of Mr Delmonico. Jessie had drawn him as an evil-looking devil, exaggerating his sharp teeth. A pointed tail grew out of his behind and a speech bubble from his mouth held the single word, "Understood?" Underneath, she had titled it, "*Demon*ico".

Samantha was torn between admiration and horror. "Be careful!" she whispered. Looking up briefly, she found Mr Delmonico's cold gaze on her and quickly bent back over her work until his attention shifted to another girl who had stuck her hand in the air.

"Yes?"

"Sir, I don't think I understand how the formula in b of your notes works. Do you mean that when we square the sum of–"

"The explanations are quite clear, Miss Armstrong. Kindly get on with the work and do not interrupt me again."

At least she was not alone in her confusion, Samantha thought, as she re-read the notes she had taken down. In desperation, she paged back in the textbook and read slowly through the explanations given there until she understood. She finished the exercise and then slumped back with a sigh of relief. Unfortunately, this movement seemed to attract Delmonico's attention.

"Finished already, Miss Steadman?" he asked, walking over to their bench.

"Watch it!" Sam breathed to Jessie and, under guise of closing her textbook, she pushed it over so that it covered Jessie's sketch.

Mr Delmonico stretched out his hand for Samantha's exercise book and she handed it over, reasonably confident that she had got the work right, a feeling which grew when he read through her answers without commenting. Surely, if she had got something wrong, he would have said something. But then Mr Delmonico placed the exercise book down, open, on the desk, picked up Samantha's ruler and with the pen in his hand, drew a bold red line diagonally across all of her work. Her mouth gaped as she stared up at him.

"As I clearly instructed this class yesterday, new exercises are to begin immediately underneath the previous exercise. You, Miss Steadman, have started on a new page. You have also, contrary to instructions, written the date in the top left-hand corner, instead of in the top right-hand corner. You will redo the entire exercise and this time you will follow instructions." He leaned over, scrawled a red circle with "–2" inside and said, "I will be deducting two marks from your book mark for this infringement."

Now Samantha's own cheeks were burning. She could feel Delmonico's gaze on her, carefully evaluating her response. She blinked fiercely and stared down at her work. Under the desk, she dug her nails into the palms of her hands, trying to focus on the pain there instead of the hot frustration which was constricting her throat and pricking the backs of her eyes.

"In the disciplines of science and maths," said Mr Delmonico, returning to his desk with a faint smile curling his thin lips, "it is necessary to get each and every last detail correct. We cannot get *original and creative.*" He said this with a contemptuous glance at Jessie. "And we cannot follow our own preferences." Samantha just knew he had directed this last comment at her, but she still would not look up at him.

"It's all about getting the details correct. I am sure that even a group such as this can understand. For example, if you were to change just a single digit in a telephone number, you would be connected to the wrong person. If a single digit change in something as trivial as a telephone number results in social chaos, how much more careful must we be with science and mathematics? Understood?"

The ringing of the bell to mark the end of the period had never before been so welcome to Samantha. They spent the whole of break roundly abusing Delmonico and when Jessie insisted that she was going to pin the Demonico caricature to the school's main notice-board, Samantha was seriously tempted to let her do so. It was only the certainty that Jessie would surely be caught (since everybody knew her distinctive sketching style) and severely punished, that made Samantha exert herself to talk her friend out of it. Nomusa tried to calm them both down by saying soothingly, "Maybe he's just coming on strong in the beginning. Once he's, you know, set the boundaries, he might loosen up." Jessie snorted at this.

"Anyway," continued Nomusa calmly, "I think we should try to fly under the radar for a bit, not attract any more of his attention. And don't let's allow him to catch us doing anything wrong."

"That's going to be difficult," predicted Samantha, "because I have a feeling he *wants* to catch us out. I think he likes it."

5

Just checking

Samantha tried hard to follow Nomusa's advice in their lessons with Delmonico: she avoided his attention and did her work exactly according to his instructions. As the work got more difficult, however, she became more and more frustrated by his teaching style, which seemed to involve no actual teaching at all – merely getting them to copy down notes and do exercises. Everyone seemed confused to some degree. Jessie rapidly gave up even trying to understand in class, and Samantha regularly found herself trying to explain the science work to her increasingly glum friend in their dorm room in the evenings.

"I just have to make it to the end of the year," said Jessie, after one of these impromptu extra lessons. "And then I can dump this dumb subject. No way am I taking Science for matric! I may not even take Maths, at this rate."

Samantha bit her thumbnail. "I always wanted to take them both all the way to matric, but I'm beginning to wonder if I'm good enough."

"It's not you that's not good enough, it's him. He's a useless teacher! Hey, don't worry, Sam," said Nomusa, gently pushing Samantha's fingers away from her mouth. "It'll come right somehow. Just don't let him get under your skin."

"Easier said than done," countered Samantha, for Delmonico was indeed beginning to get to her.

He seemed to take pleasure in critically watching her every move, and pointing out her every mistake. She had the sense that he picked on her simply because she was the top student. She spent so much energy each lesson worrying about Delmonico – his motives, his comments, his petty rules – that she sometimes missed what he was saying, and then she worried even more that she would get something else wrong. She had already lost another two book marks for leaving two lines, rather than one, before ruling off after an exercise, and the book mark for the term was only out of twenty marks altogether.

She had taken to checking, somewhat obsessively, every aspect of her work before completing or handing in an exercise, and she felt a growing impulse to check each item in every exercise, sometimes twice, just after she wrote it. Whenever she found an error, the need to continue checking was strengthened. When, as was more common, she found no errors, she wondered whether she had checked carefully enough, and reread her work to check that she had checked correctly. She had never worked as carefully, or as slowly, and she was beginning to battle to finish her work in the assigned time.

"Hey!" said Jessie, interrupting her thoughts, "There's a meeting of the Art Appreciation Society on Friday after school. Either of you want to come along?"

"I've got athletics pre-season training," said Nomusa.

"How about you, Sam?"

"I think I'd better try and get my Maths and Science up to date – especially if we're going into town on Saturday?"

"Definitely. I need a break from this prison!" said Jessie. "I'll tell you what it's like, though, because it sounds like it might be fun and we're going to need some fun!"

Jessie was full of excitement about the A.A.S. after its first meeting, and told them all about the society's plans on their visit into Izintaba on Saturday morning. They were joined at their table in the tiny country town's coffee shop by Samantha's older brother, who was in grade 11 in Clifford Heights – the nearby brother school to Clifford House. Under his unruly thatch of sandy-brown hair, Dan's blue-grey eyes were fastened on Jessie while she explained about art club to Sam and Nomusa.

"You two just have to join the Art Appreciation Society. Ms Zenobia's taking the group to some excellent San art sites this year – it'll be fun! She's really laid back, Sam, so there won't be any extra work, just some fun outings and a chance to escape school. Oh, and apparently there's also an art club at Clifford Heights, so there'll be some boys. The first field trip is planned for February. We're going to some caves with rock art near Devil's Peak and there'll be a guide to explain stuff to us. What do you think? Will you come with me?"

"It would be nice to get up into the mountains," said Samantha.

"And there would probably be some excellent hikes to get to the caves," said Nomusa. Jessie looked a little startled at this.

"Ok, sure," said Nomusa, and Sam nodded her agreement.

Dan, who had been rocking backwards on his chair while noisily slurping the last of his double-thick choco-

38

late milkshake, now tipped the chair back onto all four legs, banged his empty glass onto the table-top and spoke.

"Let me see your chest, Jessie," he said.

"*What?*"

"Show me your chest."

"*Excuuuse me?*"

"Your T-shirt," said Dan. "There's something written on it. I want to read it."

"Oh," said Jessie. She sat up, and pulled her T-shirt out taut in front of her so that Dan could read the printing: "Girls are forever, boys are whatever!"

"Hmm," said Dan, crossing his arms and leaning back to stare at Jessie. "So you're still taking strain over your unrequited love for my older brother? Still pining because you're Jessie without the James?"

"Him? Phfff!" Jessie made a dismissive sound. "No, I'm well over James Steadman, thanks very much."

"Excellent!" said Dan, rubbing his hands together enthusiastically and looking to Samantha rather like a crafty general planning a new campaign. "Well, then we must find you someone new."

"Why?" asked Samantha.

"Why?" repeated Dan.

"Yes, why? Why does a girl have to have a boyfriend? Single girls can be perfectly happy, you know."

"Now don't start your feminist bleating with me, Sammy," said Dan, in a stern voice. "Of course Jessie needs a new guy!"

"Needs?" asked Nomusa, an eyebrow raised.

"Ack! I can see my sister's starting to influence you, too. Jessie," he said, directing an engaging grin at her, "you're too good to go to waste!"

He said it so charmingly that Jessie blinked, and forgot what she had been about to say.

"Being single is not 'going to waste'!" protested Samantha.

Dan ignored this and went on, "So let's see, how about…" he looked around the coffee shop, evaluating possible candidates. His eye fell on an enormous, thickly muscled boy with a heavy brow and a shadow of dark stubble on his jaw. "I know, how about … Ronald de Vries?" he said, with the air of a magician pulling a rabbit out of a hat.

"Ronald de Vries!" exclaimed Jessie in disgust. Jessie, Sam and Nomusa turned to look in the direction of Ronald, who was standing amongst a group of students from Clifford Heights, looking a little perplexed at the conversation that was going on around him. As they looked, he burped loudly.

"Uh, not ever," said Jessie. "Besides, what's he doing here – he can't still be at school, he must be like 22 or something!"

"Nah, he's only repeating matric for the third time. He says it's his 'make or hake' year."

"Don't you mean 'make or break'?" asked Nomusa.

"Apparently, if he fails again, his father's going to send him off to a fish-packing plant in Iceland."

"Golly," said Nomusa. Jessie giggled.

"Are you sure you don't want to make a play for him, Jess?"

"Sure. Thanks ever so much. Neanderthals have never been much my style."

"Ah! That narrows the search. So if it's not brawn you're looking for–"

"I like a *little* brawn–"

40

"It must be brain! Well, then, how about…" Dan began surveying the room again and spotted his best friend – a tall boy with thick, black hair, dark blue eyes and rosy cheeks. "Apples!" he said triumphantly.

"Apples?" said Jessie and Samantha simultaneously.

"Yeah, my friend, Mark Appleton. You know, he won't be wearing SA Gate and Fence on his teeth forever, and I'm told the girls like his dimples. And … his voice has broken!"

"Which girls?" asked Sam.

"Uh-uh, I think he's a little too quiet and serious for me," said Jessie, tilting her head speculatively as she eyed Apples. "Though, he's not bad looking."

Nomusa and Sam also looked up at Apples. He must have felt their gaze, because he turned to look in their direction, saw them all watching and gave a little wave and a grin. His cheeks went redder.

"I don't think he's really Jessie's type. Do you?" Sam asked Nomusa, who was smiling.

"Besides," added Jessie, "I've gone off the dead brainy ones!"

They all grinned and Dan and Sam slumped back in their chair, remembering Jessie's crush on their intellectual older brother, James, the previous year.

"I mean, I like them smart, but not – you know – too academic. That's more Sam's bag."

"Ok, so not majorly brawny or brainy–" began Dan.

"And he must be cute. And have a sense of humour. And no hairy, stubby, pork-sausage fingers."

"Glad to see you're getting into the spirit of the thing! Ok, how about Liam O'Leary?"

"Too tall."

"George Duarte?"

"Too short."

"Zakes Rantao?"

"Too round."

"Carl Atkins?" Dan pointed at a tall, good-looking boy with blonde hair.

"He's Cindy's brother!" chimed Samantha, Jessie and Nomusa together, in tones of deep disgust.

"Just checking."

"Definitely not!"

"Sorry. How foolish of me. We're running out of guys, Jessie," warned Dan, craning his neck to see who else was in the coffee shop. "Hendrik Smit?" he asked.

"Who?" asked Jessie.

"Him," said Dan, pointing at a small boy whose nose hardly reached the counter-top.

"He's in grade 8, Daniel Steadman!"

"Picky, picky, picky," he chided. "Well, we've gone through all the other guys here – it'll have to be me," said Dan, a wide grin on his face, his eyes on Jessie.

"*You?*"

"Howzit," said a deep voice from behind Sam. She turned to see Apples standing there, two steaming cups of coffee in his hands. He seemed to have grown much taller than the last time she had seen him. "Jessie, Nomusa … Sam." He gave them each a smile.

"Hi," said Sam.

"Here's your coffee, mate," said Apples, handing one of the cups to Dan, but seeing the frown on Dan's face, he looked a bit taken aback.

"Can I get any of you anything?" he asked, looking at the three girls.

"No thanks," said Jessie, standing up and grabbing her bag off the floor. "I think we've had more than enough. Ciao."

"Cheers," said Nomusa, getting up to follow her.

"Uhm, bye. But thanks for the offer," said Sam, following a little more slowly.

"Was it something I said?" laughed Apples, dimples creasing his cheeks.

"Hmmph," grunted Dan, and then called after the girls, "See you around."

6

Devil's Peak

The few weeks leading up to the first Art Appreciation Society excursion were very busy for Sam, Nomusa and Jessie. There was an interhouse swimming gala in which it was compulsory for every girl to swim. Jessie complained about this and disputed Nomusa's encouragement that swimming was a great form of exercise, saying "If swimming is so good for your figure, how do you explain whales?"

Austen House finished stone last in the gala – a fact for which Cindy blamed Sam, Jessie and "all the other lame losers who couldn't swim fast if a shark was chewing on their butts". Nomusa, who was the most athletic of the trio, won two of her three races, but could not have cared less. She was only interested in the athletics team tryouts the week after the gala, and performed so well in the time-trials that, as she shyly told Jessie and Sam afterwards, the coach was going to enter her into the trials for the KwaZulu-Natal provincial team.

The high school awards assembly, which presented prizes for the previous year's achievements, was held on the Friday evening before the excursion. All three girls had been informed that they would be receiving an award – Jessie had been astonished at her inclusion – and the school had invited their parents. It was sweltering in the packed hall. All the parents were crammed into seats in the middle section; the teachers, wearing their long, black academic gowns, were seated in rows on the stage, facing the audience, and the award-winners sat in rows of chairs which ran lengthways along one side of the hall. From where she sat, Samantha could see Jessie and Nomusa's parents, as well as her own father.

Mr and Mrs Gule sat in the reserved VIP section of seats in the front row. Justice Gule, a tall, handsome man with a distinguished-looking face, was a member of the South African parliament, and Mrs Grieve never lost an opportunity to show off what she called "the high calibre of Clifford House girls and their parents". Mrs Gule, an aristocratic-looking woman with perfect posture and a somewhat severe face, had merely nodded graciously at the headmistress's effusive greeting, but she clapped enthusiastically when Nomusa was called on stage to receive her award for general academic excellence. Nomusa's parents, Sam knew, had great plans for her to become a lawyer and to get involved in the world of politics – perhaps they considered an award for academic excellence to be a good first step.

Cindy Atkins also received an award for general academic excellence, as well as the subject prize for accountancy. Her parents, who were seated in the front row near the Gules, applauded when Cindy collected her certificates, but the slight frown between Mr Atkins's brows made Sam think he still believed Cindy ought to be achieving better results and winning more of the awards. She remembered the conversation she had overheard the previous year, when she had discovered that Cindy craved her father's approval, but Mr Atkins gave only his opinion that his daughter ought to reclaim her spot as the top student and become the recipient of the scholarship. If he was still putting so much pressure on his daughter, then Sam reckoned she could expect Cindy to be just as revolting this year as last.

Jessie's parents had also both attended – an event which Jessie declared to be as remarkable as her winning an award. Mr Delaney spent the entire evening staring down at the smartphone in his hands, presumably sending messages, checking his mail and generally conducting his business as if he was still at the office. It was only when his wife poked a bony elbow into his ribs that he looked up, put the phone down momentarily in his lap, and applauded Jessie, who was on stage, receiving her certificate for the best art student in grade 8. Mrs Delaney, a very thin woman with an oddly tight face, applauded with her fingers straight and her arms extended, so that her long fingernails flashed crimson in the dim light and the gold bracelets on her arms jangled noisily.

Before the ceremony began, Jessie had gone over to greet them in the foyer of the hall. Sam had watched as Mr Delaney gave Jessie an almost perfunctory hug before glancing back down at the screen of his phone while Mrs Delaney kissed the air loudly on either side of Jessie's face. Sam went off in search of her own father and when next she saw the Delaneys, they were hissing at each other in angry whispers while Jessie stood off to the side – grim-faced and repeatedly winding and unwinding a piece of cotton around the button on one cuff of her blazer sleeve.

Sam's father, who was not one of Mrs Grieve's VIPs, sat in the fourth row. He looked a little tired to Samantha, and she thought he might actually be nodding off to sleep behind his spectacles during one of the more boring speeches, but he sat bolt upright when the awarding of prizes began, and beamed widely and applauded loudly as Sam received award after award. Jessie hooted noisily as Sam was given the overall top student award in addition to the awards for most of their individual subjects, and Mrs Grieve sent a reproving stare in her direction before smiling indulgently at Sam while she shook her hand and announced to the audience that Sam was the worthy recipient of the Clifford House Full Scholarship Award and was justifying the school's faith in her with her excellent results.

"Though, of course," said Mrs Grieve, smiling smugly, "excellent results are perhaps more the norm at this superior institution than they are at other schools, we do still like to recognise exceptional achievement and no-one is more pleased than I when this means that less fortunate students can benefit from attending Clifford thanks to the ongoing financial support of our parent body and generous alumni." She swept a hand in acknowledgement to the front rows.

Her face burning with embarrassment at Mrs Grieve's comment, Sam walked quickly off the stage as soon as the headmistress released her grip on Sam's elbow. Mr Delmonico sat at the end of the row of teachers, staring at Sam with a raised eyebrow and a speculative, almost disbelieving gaze. She looked down quickly at her shoes and concentrated on not falling down the stairs at the side of the stage. It was hard to see the dimly lit steps around the stack of large certificates clutched in her hands.

As she walked back to her seat, she looked over to where her father sat smiling proudly. There was the slightest hint of sadness in the glance they exchanged, and Sam knew that he wished, just as much as she did, that her mother was still alive to celebrate Sam's achievement. It had been four years since Mrs Steadman had passed away from cancer and although Sam's grief had dimmed to a dull, background sadness, there were times, like tonight, when her longing for her mother was a sharp ache in her chest.

She was so lost in her thoughts as she manoeuvred between the chairs on the way back to her seat that she did not notice the foot that Cindy Atkins stuck out into her path at the last moment. She tripped, managed to keep herself from sprawling headfirst into the narrow aisle between the award winners and the parents, but her certificates flew out of her hands and slid under some chairs. She had to grub about on the dusty wooden floor trying to retrieve them, all the while aware of Cindy's sniggering sneer of burning hatred behind her.

Eventually back in her chair, and trying to brush the worst of the dust off the certificates with a tissue, she discovered that, attached to the back of each certificate was a generous book voucher for the bookshop in Izintaba. This delighted her so much that she forgot her embarrassment and spent the rest of the awards evening in a pleasant daydream about which books she would buy when next in town.

Early the next morning, yawning and heavy-eyed from their late night the evening before, Sam, Jessie, Nomusa and about half a dozen other girls, climbed onto the bus that would take them on the A.A.S. excursion to the rock art site at Devil's Peak. Ms Zenobia, stood up at the front of the bus, her long, thick black hair streaming out over a bright purple and orange tie-dyed smock and explained the arrangements for the day.

Sam paid close attention to these, even making a few notes on the hand-out they had been given, but Jessie

48

rested her head against the windowpane and seemed to be dozing. When the bus slowed down, turned off the curving mountainous road and turned onto the gravel driveway of another school, Ms Zenobia said, "And so that's why we're stopping here at Clifford Heights to collect those boys of their Art Club who are interested in coming on today's excursion."

Jessie opened her eyes immediately, sat up straight and peered out of the window to where a handful of boys stood waiting in the school car park.

"Is that–? It is! It's Dan," said Jessie, her voice rich with disbelief.

"And Apples," said Sam.

"Who would've guessed it," said Nomusa quietly, smiling to herself.

The boys ambled over to the bus and climbed in. Dan and Apples, both in faded jeans and T-shirts, walked down the aisle and dropped into seats near the girls.

"Greetings, fellow artists," said Dan, grinning at Jessie's shocked face.

"Hi," said Apples.

"Since when are you into art?" asked Jessie suspiciously. "I've never heard you express the vaguest interest."

"Me neither," said Sam.

"Shows how little you know me," said Dan with a wounded sniff. "I am, and always have been, deeply appreciative of great beauty," he said to Jessie.

"Uh hmm?" said Nomusa, nodding.

"Phffft," said Jessie, incredulously.

"And you, Apples?" asked Sam. "Are you also an aficionado of great beauty?"

"Heck, no! He's got no taste – he just came to see–" began Dan.

"Dan dragged me along," interrupted Apples, running a hand through his black hair.

They all looked at each other for a few moments. Then Nomusa giggled, cleared her throat and said, "Well, this should be interesting."

The drive to the campsite at the base of Devil's Peak took the better part of an hour. The narrow road wound steadily higher through the foothills, passing a few small villages, their simple mud and stone huts topped with corrugated-iron roofs weighted down by old tyres and ripening pumpkins. Once the bus stopped suddenly to allow a handful of cattle to cross the road under the watchful guidance of a small boy wearing ragged clothes and carrying a long stick. He stared at the children in the bus, the expression in his eyes unfathomable. It seemed strange and made Sam uncomfortable to notice the contrast between their own privileged lives at Clifford and the hand-to-mouth existence of those living just a few kilometres down the road.

The road climbed steadily higher as they entered the uKhahlamba Drakensberg Mountains Park. Sam, Apples and Nomusa spent the time catching up on news and trading horror stories about their teachers. Dan and Jessie rapidly got involved in a discussion on art. Dan, Sam noticed, let Jessie do most of the talking, but occasionally he dumbfounded her by tossing in a phrase like, "moral ambiguity is the essence of post-modern artistic expression" or "using impasto techniques with oils permits a chiaroscuro of light". Sam did not understand a word of it, and rather thought that Dan did not either. She suspected that he had memorised the phrases from some book – perhaps *Art Appreciation for Dummies*.

When they all clambered off the bus, some swinging

small rucksacks onto their backs and pulling hats onto their heads, Jessie looked around as if in hopes of spotting the cave immediately. She groaned when Ms Zenobia handed out bottles of water and informed them that the hike to the cave would take about an hour, perhaps more. She introduced them to their guide, Khosi, a short, slender woman carrying a walking stick and dressed in the khaki uniform of KZN park rangers. Khosi said that they would be joined on their hike by some tourists who had also come to see the art and pointed to a group of five people who were walking over to join them.

Two of the group, a young man and woman who held hands and were obviously very much in love with each other, looked and sounded South African, but the other three were distinctly foreign. A tall, angular man, with thin blonde hair and the prawn-pink skin of a European who has already been fried by the African sun, had a large camera slung around his neck and wore leather sandals, with socks, on his feet. Sam stared, fascinated, at the spot where the leather thong pushed in the sock between his big and second toes.

"He's surely not going to try to climb the mountain in that?" she asked Nomusa.

Apparently the guide had the same concern and had a loud exchange with the tourist, who spoke a bare minimum of English with a strong German accent and did not understand that the word takkies meant trainers. Eventually the guide pointed at everyone else's shoes and then at the man's and then at the mountain rising above them. He nodded in understanding, said, "Ja, Ja" and changed into a pair of trainers which he extracted from his backpack. Encouraged, the guide then pointed at her own and everyone else's hats, and then up at the sun, already hot in the wide, blue sky, and then at the man's bare head.

"Nein, nein, is good, is A-OK," he said, shaking his head and rubbing his hair.

The guide shrugged, checked the remaining two tourists, a man in a safari suit and a colourfully dressed woman, with the impassive gaze of someone who has seen a great many strange things and was not about to be startled by oddly dressed foreigners, and then headed over to where a white-painted rock marked the beginning of the trail. She drew their attention to a glass-covered noticeboard where a boldly printed sign informed them that they were in a protected World Heritage Site, warned that littering, hunting, fishing and the making of fires were forbidden, and threatened dire consequences for anyone caught damaging any part of the environment. She pointed at the "no fires" sign – a line drawn through a lit match – and then looked pointedly at the man. He grinned sheepishly, then stubbed out the fat cigar he had been smoking and tossed the butt into a nearby baboon-proof rubbish bin.

"This is it, honeybuns, we're off on our adventure," said the man loudly to the woman. His accent was distinctly American, from somewhere in the South, Sam thought and had her guess confirmed almost immediately when he guffawed and added, "We ain't in Kansas, anymore, Dorothy!"

"We sure ain't, sugar," she replied.

"Holy cow," said Jessie, who had been so busy trying to quiz Dan on Impressionism that she had only just caught sight of the extraordinary couple.

The woman, somewhere in her late thirties or early forties, Sam estimated, wore a large floppy white straw hat with a broad ribbon which tied under her chin, and a giant pair of pink framed sunglasses. What little could be seen of her long face was pretty in a horse-faced way. An excellent set of gleaming, white teeth flashed beneath lips sticky with fuchsia lipstick whenever she smiled, and her jaw moved from side to side as she chewed on her gum. Occasionally she blew a large purple bubble and then popped it with one of the hot pink talons at the end of her fingers. The nails had to be false – they were longer even than Mrs Delaney's. On her feet was a well-worn pair of hiking boots. Their suitable practicality contrasted markedly with her pair of micro denim shorts and her tight, vividly coloured shirt. The brilliant oranges, reds and yellows, the lurid pink and turquoise blue of its Hawaiian design of flowers and exotic birds stood out against the muted browns and dull greens of the end-of-summer veld like a dazzling jewel against desert sand. It was as if a flamboyant jungle parrot had landed, chattering, among them.

Her "sugar", a portly man whom Sam presumed was her husband, was dressed quite differently. He wore a khaki-coloured short-sleeved shirt and shorts, scuffed and sturdy leather hiking boots, a battered knapsack and an impressive black moustache which curled at the ends. He looked like he was set for a nineteenth-century elephant safari, an impression ruined only by the twenty-gallon cowboy hat with leopard-skin trim that he wore on his head instead of a pith helmet, and the large cellphone which he stowed in the knapsack.

At the guide's suggestion, the students from the two schools went first up the mountain trail, and the tourists followed behind. They set off up a small dirt pathway which snaked through waist-high grass, dotted with tiny purple and blue wildflowers. Samantha, who frequently hiked in the Berg with her brothers and father, happily took the lead, but it soon became clear that Apples, who was walking immediately behind her, had a longer stride and so she stepped aside to let him go ahead of her. She followed, with Nomusa behind her, then Jessie, while Dan brought up the tail of their little group. Every so often Dan stopped for a few moments. When Jessie noticed and quizzed him about this, he merely smiled and said he was enjoying the view.

At first, the pathway was marked by regular white-painted rocks which had been placed on the side. Small wooden arrows pointed down other pathways which branched off to the side, signposting the way to Crystal Falls, Echo Gorge and Dragon Rock, but after a while, the markers disappeared. The guide lead them off up one of the unmarked tracks that branched off the main pathway, then took a succession of twists and turns.

"This site is sure well-hidden. I'm glad we've got a guide," said Sam. "We'd never find the cave on our own – or the way back down again!"

From behind her, Sam could hear Jessie grumbling.

"I signed up for an art appreciation society, not a mountaineering club!"

A little while later she complained, "How much further can this possibly be? We must almost be in Lesotho by now!"

When they paused for a short rest under a thorn tree, she said, "Perhaps one of you could just take a photo and bring it back to show me, and I'll rest here – in the shade."

"Suck it up, cupcake," was Dan's unsympathetic response.

The last part of the hike was very steep. Nomusa

54

scrambled over the rocks nimbly and seemed as fit and fresh at the end of the hike as she had been at the beginning. Sam was panting and was grateful when Apples leant her a hand to climb over a last enormous boulder and into the rocky overhang of the cave. Jessie emerged at the top of the great boulder – with Dan pushing her up from behind – red-faced, sweaty and too out of breath to utter more than a feeble gasp for "Water!"

They sat for a few minutes, catching their breath, drinking water and admiring the view of the valley and surrounding mountains from their high vantage point. Samantha looked around her with interest. The "cave" was really a wide hollow, which extended just a metre or two into the side of the mountain. The overhang – a large flat section of grey rock, covered in moss and multi-coloured lichen – stretched out over a level section of floor and would provide a sort of roof to anyone taking shelter under it. Right now she was enjoying its shade, but it took only a little imagination to see how, hundreds of years ago, a tribe of San hunters may have sheltered from rain, wind and perhaps even the occasional snowfall in this very spot.

The young couple sat on a log at one end of the shelter, staring into each other's faces with lovesick looks. The tall German man picked a large leaf off a nearby bush and began fanning his sun-burned face with it.

"No, you are not allowed to pick leaves or flowers, this is a reserve. Also," Khosi addressed them all, "you must not take any rocks or stones, or any kind of remains or fossils if you find them here. And no graffiti."

Was it Sam's imagination, or did the man look disappointed at this? She wondered if he had been planning to scavenge for mementos, or to carve his name into the rock-face where, she noted with disgust, some ignorant oafs already had. Some of the graffiti carried dates from the 1800s. Apparently, Sam mused, terminal stupidity was not a modern phenomenon.

"This is a heritage site, which must be protected. Take only photographs," the guide smiled at the tourists, "and leave only footprints."

"Lawdy-lawd, but it sure is hot up here. I'm missing my air-conditioning, honeybuns, and my cherry-cola," said the colourful woman, who had been the last to scramble up into the shelter though, to Samantha's surprise, she did not seem at all out of breath.

"Now, sugar, be reasonable. Y'all cain't have air-conditionin' and a mini-bar out in the middle of mother nature. Besides, this here ain't hot. On a summer day in Texas," the American man said, addressing the other hikers, "it can get hot enough to fry an egg on the sidewalk . 104 degrees – and that's in the shade! This here's just a little warm, is all. Well, lookee there!" He pointed to the back of the shelter, to the section of wall which would be most protected from the elements. "Ain't that a sight for sore eyes, Dorothy: real, honest-to-goodness Bushman paintings!"

7

Damage

Khosi, the guide, stepped in front of the sandstone rock wall where the San art was painted and asked, "Does anyone know about the San people?"

Sam nodded, but she was the only one who did.

"Why don't you tell us a bit about them, Sam," said Ms Zenobia.

"Uhm, OK," said Sam. "Well, they were one of the indigenous tribes of people who lived in southern Africa thousands of years ago. They were nomads, who moved from place to place hunting animals like impala and eland, and also gathering roots, fruits and berries for food. They sometimes took shelter in caves like this, but they didn't build permanent dwellings or keep herds of animals, or farm crops. They didn't really have any sense of ownership and so they would just hunt cattle that belonged to the Nguni tribes, and later to the European settlers, and that lead to conflict and the San were driven out of this area and hunted almost to extinction. I think some of their descendants still live in the Kalahari desert, in Namibia and Botswana."

"Very good," said Khosi.

"How do you know all this stuff?" whispered Jessie.

"Because the San had no written language," the guide continued, "the only way we can learn about this gentle, spiritual people is from these paintings which are found at many sites in South Africa: in the Berg, in Limpopo, and even in the Karoo. And every year we are finding more. Come closer and have a look at these paintings and I will explain them."

They all shuffled forward and looked at the sandstone wall where strange figures and designs were painted in deep reds and browns, mustard yellow, faded white and black pigment. Some of the paintings were clearly of animals. Samantha could easily recognise the form of the enormous eland with its distinctive horns, and one, she thought, might have been a depiction of an elephant. Most of the human figures seemed to be of hunters – carrying bows, arrows and sticks, but some were strangely formed – elongated, with animal heads and human bodies, or weird praying mantis-like limbs, or were leaping through the air with unnaturally long legs.

"For their paint, the San artists used different materials. The reds and yellows came from crushed ochre rock found in this area, black paint was made from charcoal and soot, white was made mostly from clay and other minerals. It fades the easiest. To make the paints stick and the colours last, the artist would mix the colour with animal fat, egg white, plant sap, urine and even blood."

"Cool!" said Jessie who was creeping closer and closer to the paintings.

"Here are pictures of the hunters," Khosi pointed at the figures carrying bows. "See here and here," she pointed to faint stripes, "these are the arrows travelling to the eland." She pointed to the images of the beautiful buck, with its distinctive reddish-brown back, white underbelly and face, and straight black horns.

"You can actually see eyelashes on this eland!" said Jessie, who had crouched down and was studying the fine details on the paintings with fascinated interest.

"This," Khosi pointed to one of the part-human, part-animal figures, "is called a therianthrope."

"A therianthrope," Sam repeated, committing the word to her memory.

"A therry-anne-who?" asked Dan.

"A therianthrope," repeated Khosi. "They are pictures of a shaman who is in a trance state and has become like the antelope."

"Oh my!" said the American woman. "Did you hear that, Mitch? Shamans!"

"I hear it, my darlin', and I see it. And what I see is a fine example of primitive art, damn fine." Mitch gave a long appreciative whistle.

Sam looked at the man in the Stetson hat and was amazed to see that he was now keying something into his phone. Surely he must realise that there would be no reception up here? When he then aimed the phone at the rock wall and pressed a button, Sam realised he must have been accessing the camera function on his phone. Meanwhile, the tall German tourist, who was standing next to Sam, was taking pictures with his expensive-looking camera, focusing the long lens and snapping off shot after shot. He studied the results on the digital display with dissatisfaction, however, and then began to rummage in his backpack.

"They are not very good, the colours," he said.

"Yes, when they were first painted, hundreds of years ago, they would have been very beautiful and the colours bright and strong. But the sun and the wind and the rain have faded the colours and the details. There are many ways the paintings are damaged. Some people have scratched at the paintings, sometimes Sangomas – Zulu healers – take scrapings for powerful muti and even when people touch the paintings," here she gave Jessie a warning look, "then the oils on our fingers can damage the art." Jessie inched backwards on her haunches and conspicuously put her hands behind her back. "Some paintings have even been cut out of the rock by thi-"

Just then, the man next to Sam flicked out his arm, and a spray of water flew from his bottle and splashed onto the paintings. Jessie fell backwards onto her bottom in surprise and everyone gasped in shock, staring at the painted images, their colours now brighter and more vivid beneath the water running down the rock wall, and dripping onto the dusty floor of the shelter.

"Ah, that is better. Good colour, ja? Strong!" said the man, snapping off more pictures, completely oblivious to the horrified faces turning towards him.

"You damned fool! How dare you?" shouted the Texan, knocking the camera out of the man's hands. "Hasn't Cosy just' told us how water damages and fades the paintings? What are you? Double-barrelled stupid?"

Now it was the German's turn to look surprised. Dorothy advanced on him until she stood right in front of him. She lifted her sunglasses up, the better to glare at him, poked a sharp, pink fingernail into his chest and said, "It's fools like y'all who destroy the art heritage of the world! Don't you know how rare this work is? How valuable? How many people would kill to-"

"Nein! No … I just … but … it's only a little bit of water, to make a better picture," stammered the man, edging away from her.

"What you have done has damaged this painting. I will need to report you and you will be fined," said Khosi. Her voice was stern and her face serious as she extracted an official-looking form from her knapsack, took the worried German aside and began filling in details. The South African couple took advantage of the moment to step away from the group and get in a few more kisses. A very distressed-looking Ms Zenobia fanned at the wet wall with her pages of notes, while Dan, Apples and the girls began talking quietly among themselves.

"How stupid can you get?" said Apples.

"It's unbelievable! Wasn't he listening to a word she said?" said Sam.

"It's just selfish," said Nomusa. "He wants a nice picture and can't be bothered what damage he causes to get it. It's not his problem – at the end of the holiday he goes home, and a little bit more of our heritage is lost."

"Even the Americans knew how bad that was. That man is a fool and a moron, Mitch and Dorothy are right," said Jessie, glaring over her shoulder at the offender, who was now signing the bottom of a completed form. Then she took out her sketchbook and pencils, and began making drawings of the paintings.

"Yeah," said Dan. "Though who would have figured them for such hectic defenders of art? They hardly look like the cultured type."

Sam looked at the odd couple who were standing a little bit apart, talking to each other. She, too, had been surprised at their strong reaction. Perhaps, despite their appearance, they really were nature enthusiasts and protectors of the environment. As if to disprove this thought, the woman chose that moment to extract a fresh stick of gum from the pack in her pocket. She unwrapped it, popped the gum into her mouth, then crumpled the silver wrapper and dropped it to the ground where she stood.

Sam's jaw dropped. Honestly – it was no wonder the Parks officials kept the exact location of these heritage sites hidden, and only allowed excursions with official guides, if this was how visitors treated the environment. Sam walked the few steps over to where the couple stood with their backs to her and bent down to pick up the litter.

"Ok, that's these captured," the stout man was saying. "That makes three–"

"Excuse me for interrupting, but I think you dropped this," said Sam. She smiled and spoke sweetly, but there was a steely glint in her grey eyes as she handed the wrapper to Dorothy.

"Oh my goodness gracious me! How careless of me, hon! Let me put it straight into my backpack right away. Take only pictures, leave only footprints – ain't that right?" she burbled apologetically, but Sam was not listening. She was staring at the phone in the man's hands. It looked new and modern, but was larger than the phones Sam was used to seeing her friends use, and it had a stubby aerial sticking out of the top-right corner. On the screen were two lines of long numbers, displayed against the background of what looked like a map from Google Earth.

Mitch, who had turned around when Sam spoke, now saw her looking at the instrument in his hand. He pressed a button and the screen cleared.

"What's that?" asked Sam.

"Why, it's just an old phone, sugar." He smiled widely as he spoke, but Samantha thought she had seen a brief flash of anger at her interruption.

"The numbers, I mean?"

"No numbers, honey, just pictures. It's a hobby of mine and my little lady's," he gave his wife a squeeze and she squealed and giggled. "We like to keep a record of all the places we go. We take pictures and then when we get home, we throw a big old steak on the barbeque and invite all our friends around and have us a good old picture show. And we put on a star on a hee-yuge map on the wall of the living room. It shows all the places we've been. Why, we've been all over the world, haven't we, Dorothy? Last year we went to Paris."

"That's Paris, France!" exclaimed Dorothy. "And we also went to the Lasco caves, and Morocco – though that's not in France, of course, even though they speak it – and even to Alice Springs – that's in Australia. Did you know they have crocodiles there?"

Samantha was about to ask another question, but just then Ms Zenobia called them over and told them it was time to start the hike back down to base. Again, the youngsters lead the way. The disgraced tourist brought up the rear, muttering unhappily under his breath. The incident with the water had spoiled the outing for them somewhat but, back on the bus, Dan and Jessie were soon happily criticising the tourist again.

"I mean, how would he feel if we defaced his country's art – tell me that? If we went to Germany – Munich, say, or Frankfurt – and waltzed into a museum and chucked a bucket of water onto a Van Gogh painting?"

"Van Gogh was a Dutch painter, Dan, not a German," said Jessie.

"OK, onto a Picasso, then."

"Spanish!"

"The Mona Lisa?"

"That's by Leonardo da Vinci, an Italian. And it's in the Louvre museum in Paris. Do you actually know anything at all about art?"

"I do, indeed, miss know-it-all. Did *you* know that Cubism was the vanguard of the avant-garde movement in Europe? Ha! Got you there, didn't I?"

"Oh, give me a break!" laughed Jessie, and began throwing jelly beans at him. Soon it was a free-for-all sweet-fight in the bus. Samantha, who was deep in thought, only joined in when Apples hit her in the ear with a green jelly bean. She threw it back at him, as hard as she could, but he ducked and the bean sailed right to the front of the bus where it hit the back of Ms Zenobia's head. By the time she had fished it out of her thick, black hair, examined it, and turned around suspiciously to find the culprit, Dan, Apples, Nomusa and Sam were sitting still and staring quietly over the window, and Jessie had hidden her face behind her sketchpad.

That night, at supper in the school dining room, Samantha and Nomusa were amazed to see Jessie collecting the individually wrapped butter pats from the bread baskets on the table and dropping them into a plastic bag. She twisted the top of the bag closed and then secreted the package in a handbag which she had

64

apparently brought to the dinner table for this express purpose.

"Do you think they'd give me a raw egg if I asked them nicely?" she asked Sam and Nomusa, gesturing to where the kitchen staff were carrying empty plates back into the kitchen. When she got no answer, Jessie looked from Sam to Nomusa.

"What?" she challenged, making a face at their puzzled expressions. "I'm getting the raw materials to make pigments for my rock art."

"Don't you think butter and eggs will make your paper soggy? And rot it?" asked Nomusa.

"I won't be painting on *paper*. I'll paint on a wall of our dwelling, like they did – those San artists."

"You're going to paint on the walls of our dorm room?" asked Sam.

"Don't be thick. What if I got caught? What if that snooping Cindy saw it and ratted us out again?"

"Us?" asked Nomusa.

"I'm going to paint it inside that sloping cupboard at the back of the room. I mean, it's kind of like a cave, isn't it? And I can't see Matron McKensie or The Grievous creeping and peeping about in there. And if we move rooms next year, and someone else finds it, who's to say who painted it or even when it was painted? Anyway, it's authentic art, not graffiti."

"Yeah, maybe they'll think that a San artist once attended Clifford House, and painted the walls of the cupboard where he lived," said Sam with mild sarcasm. Secretly she was just thankful that Jessie was not planning to paint surreal oily, eggy scenes onto a school noticeboard, or Delmonico's smart-board. Really, she thought, for Jessie, this was quite a tame plan. Her relief was short-lived, however.

"So the butter will be my fat, and I can probably get an egg from the kitchen. I'll nick some white clay from art class. And that just leaves… Well, that's easy enough," said Jessie, picking up a sharp knife and bending under the table where she rolled one leg of her jeans up over a knee and muttered, "Hey Sam, got anything I can put the blood in?"

8

Good news

"Catch!"

Startled out of deep concentration, Sam only just managed a fumbling catch of the blur of colour before it hit her head. It was a cool Sunday evening in March. Through the window, the sunset was staining the sky with scarlet and coral sweeps of cloud, but Sam had her back turned to the beauty. She was sitting cross-legged on her bed in the dorm room, and had been staring hard at the science textbook lying open on the bedspread in front of her, without taking in a word of it, when Jessie came into the room, throwing what she now saw was a tube of Smarties at her.

"Eat those instead of your fingernails, will you? No offence, Sam, but your hands are starting to look gross."

Samantha stared down at her hands. Jessie was right, they did look pretty awful. She had bitten every nail down to the pink bit, and two of her nails had painful whitlows – a consequence of her habit of tearing off bits of skin to the side of her nails when she was worrying.

She had been worrying a lot, Sam admitted to herself, as she popped the lid on the tube and poured the colourful, sugar-shell-coated chocolate buttons out into a pile on her bedspread. So far this year, school had not been going well. It was not, she reflected, that everything had been going *badly*, precisely. In fact, most things were just fine. She still enjoyed Biology and Geography lessons with the competent Miss Stymen, who had taught the same subjects to them the previous year, and Mr De Wet was his usual sweet and funny self. She had nothing like Jessie's talent, but Sam still looked forward to art classes with Ms Zenobia as a welcome and creative break from the more academically challenging subjects. She was even finding accountancy, a subject which usually bamboozled her with its debits and credits, its journals and ledgers and cashbooks, to be comparatively easy. When she tuned out Mr Dlamini's constant rhythmic drumming on every surface in his classroom – including, occasionally, on a student's head – she found she could follow his explanations quite well.

She had only two new teachers this year. Mrs Pillay now taught them English and History, instead of Mrs Borman – the large, loud and melodramatic teacher of the previous year. Mrs Pillay was pretty, sweet and nice – too nice for the high school students who had taken a mere half-hour lesson to establish that here was a teacher who would never order instead of ask, never suspect the worst when she could believe the best, never punish when she could forgive. Every week, the class grew more restless and less well-behaved. Samantha suspected that a blowout and a clampdown were on the way soon. Either Mrs Pillay would have to take charge, or she would have a nervous breakdown – one of the two. Sam hoped it would be the former, rather than the latter, because Mrs Pillay was really very kind, and Sam wanted to hang onto all the kindness she could get right now. And that was due to the other new teacher.

Mr Delmonico – The Demonico as they all now called him – had turned Maths and Science classes into living nightmares for Sam. He was petty, pedantic and arrogant and, Sam thought, he seemed to take particular pleasure in picking on her. The worst part was that because she was so stressed in his classes, she was not concentrating well and so she often missed what he was trying to explain, or misunderstood his ridiculously complicated instructions. The result was that she got confused, made silly mistakes, and gave him even more reason to point out her faults.

Her dread of the hours of feeling stupid and inadequate in his neat and sterile classroom had grown until she now only had to see *Maths* or *Science* written in the next timetable slot in order to start feeling queasy. He had deducted several more marks for the state of her books and files, and she just knew that he was giving her a poor score for "classroom participation". This was even more reason why she had to do exceptionally well in Tuesday's Science cycle test, in order to pull up her marks. She *must* focus. She must study, and not allow her mind to wander off like this!

"What are you doing?" Jessie's voice sounded both perplexed and mildly concerned.

Sam looked down at her fidgeting hands. As if of their own accord, they had sorted the Smarties into their different colours, arranged them in exact, matched rows, and in descending order from the longest column on the left (the browns of which there were the most), to the shortest column on the right (the yellows).

"I don't know," said Sam absently. "Sorting, I guess."

"Is there any point in asking you why?"

"Because they're all mixed up! It bothers me. There's no order to them. Look – they don't even put the same number of each colour in the tube."

"Sam – chillax already!"

Sam used her ruler to edge away the extra Smarties. Now each column had exactly the same number of
candies in it. She straightened the rows and columns
so that they formed a neat, perfectly symmetrical grid,
and, for a brief moment, she felt a sense of relief, like
things were under control. Then she spotted the pile
of leftovers – uneven numbers of different colours that
could not be matched or formed into any kind of well-
ordered pattern – and she frowned crossly at them.

"What are you supposed to do with the odd ones
that are left over?"

"Uh, I don't know, Sam. Maybe … eat them?"

"I can't eat those, there aren't even numbers of
them," Sam muttered.

"What would happen if you ate uneven numbers?"

"I don't know… Anything could happen… It feels
like something bad…"

"Sam, what on earth are you talking about?"

"Besides, I couldn't eat anything – I feel sick."

She pushed the ragtag pile of candies away and carefully scooped up the grid of Smarties into the tube, first
a row, then a column, first a row, then a column. She
was a little worried that there would not turn out to
be the same number of rows and columns, and sighed
with relief when she counted off the last row. There had
been exactly eight rows and eight columns. That felt
good – safe, somehow. But then she realised the colours
were all mixed up in the tube again. For a moment she
wanted to pour the candies out and start separating and
arranging them again, but she stopped herself and made
her hands put the tube down on her bedside cupboard.

"Why do they have to mix up all the colours like that? Why do they do it?"

"So nutters like you can separate them of course," said Jessie. She was not smiling; she was looking at Sam with something like real concern in her expression.

"Listen, Sam, are you alright? I mean, I know Demonico's getting to you, but are you OK? You're not cracking up, or anything, are you?"

Samantha was spared having to answer. At that moment, Nomusa bounced into the room with a wide grin on her face.

"Do you want the good news or the good news?" she asked, waving two pieces of paper at them.

"Surprise me," said Jessie dryly, casting a last, worried look at Sam before turning her attention to Nomusa.

"The St John Ambulance people are coming on Saturday morning to do a first-aid course – here at the school!" Nomusa was beaming from ear to ear.

Jessie looked like she was still waiting to hear the good news part of this, but Sam said, "That sounds like fun."

"Yes – there'll be three real paramedics training us. And it will be practical, not just theory. We'll learn wound dressings, infection control, even CPR – we get to practise on dummies," said Nomusa, reading off the paper. "It starts at eight, and I know it's your birthday on Saturday, Sam, and you probably want a lie-in, but are either of you interested in joining me?"

"Are students from any other schools coming – Clifford Heights, or anything?" asked Jessie.

"I don't think so – why do you ask?"

"No reason, I just wondered."

"So how about it?" asked Nomusa.

"Pus and blood and kissing dummies? Tempting ... but no, thanks," said Jessie, flopping back into her pillows.

"You can sign me up," said Sam. "What was the other good news?"

"Oh, right, yes. There's going to be a social – a dance – right here at the school, and," she cast a glance at Jessie, "Clifford Heights *are* invited to that!"

"Awesome!" said Jessie, sitting up straight. "Are we supposed to invite partners?"

"It doesn't say so, but I guess you could. If you haven't got Dan's number, Sam will give it to you," said Nomusa, smiling.

"What do you mean? I didn't say I– I'm not–" stammered Jessie.

"What?" said Sam, looking in amazement from Nomusa to Jessie. "Do you like Dan, now? Since when?"

"No! Dan? Me? As if! Phfff!" said Jessie, ducking her head.

Sam felt as though a bucket of cold water had just been splashed on her face. Was it true – was Nomusa right? Had she, Sam, been so preoccupied with her own worries that she had not noticed that one of her best friends was interested in her own brother? And did Dan feel the same way about Jessie?

"I'm supposed to give you a message from Ms Zenobia, Jessie," a voice interrupted Sam's astonished thoughts. She looked up to see Cindy Atkins and Kitty Bennington standing at the doorway. Sam wondered how long they had been there and what they might have heard. Cindy, whose long, blonde hair fell in soft curls over her shoulders, was wearing a shocking-pink T-shirt with the words "Killer Barbie" printed in big glittery letters over the chest, and was looking intently at Jessie.

"So give it to me, Barbiegirl," said Jessie.

"Come and get it," sang Cindy, leaning against the doorjamb and waving a folded piece of paper at Jessie. Her eyes swept derisively around the room, pausing briefly on the small pile of Smarties on Sam's bed and then coming to rest on the notice Nomusa was holding.

"So, you've heard about the dance. What are you planning on going as?"

"What do you mean?" asked Nomusa.

"It's a *fancy dress* – can't you read? Perhaps you should go as the local village idiot. You–" she pointed a finger at Sam, "should definitely go as poor little Cinderella – no mummy and no money, see? And you," she sneered at Jessie, "would be perfect for one of the ugly sisters, who can't get a date. Oh, no – wait. I'm sorry," she said in a falsely sweet voice, "it's a *fancy* dress. That means you're supposed to go as something you're *not*." Cindy sniggered and, beside her, Kitty laughed as if this was the funniest thing she had ever heard.

"Oh, get lost!" said Sam.

Jessie jumped up from the bed, snatched the note from Cindy's hand and closed the door in her face.

"One of these days…" she said warningly. She grabbed her cellphone and began to type madly, her thumbs flying over the keyboard.

"What are you so busy with, there?" Nomusa asked Jessie.

"I'm putting in a rush-order for a new T-shirt."

"I guess I'd better do some studying for the cycle test, too," said Nomusa, walking to her schoolbag and extracting her Science file.

"Yes, and so should you, Jessie, I think it's going to be a stinker," said Sam. Jessie ignored this advice. "And I don't get this section at all. I've never felt so stupid in my life. Do either of you know exactly – I mean, for sure and for definite – how to calculate the mass of a proton?"

Jessie looked up from her phone and said, "Protons have mass? I didn't even know they were Catholic!"

9

Shattered

The next week was one of the worst in Sam's life at Clifford House. Everyone else seemed abuzz with speculation about the upcoming social, and seemed to be enjoying discussing the options for fancy dress outfits, but Samantha's whole focus seemed to have narrowed down to the cycle test. In the last Science lesson before the cycle test, she asked Mr Delmonico to explain how to calculate the mass of protons. He had never, she realised, actually taught them exactly how to do it, he had only provided a brief overview, assigned exercises and then referred them to the textbook for further reading.

"I have already explained that to this class, Miss Steadman, and I am not in the habit of repeating myself. I suggest everyone make sure they understand the process, however, as that section is sure to come up in the test."

"But, sir," said Sam, forcing her voice to stay calm even though frustration was beginning to prick at the back of her eyes, "I don't understand. I've read the notes and the textbook several times, but it would really help if you would just take us through *how* to actually do it, step by step." Around her several other girls were nodding their agreement.

"Miss Steadman," said Delmonico, walking right up to the other side of the lab bench from her, leaning forward and narrowing his dark eyes at her. She could see the thin threads of blue vein through the white skin at his temples.

"The reason you fail to grasp simple processes is because you always get upset, and allow emotion to cloud your reason."

Sam could feel the traitorous tears building in her eyes, and anger at herself rose to join the rage at him. A brief smile flickered over his thin lips, as if her reaction were some sort of victory for him, one he had anticipated. Sam snatched up her ruler as he turned from her to address the class. She wanted to hit him with it – smack in the middle of his neat little head – but instead she began mangling it under the desk, thankful that it was a shatterproof model.

"Not everyone has an intellect suitable to the hard sciences," said Delmonico, as he stepped back to his desk. "Those who are emotional and oversensitive are unsuited to the pure rationality and solid logic of science. I am not particularly surprised at your distress and your incomprehension, Miss Steadman. It is not unusual to find this, in a class of girls. The female brain is, perhaps, ill-equipped for hard facts and figures."

"What!" burst out Sam. Under the desk, the ruler splintered into shards into her hands. She stood up. Cold fury had driven out all thought of tears, and she ignored Jessie and Nomusa who had each grabbed a fistful of her skirt and were trying to tug her back into her seat.

"Did you just say that–"

"Sit!" said Delmonico, his dark eyes glittering, his lips pinched in his pale face.

"I just want to–"

"I said *sit!* Not another word, Miss Steadman, unless you want a demerit added to the ignominy of your falling marks. Sit down and review for your test tomorrow. Heaven knows that you can surely use a little extra study time to improve your substandard performance." He glowered at Samantha, until she sat back on her stool. She glared back mutinously at him.

"Breathe," she heard Nomusa whisper from beside her, "just breathe."

Sam looked down at the notes in front of her. She felt hot and cold at the same time. She felt like killing and she felt like crying. And the printed black words and numbers and function signs on the page in front of her danced like meaningless squiggles, as indecipherable as ancient painted symbols on a cave wall.

The cycle test, the next morning, was as bad as she had expected it to be – perhaps even worse. The questions were difficult, requiring them to have memorised lists of formulas, and they were worded in confusing ways: half the time Sam was not even sure what was being asked, let alone whether she had answered correctly.

Worst of all was her anxiety. It seemed to have grabbed her by the throat at the start of the test, and had not let go. She could not seem to stop her eyes from flashing forward to the next question, even as she struggled with the current one. Every time she finished the answer to a question and ruled a line beneath it, as the Demonico had insisted they should, she began to worry whether she had read the question correctly and answered it right, and she felt compelled to go back and check her answers. Twice, her mind went completely blank and she seriously considered simply walking out the room and going to the toilet to let her roiling stomach have its way. She remembered Nomusa's advice, though, and breathed deeply until she was marginally calmer and could focus on the test again.

Near the end of the test, the idea popped into her head that she had written, somewhere in one of her answers, "You are a demon who tortures children for fun, you sicko!" She spent so much time reading and re-reading each line of her pages of answers, searching for these words, that she didn't finish in time and was still trying to answer the fifth-last question when the invigilating teacher pulled her answer paper away from her.

Nomusa and Jessie cast one look at her tight face after the test and then exchanged a speaking glance in which they silently resolved not to mention the test.

"Tuck-shop!" said Jessie, pulling Sam away from the classroom.

Even chocolate, which Jessie swore was a cure for everything, could not help Samantha feel any better the next day, though. Mr Delmonico singled her out in the Science lesson to inform her he had marked her test paper already; apparently he had not yet looked at anyone else's.

"Your performance was abysmal. You will attend an extra lesson on Saturday morning, between nine and twelve o'clock to review where you went wrong and to try to gain some understanding of this work, before you fall hopelessly behind."

"But, sir!" said Jessie and Nomusa at the same time.

"She's booked on the St John's first-aid course, sir – it's on Saturday morning," said Nomusa.

"And it's her birthday!" said Jessie.

"Be there," said Mr Delmonico.

So on the morning of her fifteenth birthday, Samantha sat through three hours of solitary torture – you could not call the silent, unexplained revision session "teaching", she thought – in the Demonico's classroom, alternately trying to focus on proton-to-electron mass-ratios, and daydreaming about the presents she had received. Nomusa had presented her with a generous voucher to her favourite book shop and Jessie had given her two printed T-shirts: one said *Don't worry – be happy* while the other read *It's all geek to me!* Her mind also kept returning to the unexpected text message received that morning and wishing her a happy birthday. It had been signed, "See you at the dance. Apples".

10

Zombies

It was almost lunchtime when Samantha returned to the Austen House dormitories from the session with Delmonico. Just inside the entrance, she saw Jessie lying at the base of the stairs with Nomusa leaning over her, a large first-aid box at her side. Nomusa was winding a bandage around Jessie's head while Jessie's arms where extended into the air holding her phone.

"Don't cover my eyes, I want to be able to read my messages," Jessie complained, pushing a piece of the stretchy white bandage back up above over her right eyebrow.

"Quit bleating," said Nomusa, "and lie still – you're supposed to be unconscious. Oh, hi Sam, how was the extra lesson?"

"Don't ask," said Sam. "Are you practising your new first-aid skills?"

"Yeah, the course was great. I just wish you could have been there with me."

"Me, too, believe me," said Sam as she perched herself on the lowest step, watching as Nomusa fastened the end of the bandage neatly with a stretchy clasp.

"OK," said Nomusa, patting the thick wadding of bandage on Jessie's head, "that should stop your brains from falling out your skull–"

"Charming," said Jessie.

"–and now I want to try a full leg splint and bandage. Stick out your leg, OK?"

"Whatever." Jessie seemed to be trawling through her emails and text messages.

"What are you going to use for a splint?" asked Sam. She rummaged around in her pockets, brought out a packet of big black gobstoppers, and offered them to her friends before popping one into her own mouth.

"They said we should learn to improvise. You know – use whatever we could find," said Nomusa, looking around at the common room on the ground floor of the dormitory. She spied a hockey stick leaning against the wall behind a large potted palm and fetched it. "This will do nicely."

"I hope you don't expect me to stay in this for long," said Jessie, speaking indistinctly around the gobstopper and watching dubiously as Nomusa began attaching the hockey stick to the side of her leg with an enormously long bandage wound from above her knee all the way down to her ankle.

"What did you do all morning, Jess?" asked Sam.

"Art Appreciation Society meeting with Ms Zenobia."

"Did you tell her about your latest, er, project?" asked Sam, thinking about Jessie's painting forays into the cupboard in their dorm room.

"Not exactly. Anyway, we were learning about rock art in other parts of the world."

"There you go Jessie, done! It's not very neat, but I think it would hold. Now for an arm sling," said Nomusa, but Jessie, who tried several times, and failed, to stand up with her stiffly splinted and bandaged leg, baulked at this.

"You practise on Sam for a while, go on."

"Sure," said Sam, "what do you want me to do?

"Just hold your arm so," said Nomusa, bending Sam's left arm across her chest, "and keep still. I just need to find the sling thingie. It must be in here somewhere." She rummaged in the large, untidy first-aid chest, unpacking tweezers, safety pins, tubes of ointment, blister packs of aspirin, and a couple of small bottles. Jessie picked up one of these, held it against the light to examine it, and began fiddling with it while Nomusa, who had found a triangular piece of cloth, attempted to fasten a sling around Sam's shoulder.

"One thing was really interesting, though. Ms Zenobia said that there was a real problem with the theft of rock art from sites around the world.

"How on earth do you steal art that's painted on a rock wall?" asked Sam.

"She says they chip and chisel out chunks of the rock on which the pictures are painted. Sometimes they even use explosives to blast it out."

"Explosives! Wouldn't those just blow the art to smithereens?" asked Nomusa. She was battling to make the sling fit on Sam. "I don't know – it just seems too small. Unless you're just too tall, Sam."

"Nice, Nomusa, thanks!"

"No, apparently they use it in small amounts in controlled explosions placed in exactly the right spots on the rock to break away entire panels. And then they carry those off."

"Nomusa, some of this stuff is really old – this bottle expired in 1989," said Jessie. Using her teeth, she finally succeeded in opening the little bottle. She lowered her nose to the opening, took an experimental sniff and said, "Ah, mercurochrome. I haven't seen this stuff in forever. My gran always used to put it on Cassie and me when we grazed ourselves."

"But that's terrible!" said Sam.

"I know – we had to walk around with red-stained knees and elbows for weeks at a time. Didn't look half-weird, I can tell you."

"No, I meant about the paintings. It's theft of some of the oldest and most valuable art a country owns. In fact, since the art predates when countries were established, you could say the art belongs to the world. It's a treasure."

"That's why they do it. Seems it's very rare and incredibly valuable, and there are private art collectors all over the world who will pay a whack of money to own authentic rock art. So these international theft syndicates keep stealing and smuggling... Hey, look at me – I'm mortally wounded."

Jessie seemed to be oozing blood from severe wounds. She had poured mercurochrome over one side of her head bandage and had dripped more of the red liquid on her bandaged knee and leg. She was also sticking her tongue – now stained black from the sweets – out of her mouth, whose lips were also smeared with vivid red from when she had opened the bottle. She looked like a rotting zombie.

"Very impressive," said Nomusa, tightening a final knot on the sling on Sam's arm, "but not as impressive as my medical skills."

"Uhm, yes," said Sam. Her arm was now stuck bent double and tied up close to her opposite ear with the too-small triangle of fabric. It was very uncomfortable.

"Your lips are good and black, Sam, but you need some colour, too," said Jessie. She rolled over onto her stomach and then pushed herself upright by walking her hands back along the floor to her stiff legs. She twisted around clumsily, staggered over to Sam and enthusiastically doused the part of the sling nearest Sam's wrist with the remaining drops of mercurochrome.

"Muuccchh better! Much more realistic," she said approvingly. "We could be survivors of an apocalypse. Calls for a photo, I think. Here Nomusa, take a pic with my phone, will you?"

As Jessie hobbled the few steps back to Nomusa, her unbandaged foot twisted under her and she tripped, falling hard to the floor, where she lay cursing and groaning and clutching her "good" ankle. Sam tried to reach over to help, but yelped as she felt a hard tug on the hair at her neck. She realised instantly that the knot of the sling had caught in her hair, "Ow!" she complained, "Ow, ow, ow!"

It was at this precise moment that Matron McKensie walked into Austen House. She clapped eyes on the spectacle of injured, bloody, black-mouthed girls whimpering in obvious pain, and cried, "Help me boab!" She took an uncertain step forward, dropped her clipboard onto Nomusa's sandaled toe, and promptly slumped heavily to the ground in a dead faint.

"Oh, good," said Nomusa, smiling gleefully even while she hopped about on one foot, clutching her wounded toe in the other. "A real patient!"

The weeks running up to the dance were spent by most girls at Clifford House in happy anticipation of the social, and in planning, buying and making costumes. Sam's thoughts were still dominated with worry about Maths and Science and Delmonico, but she tried to get into the spirit of things by chatting to Jessie and Nomusa about their costumes.

"What are you going as, Jessie?"

"I've added some excellent accessories to my T-shirt order. I've got a killer costume planned – just you wait and see," Jessie said with a dramatically evil chuckle, and neither Sam nor Nomusa could get her to say another word about it.

"And you, Nomusa?"

"Well, I've been put in charge of reorganising and restocking the school's first-aid boxes."

"Nice one!"

"Yeah, I really enjoyed that course. I think I might like to take it further – as long as it doesn't interfere with my athletics training and competitions. Anyway, Jessie was right – most of the medical supplies in the first-aid kits are old and expired, and have to be chucked away and replaced. So I wondered if I could make a costume out of the old stuff: there are some surgical masks, bandages, plasters and even a neck brace. I could maybe go as a patient, or even a doctor."

"Go as the doctor, definitely. How about you, Sam?" said Jessie.

"I don't know – I haven't decided, yet," said Sam.

She had not shared with her friends that her main concern about her outfit was that of cost. All around her, girls were ordering costumes, or planning shopping trips with their parents on the weekends. But Sam's pocket money was not enough to buy a pair of socks, let alone a fancy costume, and she did not want to bother her father for money. She knew he struggled to keep them in the private schools and to pay James' university tuition fees; it was only her scholarship that made it possible. The decision to send the Steadman children to excellent – and expensive – private schools had been made when Sam's mother was still alive and earning a good income in her legal practice. Now, with only her dad's salary to support them, times were much tougher and there was no money to spare on frivolities. She would simply have to think of a costume that cost her nothing to assemble, that was all. So far, though, no ideas had occurred to her.

"You'd better get a move on, the dance is next Saturday," said Jessie.

By the time the dance rolled around, Sam had managed to fix herself a costume, but she knew it was a very dull and not very attractive one. She had decided to go as "Lady Justice" a character whom she privately felt would have pleased her mother. Sam had stripped a white sheet off her bed, draped this over one shoulder so that it fell in folds down to the floor, and secured it in place with a belt at the waist. She brushed her hair until it shone, and then left it falling loose down her back. Miss Stymen had very kindly agreed to fetch and lend Sam an old-fashioned set of metal scales – the sort with brass bowls dangling from thin chains – from the Science storeroom, seeming instinctively to understand Sam's reluctance to ask Delmonico for the favour. Sam had borrowed a white silk scarf from Jessie's huge collection of accessories and tied this over her eyes.

"I don't get it," said Jessie, when she saw Sam in her outfit just before they were all to set out to the hall, where the dance was being held. "What are you?"

"I'm Lady Justice. I weigh justice evenly and fairly, see?" Sam held the scales up in one hand, "and I exact punishment for crimes." She held up a rather flimsy, grey, cardboard sword (which she had constructed herself) in the other.

"Oh, OK – I get it!" Samantha could tell she didn't. "But why are you wearing a blindfold?"

"Lady Justice always wears a blindfold, because justice is supposed to be blind – you know, impartial, the same to everyone, not play favourites?"

"Well, just peep over the top, or something, will you? So you can see where you're going. We don't want to give Nomusa another chance to practise her first-aid skills. Speak of the devil – look at *you*, girl!"

Samantha pulled down the blindfold and saw Nomusa had returned from the bathrooms where she had been getting dressed. She was dressed in green surgical scrubs under a white coat, and wore latex gloves, a green surgical cap, mask and matching booties. A real stethoscope was slung around her neck and she was holding a black doctor's bag with a red cross stamped on the outside.

"Dr Gule, I presume?" said Sam, smiling.

"Correct," said Nomusa. "You look good, Sam, just like the picture you showed me."

"Hmm," said Sam, who knew her costume was dead boring. Nomusa was only being her usual, kind self.

"Jessie, you look fierce!" said Nomusa.

"And I feel it, too. Cindy had better not cross me tonight," said Jessie.

"Yeah, I can't wait to see killer Barbie's face when she sees you," laughed Sam.

Jessie looked like a mix between a Goth and a tomb-raider character from a PC game. She wore skinny black jeans and knee-high black leather boots with stiletto heels. A series of realistic-looking replica bowie knives and guns hung from a wide leather belt worn low on her hips. She had gelled her normally curly, short auburn hair and styled it up in sharp spikes, and she wore black lipstick, black nail polish and thick black eyeliner.

The only colour in her whole outfit was the scarlet red where the jagged letters emblazoned diagonally across her ragged black T-shirt spelled out: "Barbie Killer!"

11

Vampires and werewolves

"Let's go," ordered Jessie and they set off for the school hall, where the dance was being held.

Of the three of them, only Nomusa looked truly comfortable in her costume. Jessie was struggling to stay balanced on the killer heels – Sam hoped Nomusa had an ankle brace tucked away in her medical bag, just in case – but she seemed to enjoy snarling at passing students. She even succeeded in scaring a group of younger girls, who were wearing blue face-paint and were dressed as Smurfs, into running away screaming when she lurched out at them from the shadows wielding the largest of her fake knives.

It was fun to see how all the others had dressed up. Poppy Katakouzinous was wearing an angel costume, complete with gauzy wings and a tinsel halo, while Uvani Moodley was almost unrecognisable as Lady Gaga, wearing a dress made from reams of tin foil and a sleek, platinum blonde wig over her own glossy black hair. Mercy Tshabalala was dressed in a long black robe, with a pointed witch's hat perched on her head. When she saw them walking by, Mercy climbed astride the straw broom she had been dragging behind her, pointed a wand (which looked a lot like a chopstick) at Sam, and yelled a series of spells in a screechy, cackling voice.

"Who knew?" said Nomusa, sounding impressed.

As they neared the hall, they began to see some of the boys from Clifford Heights. The sight of hulking, hairy Ronald de Vries in a WWW wrestler's leotard made them all laugh, but Gabriel September, a grade 11 boy with a mischievous grin and a real talent for imitating accents, made a convincing Sherlock Holmes, complete with deerstalker cap, wooden pipe and posh British accent. It looked very odd to see him walking along chatting to someone dressed in a hairy, black gorilla suit.

Carl Atkins – Cindy's brother – was undeniably handsome in swashbuckling pirate's garb. He wore a fake, stuffed parrot on one shoulder and swished a rapier around in the air at them as they approached, calling out: "Ahoy there, wenches!"

"That looks real," said Nomusa disapprovingly, pointing to the weapon.

"I nicked it from the fencing team," said Carl, winking at her. "If I injure anyone, I'll call you, nurse."

"She's a doctor – you sexist git!" said Sam grumpily.

She was already heartily sick of her own costume which, she now realised, was not only boring, but was uncomfortable, too. The scales, heavier than she had first thought they would be, clanked noisily and kept swinging painfully into her ribs, while the sword did not look like it would survive the night. The blindfold was a nuisance – she either had to pull it down to see where she was going, or be lead around by Nomusa like a truly blind person. Jessie was not to be trusted – she would most likely lose focus and lead Sam into a ditch or walk her into a brick wall. Worst of all, nobody seemed to understand her costume: she had to explain over and over again who she was and why she was carrying scales and a sword, and wearing the wretched blindfold.

"It's like nobody has ever heard of Lady Justice," she grumbled to herself, pushing the sheet back onto her shoulder, from where it kept slipping off. Sam saw a student, walking stiff-legged and with arms extended straight in front of her, wrapped from head to toe in white toilet paper, and wondered bitterly to herself why she had not thought of dressing as a mummy.

As they turned the last corner, and began to cross the last stretch of car-park in front of the hall, Jessie pointed and said, "Will you look at that."

Cindy Atkins and her friend Kitty Bennington were standing on the kerb, examining all the girls coming into the hall and eyeing the boys from Clifford Heights, the last of whom were just getting off their school bus, parked a short distance away from the entrance of the hall.

Cindy was wearing a dramatic Cleopatra costume made of shimmering gold fabric. She had styled her hair perfectly straight and beads were intricately woven into the strands bordering her face. A green and golden cobra headdress circled her forehead, and there was a matching circlet around her neck, while a sinuous, golden bracelet in the shape of a snake wound up one arm, from wrist to elbow. She had outlined her ice-blue eyes exotically with slanting lines of black eyeliner, and she looked – there were no other words for it, Sam reflected – stunningly beautiful.

"Look how she's made her friend dress," said Jessie.

Sam now saw that beside Cindy stood Kitty Bennington, and the contrast between the two girls could not have been greater because Kitty was dressed, of all

91

things, as SpongeBob Squarepants. As they drew nearer, Sam could hear what the two were saying.

"Are you sure I look OK, Cindy?" said Kitty, tugging on the goofy-faced rectangles of foam rubber which surrounded her. "I feel a bit silly."

"I've told you, Kitty, you look just lovely! Oh, look, the three mouseketeers," said Cindy, looking at Sam, Nomusa and Jessie.

"Well hi there, Steadman, you look totally lame," said Cindy. She looked Nomusa up and down, but could apparently think of nothing scathing to say, but she did a double-take as she saw the writing on Jessie's shirt.

"And just what is that supposed to mean? 'Barbie Killer' – is that supposed to be directed at me? Because of my shirt?"

"Be afraid, be very afraid. My presence signals death to Barbie girls," said Jessie darkly.

"Oh, pul-leez. I hardly think I need to feel threatened by the likes of *you*. C'mon Kitty, let's go see who's inside."

Cindy sent one last, contemptuous look at the three of them before walking off. She walked sinuously, with a slow, hip-swinging movement while, just behind her, Kitty shuffled along in little paces – her constricting costume apparently did not permit her to take proper steps. They were still gaping after this odd procession when they heard a loud shout.

"Jessie! Watch out! Get back, you three!"

They looked around to see Count Dracula gesturing furiously at them, and stepped back – just in time – out of the path of a van which was careening through the lot. As it screeched to a stop in front of the hall entrance, Sam could see that the words *DJ Dave & the Midnite Toonz* were stencilled on the side of the van. A young man, wearing a black leather jacket and ripped jeans, sprang out of the van and sped into the hall, a stack of CDs wedged precariously under each arm.

The student dressed as Count Dracula ran up to the girls, his red-lined cloak billowing out behind him, and Sam saw to her surprise that it was Dan. Beneath the cloak he wore black jeans and a black shirt, with a white bowtie around his collar.

"Jeez – you gave me a fright! I thought you'd be knocked over. You need to look where you're going, ladies!" This all came out very quickly and quite indistinctly because Dan was also wearing a pair of false, plastic teeth with elongated fangs.

Then Dan got his first good look at Jessie. He flinched, made a noise that sounded like "mmmha!" and took an instinctive step back.

"Wow – scary Jessie!" he said. "I wouldn't want to bump into you down a dark alley."

Jessie's mouth pinched beneath the black lipstick. She looked Dan up and down and then said, "Well, you're no Edward Cullen yourself!" Then she marched off into the hall with her chin in the air, slapping her thigh threateningly with one of the guns, and wobbling only slightly on the stiletto heels.

"Wait! Jessie! I meant you look dark and emo, in, like, a good way," yelled Dan to her. "I mean, I like it!" But Jessie had already disappeared into the throng of people making their way into the hall. Dan cursed and extracted the false teeth from his mouth.

"Edward Cullen?" he asked, looking from Sam to Nomusa.

"He would have leapt out in front of her and saved her by stopping the van with his bare hands," explained Nomusa kindly, before setting off after Jessie.

93

Just then, Dan's friend Apples strolled up to them. He was not wearing any kind of fancy-dress costume that Sam could see – just a pair of old jeans and a white T-shirt – though a badge stating *Mutants Rule* was pinned to the shirt

Patently perplexed, Dan called after Nomusa "Stop the van? How in the heck am I supposed to stop a speeding van with my bare hands?" Then he laid a restraining hand on Sam as she made to follow her friends, and said, "Wait, Sam, hang on a sec – you've got to help me. Who is this Cullen guy? Is he at Clifford? Is he here tonight?"

"Google it," said Sam, laconically. She was still trying to figure out Apples's costume.

Dan held his hand out to the side, like a surgeon demanding a scalpel, and said, "Apples? Smartphone, stat!"

Apples switched on his phone and handed it over, all the while looking at Sam.

"So, Sam, what's news?"

"Oh, nothing much, you know." She sounded, she knew, about as dull and insipid as her costume.

"So how do you spell it?" interrupted Dan, looking expectantly at Sam.

"C-U-L-L-E-N," said Sam, then to Apples: "What's up your side?"

"Nothing exciting. I've decided that rugby is officially the stupidest game on the planet."

"Agreed, mate," said Dan, nodding while his thumbs flew over the keyboard of the phone. "Jeez, there's like a gajillion hits for a search on him. Who *is* this dude?"

"Rugby season started then?" said Sam, ignoring Dan.

"The training sessions have, and they've made it compulsory for all of us."

"Wait, wait, wait – here's a wiki on him! Give me a minute," muttered Dan.

"I like your costume. You're Lady Justice?"

"You got it! You're the only one so far," said Sam, amazed and inordinately pleased. She smiled back at Apples's dimples. "I have to admit, though, I don't get yours."

"I'm a werewolf."

"But you're not dressed as one. I mean, you don't look like one at all."

Apples shrugged and looked up into the night sky, "It's not a full moon."

Samantha laughed out loud at this. "That's so clever – I wish I'd thought of it."

Apples smiled shyly back at her and she saw that he no longer wore braces. His teeth were very white and even, and she noticed for the first time that he had a tiny crescent-shaped scar at one corner of his mouth.

Dan, who had been snorting and making a variety of other sounds indicating strong disgust, now spluttered: "He doesn't even exist! I mean, are you kidding me?" He turned to Sam as if appealing to her common sense. "Is she kidding me? He's not even a real guy – he's a fictional character in a romantic novel. She's cross with me because I'm not like some fantasy blood-sucker!"

"No," Sam said, speaking slowly and clearly, as if to someone of limited intelligence. "She's cross with you because you insulted the way she looked."

This brought Dan up short. For a few moments, he simply stared at Sam.

"You think?" he asked eventually.

"I think," said Sam.

"Huh."

"And I think you've got some *sucking up* to do, mate," said Apples. This time, they both laughed. Dan merely looked stunned.

"See you two later," said Sam and headed off in search of Nomusa and Jessie. She was just a few steps away when she heard, "There you are, Danny-boy!" Looking over her shoulder, she saw Cleopatra descending on Count Dracula. SpongeBob Squarepants was nowhere to be seen.

12

Challenge accepted

Sam bought her ticket in the foyer and had her hand stamped. As soon as she entered the dimly lit hall, she ditched the scales and sword, kicking them under a chair in the back corner, then she turned the scarf into a headband. She felt cooler with her hair pulled back from her face, and this was a good thing, because the hall was already hot and crowded.

Big bunches of purple and black helium-filled balloons were tied at intervals around the room, while some had escaped and bounced against the ceiling, trailing long spirals of ribbon over the heads of dancers. Purple lights pulsed in time to the deafeningly loud music. Every so often, when ultraviolet lights were switched on, white shirts, bowties and gloves glowed with eerie luminescence and teeth gleamed unnaturally white as people smiled. A large disco mirror-ball hung above them in the centre of the ceiling. It was rotating slowly, casting diamonds of light onto the faces of the boys and girls lined up against the walls of the hall, eyeing each other with expressions that were a peculiar mixture of hope, desperation and anxiety.

Sam found Jessie and Nomusa standing along one of the walls, chatting to a gypsy and a clown about their costumes. An angry look flitted across Jessie's face. Following her gaze, Sam saw Dan dancing with Cindy. Dan could not have known it, but the indie-rock song playing just then was Jessie's current favourite.

"C'mon," said Jessie, "let's dance. Who says we have to wait for the boys?"

So a large group of girls stepped into the moving throng and began dancing in a big circle. Sam's bedsheet was still intent on parting company with her shoulder, so she either had to hold it in place while she danced, or else hitch one shoulder higher than the other. Soon, she thought, people would start asking her if she was the hunchback of Notre Dame. Nomusa was clearly enjoying herself but, after only a couple of songs, Jessie started grimacing.

"What's wrong?" Sam mouthed over the loud music.

Jessie pointed down at her pointy-toed boots, and pulled a pitiful moue of pain. Then she gestured to the door.

Sam peeled away from the gyrating crowd and Jessie followed her outside. There was a small garden alongside the hall, where fragrant rose bushes bordered a square of grass, at the centre of which stood a flagpole. Sam lifted her hair off her neck to catch the wonderfully cool breeze which was blowing across the garden, and sighed while Jessie plonked herself onto a stone bench.

"Nomusa's having fun," said Sam, catching a glimpse of their friend through the open hall doors.

"That makes one of us."

"Ooh, look – she's dancing with Liam O'Leary!"

"Just the word 'dance' makes my toes ache. I need the loo."

The toilets were crowded with cliques of girls, each jostling for a place in front of the mirrors over the basins. Judging from their giggled conversations, more than half of them were crushing on the DJ. Sam sat down on the slatted wooden bench which ran the length of the wall opposite the basins to wait for Jessie. Just then, Cindy Atkins came in. She elbowed aside a few younger girls to get to the mirror, where she fiddled with her already perfect hair.

When Jessie hobbled out of a cubicle, she was wearing only one boot, the other was tucked under an arm. She sat down next to Sam and began to rub her foot, groaning.

"I see now," she said, "that the boots were a mistake."

"Only the boots?" said Cindy, her blue eyes scanning Jessie from head to toe. She turned back to the mirror and added a little extra to the thick line of kohl at the edge of her eyes, which looked more than ever like the slanting eyes of a cat.

"Ooh, a snarl – that really improves your face, Delaney. Should have the boys queuing up for dances now. And as for you, Steadman," said Cindy, her eyes meeting Sam's in the mirror, "just what are you supposed to be? A ghost? A roman in a toga? The ghost of a roman in a toga?

"No, I'm not. I'm Lady–"

"I'm really not interested. Just amazed that you came from the same gene pool as your brothers. Much as it pains me to say anything complimentary about your family, Steadman," said Cindy, now applying crimson lipstick and smacking her lips at her reflection in the mirror, "I've got to admit that Danny-boy is an absolute cutie-pie. And your brother James, of course, is also just gorgeous!"

Cindy turned away from the mirror and said to Sam, "They must have run out of the good DNA by the time they got to you."

"That's hilarious, Cindy. Did you read it in a joke book?"

"Well, I'm off – I promised a dance to Dan." Cindy looked straight at Jessie. "He's so cute, and so funny! You should have heard what he said about your outfit, Jessie."

As Cindy swept out in a swoosh of glimmering gold, Jessie threw the stiletto-heeled boot at her, and missed – they heard it clattering onto the corridor outside.

"Careful!" they heard Cindy warning others in a voice of mock-alarm. "The stink could kill you."

Jessie, now noticing that the girls in the bathroom were staring at this altercation, said, "What are you lot gawking at? Get back to your primping."

As they left the bathroom, Sam tried to console Jessie. "I'm sure Dan didn't say anything unkind about you, she's just stirring."

Jessie said nothing except, "Where's my boot?"

They had expected to find the boot lying in the corridor outside the girls' toilets, but it was nowhere to be seen. Jessie's killer mood was not improved by limping unevenly up and down the corridor, peering around corners, searching for the missing boot.

"Why don't you just take off the other one and go barefoot? It would be more comfortable," Sam suggested.

"I think my foot is so swollen inside that I wouldn't be able to get this boot off. I had to really yank to get the other off. It was already a bit of a mission to get them on, to be honest. When I get my hands around Cindy's skinny throat …"

Eventually, they gave up hunting for the boot. Back near the hall, they bumped into Nomusa.

"Hey, Jess, are you missing a boot?" she asked.

100

"Yes! Do you have it?"

"No, but I think someone has hung it on the flag-pole."

They hurried to the hall gardens where they had rested earlier on. Sure enough, there at the top of the pole, tied to the bottom of the South African flag, was a pointy-toed, stiletto-heeled black boot. Muttering oaths and threats under her breath, Jessie tried to unwind the chords which were wound around a metal cleat on the pole, but only succeeded in getting them knotted.

"Here, let me," said Sam, sweeping aside Jessie's hands and soon the flag was lowered and Jessie's boot rescued. While Sam raised the flag back up and secured the chords, Jessie put the boot back on. She did this with great reluctance and considerable cursing. Then the three of them made their way back into the hall.

Liam O'Leary immediately swooped down on No-musa, saying, "There you are!" and pulled her back on-to the dance floor.

A matric boy wearing a tuxedo and a wide red ribbon tied in a bow across his chest approached Sam.

"Heaven," he said, looking at her with an intense gaze, "must be missing an angel". He drew her out onto the dance floor, but not before Sam heard Jessie mutter, "And the village must be missing an idiot."

Sam's partner was an energetic dancer and they moved all about the dance floor. Sam noticed Apples dancing with a pretty girl wearing a crown, Cindy danc-ing with Dan, and a grinning Mr De Wet who was boogying alongside Mademoiselle Abeille. Jessie, she saw, was slumped against the wall staring at the danc-ers and scowling darkly. The music changed and a slow, romantic song came on.

101

"Aha," said Sam's partner and he crushed her against his chest. She saw that, attached to the red ribbon, was a large gift tag. It read: "From: God. To: Women."

"Mind if I cut in?" she heard and she immediately stepped away from her partner to see Apples tapping him on the shoulder. Without waiting for an answer, Apples slid one hand behind Sam's back, took her hand with the other and whisked her off.

"Sorry if you were enjoying your dance with God's gift to women," he said, grinning down at her. He was much taller than she was, Sam, realised. She had to crane her neck to look up into his teal-blue eyes.

"No, really, I'm grateful for the rescue," she said

The tune which played was a slow and wistful song about unrequited love. Sam laid her head on Apples's chest as they shuffled about slowly. She was very aware of placing her feet carefully so that she did not tread on his toes. She was even more aware of the warmth of his chest under her cheek, and the slow thudding of his heart against her ear. The sheet slipped down for the umpteenth time and Apples ran a finger over the skin of her shoulder, leaving a trail of delicious goosebumps.

As they danced past each other, Sam and Nomusa exchanged a silent conversation. Sam asked a question with her eyes, which Nomusa answered by pointing at Liam's back and then rocking her hand from side-to-side in a so-so gesture. Then she pointed at Sam and Apples together, gave a thumbs-up signal and a big wink, which made Sam want to giggle. She stopped smiling though, when they passed the next couple. Cindy had her bejewelled arms wrapped tightly around Dan. He was peering over her shoulder and seemed to be trying to look at something, or someone, at the side of the hall, but every time his gaze wandered from herself, Cindy laid the long, painted nail of one finger against his jaw and turned his head back to face her. She cast a triumphant smile at Jessie whenever they danced past where she stood. Jessie, Sam could see, was seething. A pointed toe was tapping on the floor and her hands fingered the assortment of weapons at her waist while she glowered at Dan and Cindy. Sam wondered briefly which of them was in greater danger from her wrath.

Just then, the song stopped and, after a moment, Sam took a step back from Apples.

"Another?" he asked.

"Huh?" Sam could not seem to stop herself from staring at the fascinating scar which curved at the side of Apples's mouth.

"Would you like another dance?" he asked, as a fast, popular song started up.

Sam glanced guiltily at where Jessie stood alone, but when she saw Dan walking quickly up to her, she relaxed and nodded at Apples. She saw Jessie shaking her head firmly and Dan holding his hands up in the air, and she wondered what the two of them were discussing, but then the view of her friend and her brother was obscured as more and more couples poured onto the dance floor.

Sam felt all arms and legs as she danced, but was consoled by the fact that Apples was not the world's greatest dancer either. He seemed only too aware of the fact himself, and soon leaned down to her ear to ask if she wanted a drink. They pushed through the dancers to a line of tables at the back of the hall at which a group of prefects, dressed as penguins, were selling drinks and snacks, and Apples bought them each a cool drink.

To Sam's disgust, Cindy and Kitty were also at the table; it seemed she could not get away from them. A grade 9 boy, a little shorter than Cindy, was trying to strike up a conversation with her. Sam saw Cindy nudge Kitty with her elbow, then she looked sideways at the boy from under slightly lowered lids and said, "If you ask me, I'll dance with you."

"O-oh, y-yes, please! W-w-would you dance w-w-with me, Cindy?"

"As if!" said Cindy, snorting with laughter as she walked off arm-in-arm with a giggling Kitty.

"What a charming girl," said Apples dryly.

"Let's take a drink to Jess and Dan," suggested Sam and before she could get the attention of one of the penguins behind the tables, Apples had ordered and paid for the drinks.

They squeezed and pushed past the crowds back towards where Jessie and Dan were standing and talking. "Uh-oh," said Sam. Even from a distance, she could tell by their body language that the two were having a row.

"Well, I didn't want to interrupt you. You were getting so cosy with Cleopatra," Sam heard Jessie say, as they got close. Jessie's black lipstick had worn off, her cheeks were pink with anger and she looked very pretty.

"I only agreed to dance with her because you said no when I asked *you!*" said Dan.

"I can't dance in these shoes."

"Then you can't blame me when I dance with someone else!" Dan sounded completely exasperated.

"Yeah, but with Cindy Atkins! That doesn't say much for your taste! And you looked like you were enjoying it, too."

Sam and Apples exchanged worried glances. Sam thought she should maybe interrupt them before things got really nasty, and so she stepped up to Jessie, holding out the can of cool drink. Just then, the loud song ended, and over the soft beginning of the next number, Jessie and Dan's blazing exchange could be heard clear across the hall. Heads turned, and soon there was a crowd of onlookers gaping at them as they traded insults.

"Jessie–" Sam tried to intervene, but Jessie was saying loudly, "She calls you her squeezie-pie – did you know that? How totally lame! What do you call her when she smiles at you – your Cindy-snookums?"

"At least she's capable of smiling."

"Oh shut up!"

"No, you shut up!" shouted Dan, taking a step closer to Jessie.

"No, *you* shut up!" Jessie yelled back, stepping right up to him.

"Why. Don't. You. Make. Me?" Dan spoke slowly and quietly as he closed the remaining distance between them, glaring down at Jessie. They were now almost nose-to-nose.

"Challenge accepted!" said Jessie, fiercely.

Then suddenly – Sam was not sure how it happened – they were kissing. Dan had one hand behind Jessie's waist and another cupping her cheek. Jessie had both her hands up around his neck, her fingers knotted in his hair. They stayed locked together for what seemed a very long time as the crowd went, "Oooh-oooh!", and when they broke apart, they were smiling at each other, looking both sheepish and slightly dazed.

"Mission accomplished," said Dan and he took Jessie by the hand and lead her out the hall into the cool evening outside.

13

An announcement

During the last week-and-a-half of term, the teachers piled on the work in the classroom, and the girls piled on the gossip about the dance. Everyone was agog with the news that Jessie Delaney and Daniel Steadman were now dating, though opinions were divided about the match.

"I think they make a great couple," said Stephanie Armstrong.

"Did you see that kiss!" said Mercy Tshabalala.

"I don't see them lasting long. Personally, I fail to see the attraction – it's not as if Dan Steadman's cute, or anything. And Delaney! They must both be pretty desperate," said Cindy to anyone who would listen.

"She's just jealous," Sam laughed, but she was less happy when she was given her term's report card to take home on the last day of school.

None of the girls had done as well in Maths or Science as they usually did, but only Sam seemed really worried about it. Nomusa said she had a good plan for breaking the bad news to her parents.

"I'm going to tell them that I didn't do well because we're being taught Science and Maths by a tyrannical white oppressor," she said, with a mischievous grin.

"Nomusa!" said Sam, scandalised.

"What? It's true – he *is* an oppressor."

"Yes, but that's not because he's white."

"I know that, but a 'short-man-oppressor' wouldn't carry the same weight with my folks. Besides, my version of events will give them a thrill and bring a light to their eyes. They'll exclaim that The Struggle isn't yet over, and they'll be delighted that I still have battles to fight in bringing equality to all. I'll be doing the fossils a kindness, really, bringing some joy to their lives."

"I don't think my folks will even notice – they're got other things on their mind. Anyway, a couple of D's just make my A for Art look even more spectacular," said Jessie.

But Sam was not used to getting anything other than A's. The B for Maths and the C for Science which she had achieved seemed to press down on her chest like a heavy rock, and she felt that if she had had to grade herself for her ability to deal with Delmonico, to stand up for herself and her friends, she would have given herself an F. Her face must have shown some of what she was feeling, because Jessie said, "Don't freak out, Sam. A little bit of failure now and then builds character. You can't always be perfect, you know. Actually, you can't *ever* be perfect – no-one can."

Nomusa said, "Don't let it worry you Sam. They'll have to lift the marks – the whole grade seems to have done badly. Surely Grieve will smell a rat."

"She'll probably just think we've been marked too leniently until now. Demonico will say he's raising the standard and that's why we've done badly. Argh! Does no-one see how really bad he is at actually teaching?" said Sam, then she changed the subject to distract herself because she felt a rising need to start tapping on the doorframe with her fingers – an equal number of times with each finger. It was a habit which had begun to emerge in just the last few days.

"It's a pity we can't spend the hols together."

They all agreed. Nomusa, at least, was looking forward to visiting an aunt in the Eastern Cape with her mother, but Jessie's expression said she was looking forward to this holiday about as much as a criminal anticipates a stay at the local prison. When Sam had invited her to spend a few weeks at the Steadman house in Pietermaritzburg, Jessie had shaken her head.

"I can't."

"Dan will be there," Sam tempted.

"No, I mean, I'd like to – I really would. But I've been ordered home for some 'family time'."

"What?" Both Sam and Nomusa were surprised. Jessie's family was not in the habit of spending much quality time together.

"Something's wrong. The Delaneys don't do family holidays unless there's a spa and a golf course nearby to keep the old fogies apart, and a kiddies club to keep Cassie and me out of their hair. Do you know when last we all had a holiday together at home in Jo'burg?"

"No."

"Neither do I. I fear the worst."

So Sam had planned to have a holiday at home in Pietermaritzburg with only her father and Dan for company, but when Dan heard that Jessie would not be visiting, he decided to spend the holidays with Apples's family instead. Sam packed all her Maths and Science books into her bag – which now felt almost as heavy as the weight on her chest – and planned to spend lots of time in the holidays going through the work until she was sure she understood it and knew it backwards.

Maybe James, if he popped home for a visit, would be able to help her; she was pretty sure her father would not have a cotton-picking clue about the work she was doing. Still less would he be able to advise her about how to cope with Delmonico – what did adults know about the helplessness of being fifteen and at the mercy of freak teachers?

In the end, the April holidays passed without Sam doing any work. She spent the weeks at home, alone for the most part, while her father was at work, making fudge and immersing herself in reading book after book. Each time she escaped into a fantasy fictional world, she forgot about her worries, but whenever she finished a book, the unease was back again, waiting and growing, like some hulking shadow. Whenever she thought of school, her mind leapt immediately to Delmonico, and her fingers began tapping, tapping, tapping, or else she felt the urge to arrange things in even numbers.

James came home for the Easter weekend, and Sam spent some time with him, catching up on his news. He was enjoying the English and Communication courses at university more than the legal ones, and was considering switching from law to journalism. Sam did not ask him to help with her Maths and Science – she just could not face opening the books. They were still lying unopened in her bag, like a reproachful reminder of her failure. When she returned to school the night before term started, it felt as if the heavy rock had shifted down to her stomach.

The rooms and corridors of Austen House were full of girls lugging in bags and suitcases. Everyone was wearing sweaters and scarves and gloves because the holidays had been blown out on the wings of an icy cold snap, as if the weather was emphasising the fact that the fun and games were over, and it was now time to get down to work. There was even a dusting of snow on the distant Devil's Peak visible from the window of their dorm room as they caught up on each other's news.

Nomusa had had a good holiday visiting with family and swimming on the golden beaches of the Wild Coast, but one look at Jessie and her younger sister Cassie's faces told them that something was wrong. Jessie's face was set in grim lines and her jaw was clenched; Cassie merely looked sad.

"What's the matter? Is something wrong?" Sam asked.

"Didn't I tell you it would be bad news?" said Jessie. "Our folks have separated and have decided to divorce. Actually, it turns out they decided quite a while ago, they just got around to telling us now. It'll be finalised in May."

"That's terrible," said Sam. "I'm so sorry."

"I don't like it that my mommy and daddy won't be together. I tried and tried to tell them not to divorce, but they wouldn't listen. And I won't call Cynthia 'mommy'. I won't! I'm very sad."

"Cynthia?" asked Sam.

"She's my daddy's new friend. But I don't want her to be," said Cassie, tears swimming in her big eyes. Over her head, Sam, Jessie and Nomusa exchanged meaningful glances.

"That's just awful, Jess, I'm sorry," said Nomusa, giving her friend a hug.

"I'm not. I think it's a good thing," said Jessie, pulling out of the embrace. "Not the Cynthia-daddy's-new-*friend* thing, obviously, but the divorce is."

"What do you mean?" said Sam.

"They were always fighting, always at each other's throats. I'm sick of it. Maybe it'll be better now – it can hardly be worse, can it?" Jessie spoke in an offhand way but Sam was not fooled. There was a tough bleakness to her friend's voice.

"And," said Jessie, yanking a bundle of clothes out of her large suitcase and waving them at the others, "there's always parental guilt to look forward to." Some of the clothes, Sam could see, still had price tags attached.

It was a grim way to start the term, but there was one good thing which they now discovered: the exposed pipes which ran the length of one of the walls in their room were piping hot to the touch. It turned out that they carried oil from the boiler in the ceiling to the radiators in all the dorm rooms below. Their room might be tiny, but at least it would be cosy in the winter.

It was certainly warmer than the hall was at the first assembly of term, held the next morning. They sat on the wooden floor, shivering in the unheated room as Delmonico lead them through the usual school song and a Bible reading. He finished with a verse from Isaiah which, he said, "Some of you would do well to take note of." He stared directly at Sam when he recited the words, "See, the Lord Almighty, will lop off the top boughs with great power. The lofty trees will be felled, and the tall ones will be brought low."

"What is his problem?" whispered Sam crossly.

"It's 'cos he's not a lofty tree. He wants to cut you down to size so he doesn't feel so little," said Jessie sagely. "I mean, you're taller than him, aren't you?" she added. "Smarter, too. And I reckon he knows it, the poison dwarf."

Their Physical Training teacher, Miss Gamion, now walked up to the microphone. Perhaps she had been running about in the autumn wind, because her hair was even more unruly than usual.

"She looks like she just saw a ghost," said Jessie, tilting her head to the side to study Miss Gamion. "Or maybe she stuck her finger in an electrical socket."

"Shh," said Nomusa, who was craning her head forward to catch what Miss Gamion was saying.

"... So the trials for the Kwa-Zulu Natal provincial athletics teams will take place on the last Saturday of May. Those of you who would like to try out, please come to a meeting in my office at first break."

"Are you going to try?" Sam asked Nomusa.

"I don't know. It's such a long shot; I doubt I'd make the team."

"You'll never know if you don't try. Go for it!" said Sam, but then she stopped her whispering. Mrs Grieve was now at the podium and as her sharp eyes scanned the girls sitting in the hall, everyone fell silent.

"I have two important announcements for the grade 9's, so will you please remain behind. All the other grades may now leave the hall."

All around them, there was muttered speculation about what the news might be.

"Maybe Delmonico's leaving," said Mercy Tshabalala.

"I wish you were," Cindy Atkins retorted.

"I heard Mrs Pillay saying something to Miss Stymen about a field trip. Maybe the announcement's about that," said Uvani Moodley

"Whatever it is, I just hope it doesn't involve more work," said Sam.

"Or more exercise," added Jessie.

112

Mrs Grieve cleared her throat, waited a few moments for the girls to stop talking, and then spoke.

"I am sure you will all be glad to hear that, next Friday, all the grade 9's will be going on an outing, by bus, to the Didima San Art Interpretation Centre at Cathedral Peak," said Mrs Grieve.

There were a few excited whispers among the girls at this, and Jessie smiled happily at Sam and Nomusa.

"I need hardly say," continued Mrs Grieve in a louder voice, "that the outing will be of an educational nature. There will be tasks and worksheets to complete on the day, and the learning will be incorporated into your English, History and Art syllabuses in the weeks afterwards."

Jessie's face fell at this, and there were a few disappointed groans. Sam thought a few worksheets and some class exercises would be an easy price to pay for getting away from the school, and missing their usual Friday double-Maths and double-Science periods with the poison dwarf.

"Please remember that anytime you appear in school uniform in public, you are ambassadors for Clifford House and need to behave impeccably."

"We have to wear school uniform?" Sam heard Cindy complain.

"The other announcement concerns an exciting event which takes place in July, in the first few days after the end of term. And, even though it takes place in the holidays, and is therefore not compulsory, I fully expect each and every girl to make the effort to participate, or to provide me with an excellent reason why she cannot."

"In other words," whispered Sam, "it *is* compulsory."

113

"Although, when you hear more about the competition, I'm sure you will *want* to sign up immediately. The Giant's Castle Survivor Games will be a contest between teams of girls in which you will compete on tasks such as map-reading and orienteering, obstacle courses–"

"Cool!" said Nomusa, at the same time as Jessie groaned.

"–as well as various team-building exercises. The Games will occur over the course of three days, which means that you will be spending two nights in the guest chalets at Giant's Castle in the central Drakensberg. The Games will be challenging and will bring out strengths you never knew you had, girls, and we, the staff, will be closely observing your cooperative and leadership skills all the way through the tasks. We will make an effort to get to know each and every single one of you."

"That sounds like a threat," muttered Sam.

"I will be posting more information on the grade 9 noticeboards later this week. Entry forms are available from the office. I suggest you choose your teams soon and enter as quickly as possible. Each team will comprise three girls, all of whom must be from the same house as this is both an interhouse as well as an individual competition. Right, that will be all – you may proceed to your classes."

"What do you think? It sounds like fun," said Nomusa as they joined the throng exiting the hall into the blast of cold wind.

"Easy for you to say," said Jessie. "I don't like the sound of those obstacle courses, and the only orienteering I want to do is to help me find the nearest cup of coffee."

"The way she said it, I don't really think we've got much of a choice. It sounds like it's a case of participate or be prepared for the consequences," said Sam. "At least we three can be a team. I'll get us a form from the office."

"I never said yes," protested Jessie.

"You've been outvoted," said Sam.

"Besides, it'll be three days less you'll have to spend with your parents," said Nomusa.

"It's a deal!" said Jessie, with a reluctant grin.

14

Red pins

By the time the day of the field trip arrived, the girls were desperate for a break: it had been a hectic two weeks. Mrs Pillay, their kindly History and English teacher, had broken down in a storm of tears during one lesson on the rebellion of peasants in the Russian Revolution, and ran out the classroom like Tsar Nicholas fleeing St Petersburg. Minutes later, a wrathful Mrs Grieve had stormed into the classroom and, with the tact and gentleness of Lenin, or perhaps even Stalin, Sam mused, she had proceeded to scold the girls for a full half-hour.

Prowling up and down in front of the class in a severely cut grey suit, her hair pulled back into a tight knot at the back of her head, her eyes narrow with anger, Mrs Grieve told them they were spoiled brats. She said they were ungrateful for the privilege of education offered to them by such excellent teachers at as fine an institution as Clifford House, when just down the road children without desks or chairs had to sit beneath trees in classes of forty or more. She said that she would be doing a spot-inspection of their books and "woe betide anyone who has been turning in inferior work", then ended by vowing to deal harshly with anyone behaving disrespectfully towards Mrs Pillay in future.

Sam, who had never been mean or rude or anything other than perfectly polite and cooperative in her interactions with Mrs Pillay, immediately felt guilty, but she seemed to be one of the few who did. Most of the others seemed merely resigned to the fact that goofing off in English and History was a thing of the past. They burst out in nervous laughter and whispered discussions when Mrs Grieve left the room but, under her desk, Sam's hands were tapping – as if of their own will – a pattern of equally numbered beats on each knee.

When Mrs Pillay returned to their class, a little red around the eyes and tip of the nose, she seemed unnerved by their silence and good behaviour, and was positively round-eyed with surprise when she gave them a project comparing the Russian Revolution to the South African struggle against apartheid, and no-one protested or even argued the deadline.

Nothing could unnerve Delmonico. At the start of term, he lectured them about their laziness and lack of aptitude for the "hard sciences", and then said that he believed a regime of extra homework would be of benefit. As a result, they were now doing double the amount of homework for Maths and Science, in addition to all the work they were getting from their other teachers. They had to prepare a speech on crime in Afrikaans for Mr De Wet and germinate bean seeds in cotton wool (for what felt to Sam like the umpteenth time in her school career) while doing daily diagrams of the plants' growth for Miss Stymen.

There was no way that any individual could keep on top of the heavy load of work and so, little as she liked it, Sam agreed that they should share out the homework each day. She, Jessie and Nomusa each did a chunk, and then would copy from the others since copying was faster than each of them actually doing the work for themselves. Nomusa and Jessie benefitted from this arrangement, but Sam found that the other two's work contained too many errors for her to be satisfied with submitting it, and so she usually wound up redoing it for herself anyway.

Between all the homework, and all her slow and thorough checking, Sam was getting to bed later and later, and feeling more and more tired in class as a consequence. It was not surprising that she fell asleep on the bus en route to Cathedral Peak on the Friday of their field trip. She awoke to someone shaking her shoulder.

"We're here," said Jessie.

Sam sat up and looked out of the window at the San Art Interpretive Centre, rubbing the sleep from her eyes and trying to yawn some oxygen into her tired brain. The Didima Rock Art Centre was a little way down the road from Cathedral Peak, a high bell-shaped ridge on the escarpment. It was a long, low, curved building, topped with rippling folds of thatch and guarded by a massive statue of a kneeling eland on an oval of rock.

The grade 9 girls made their way through the entrance into the display hall where they milled about, looking at the variety of exhibits in glass-fronted cases, that showed the lifestyle, culture and art of the San people. Before Sam had had a chance to examine all the exhibits, their tour guide was calling them into a group. He explained that there were more than 600 known rock art sites in the uKhahlamba Drakensberg mountain range and reminded them that the greater area had been declared a UNESCO World Heritage Site in 2000.

"Hmm!" said Sam, impressed.

"Whoopee," said Cindy, sarcastically.

118

The guide lead them from the display hall, through a dimly lit "cave" with low ceilings and rough rock walls, in which there was a lot of pushing and shoving and protestations of claustrophobia from the girls, until they emerged into a large auditorium. This, too, looked like it had been cut out of rock, and images of San art were projected onto a large overhang much like the one Sam had seen on the hike to Devil's Peak earlier in the year. They took their seats and soon the lights dimmed and a vivid and loud audio-visual presentation took them through the myths, legends and facts of San rock art. It was great fun, especially when smoky fog effects clouded the room (Cindy and Kitty took to coughing loudly), and a fine mist of water sprayed down from the ceiling during a scene about a thunderstorm (Cindy and Kitty squealed irritatingly at this).

As she gazed at the spectacular images of San paintings, Sam felt awed at the ancient beauty and spiritual significance of the art. It was amazing to think of these gentle people, living right here on this land for centuries, and leaving behind only these mysterious and enigmatic symbols. Beside her, Jessie was staring at the paintings, mesmerised; perhaps she, too, felt a connection with those ancient artists. Cindy, however, made sure everyone understood just how unimpressed she was.

"This is pathetic," she in a loud voice which carried all the way from the back row of the auditorium where she sat, to the front where the guide stood.

"Do you call this art? It's just stick figures and the same old manky bucks, over and over again. I mean, seriously, my five-year-old cousin could do better scribbles than that. I expected it to be much more spectacular. Next time, just send me to the website and save me the effort of coming, thanks. I'd rather be shopping."

A few girls giggled, but Sam could see that the guide had heard her dismissive comments, and was offended by them. After the show was over, they filed back out of the auditorium and had more time to browse the displays. Jessie immediately headed over to those cases where the art and painting materials were displayed, and Sam supposed that more paintings would soon be covering the walls of their dorm-room cupboards. Nomusa was fascinated by the cabinets exhibiting medicinal plants, and the role of the tribal shamans in healing rituals.

"This is soooo boring," said Cindy, who had read none of the information in the displays. "Let's go outside onto the deck and check out the curio shop, Kitty. Hopefully it won't all be primitive and pathetic."

"Maybe she'll fall off the deck into the river, and be carried away to the ocean to be eaten by sharks," said Jessie hopefully.

Sam smiled. She was enjoying the displays on daily life within the tribe – the heavy digging sticks, weighted by doughnut-shaped rocks, which had been used as spades; the quivers of slender, poison-tipped arrows which were used for hunting; and the delicate jewellery made from the shells of ostrich eggs. She wandered half absent-mindedly along the wall of cabinets to the back of the display hall, and there saw something which immediately got her full attention. It was a temporary display on "Rock Art Sites of the World". A large map of the world was stuck on the wall and on a table beneath it was an exhibit that included photographs of different examples of rock art, a thick red-leather bound book, and loads of information about these magnificent sites.

Sam studied the map for a few minutes and saw that areas all over the world had been highlighted. There were several rock art sites in Europe, especially in Spain, France and Italy, but also as far afield as Portugal, Sweden, Ireland and Finland. Most of Asia's rock art was clustered in the Middle East – Iran, Israel and Saudi Arabia – but there was also a smattering of sites in China, India and somewhere called Uzbekistan, which Sam thought might be in Russia. There were scores of sites in North and South America, as well as in Mexico and, on the other end of the world, in Australia, too. But Africa had the most rock art sites by far. Ancient rock art, both painted and engraved, had been discovered in Egypt, Libya, Algeria, Somalia, Zambia, Uganda, Botswana as well as in sites scattered throughout the length and breadth of South Africa.

Sam noticed that a series of red pins had been stuck into the map at many of the sites, including a few in South Africa. She read the labelled names to herself: Burrup Peninsula and Alice Springs, Australia; Morocco and Somalia in Africa; Reno, Nevada in the US; Lascaux Caves in France. The names sounded familiar somehow, and she wondered what they had in common.

"Can I help you?" Sam looked up to see a pretty young woman, wearing jeans, a T-shirt with the logo "We're all children of Africa", and dozens of grass bracelets up her arms.

"Yes, actually. Do you know anything about this display?

"I certainly hope so. I'm Bongi, and this," she tapped the thick red book, "is my doctoral thesis: a comparison of rock art sites around the world, looking at petroglyphs – those are scratchings and carvings into the rock itself – and pictographs, which are the pigment paintings onto the surface of the rock."

"Hi, I'm Sam." Sam gestured at the map on the wall. "This is all so amazing. I didn't know there was rock art in so many places."

"Yes, it seems that from our earliest days, humankind has wanted to decorate and communicate, and has done so through the medium of art."

"What are these red pins for?" asked Sam.

"They show the sites where rock art has been stolen, or damaged in an attempt to be stolen. It's not really the focus of my study, but I thought it would add interest to the display."

Sam looked at the red pins again; there were so many of them. "Is there a lot of theft?"

"You bet. There's big money to be made. I read in a recent study that the illegal trade in antiquities is estimated at about 8 billion dollars per year. Only the international trades in illegal arms and drugs rank higher. Of course, the antiquities include items stolen from museums and archaeological sites, such as clay pots and figurines, bronze statues, Iron and Stone Age weapons, ancient jewellery – even fossils, not just rock art."

"Wow! I didn't know that it was such an international problem, or that it had happened in South Africa."

"Oh yes, we're what they call a *donor country*, because so many of our artefacts are pillaged and smuggled out of the country. In fact, this needs updating," said Bongi, picking a red pin out of a small container on the table and pinning it into the map. "There was a bad theft not far away just a month ago."

Sam peered closely at the map. The pin was stuck into a section of the northern Drakensberg.

"Where exactly was this?"

"Devil's Peak," said Bongi.

"Devil's Peak?" Sam repeated, stunned.

"Yes, at the cave there. They prised the entire panel off the rock face – it looks like they got it off in two massive pieces. Someone's doing a really professional job of looting our heritage. Somehow we have to do a better job of protecting it." Her face was troubled as she spoke to Sam.

"Have a look over here, you might find this interesting. I've collected some news articles about thefts and vandalism at rock art sites around the world. Maybe you'd like to look through it? Just please put it back on the table before you go," Bongi said. Then she excused herself to talk to a few other students.

Still reeling from the news that the magnificent paintings they had seen on their A.A.S. hike were lost, Sam began to page through the flip-file which Bongi had handed her. She was horrified to see the number of ways in which rock art around the world had been permanently damaged by vandalism, and not just of the sort of graffiti they had seen on the hike. Vandals had spray-painted names and slogans over rock art panels, lit fires underneath them so that they were destroyed by smoke and soot, chipped initials into the rocks, and even used the rare and fragile paintings for target practice – of paint-balls and live ammunition!

"Morons!" said Sam, crossly.

"Excuse me?" Nomusa had come to fetch Sam.

"This – you've got to read this. It's shocking!" said Sam, but Nomusa had grabbed her by the elbow and was steering her out of the display hall onto a wooden deck where the girls were eating lunch.

15

These boots were made for hiking

Jessie was already sitting at one of the small tables, drinking a cappuccino. The restaurant deck was built on a slope under the shady canopy of several large trees, and just below, a clear mountain stream was burbling over a rocky patch. At one end of the deck, local crafters were selling their wares: soapstone carvings of heads, bracelets woven from grass and copper wire, brightly coloured beadwork, bent wire models of cars and chameleons and lizards, tall wooden giraffes with delicate tails, and piles of woven baskets in every shape and colour. It was a cool and relaxing place – a bit like being in a tree house – but Sam was indignant and irate, and in no mood to relax and enjoy the view.

"You need to hear this," she said and filled them in on what Bongi had said about art thefts around the world.

"Hmm," said Jessie. "Here, have a sandwich – we ordered you toasted cheese and tomato – hope that's OK."

Sam grabbed a piece of the oozy, cheesy sandwich with one hand and continued flipping through the pages of the file with the other. Between bites, she read out excerpts to her friends.

"These are articles on thefts of rock art from around the world. It's incredible! Like here, see?" She held up the file to show them a picture of an engraving on a rounded boulder. "This is from Alaska, it's an engraving of an orca – you know, a killer whale. Isn't it gorgeous?"

Without waiting for a reply, she continued, "Well, some idiot removed a bunch of these from near a beach – just loaded them up and carted them off – and used them to make a ring of stones around the bonfire in his yard! And this article here is about two men in Nevada in the USA who were arrested for stealing rocks with 1000-year-old rock art on them, and using them as garden ornaments. Garden ornaments! I kid you not. And this one is about someone who tried to sell Australian Aboriginal rock art on eBay. It's looting, that's what it is!"

The talking was making Sam thirsty, so she paused for a slurp from her cool drink.

"And these muppets are just the amateurs who have been caught. The bigger problem comes from organised and professional international theft syndicates – sophisticated gangs of crooks who take what they want, smuggle it out of the country of origin and then sell it to rich private collectors. All this precious art, the heritage of thousands of years, is just disappearing and no-one is getting busted."

"That's really bad. But what would anyone want with a giant rock panel? You can hardly hang it up in your living room," said Nomusa, spearing a chunk of pineapple from her fruit salad and popping it into her mouth.

"These private collectors apparently have their own viewing rooms – like mini-museums. And they collect not just to own the beauty, but because it's a valuable collectable. We're talking big bucks here," said Sam,

125

tapping one of the articles with her finger. "A decent rock painting, proved to be authentic, can sell for anything between a couple of hundred thousand – that's US dollars – and a couple of million!"

"Wow," said Jessie, amazed.

"But, but, but …!" said Sam, rushing on. "That's not even the worst of it. Many of these thefts happen in South Africa and Bongi told me that just last month there was a theft at Devil's Peak. That panel of San paintings we saw in the cave? Gone!"

"What?" said Jessie and Nomusa together.

"Gone," repeated Sam. "Apparently the entire panel was removed in two massive pieces."

"The elands? The therry-whatsits?" said Jessie in a forlorn voice.

"The whole lot."

"But how did they get it off?" asked Nomusa.

"I don't know specifically about the panel at Devil's Peak, but this article says that the thieves generally use chisels and claw hammers for the smaller bits. For the large panels, they might use small controlled explosions like Ms Zenobia told Jessie, but also jackhammers, wedges and crowbars. Sometimes they make cracks in the rock behind the art, pour in liquid resin and then it expands when it sets, and widens the crack so they can lever it off. They even do something called thermal shock: they make fires on the rocks, then douse them in cold water, which makes the rocks split. If the pieces are very large, they use cranes to load them onto flatbed trucks and then just drive off with them. And they do a lot of damage, even when they're not successful. They often destroy the paintings trying to get them off, and leave the shattered pieces behind."

At a nearby table, Cindy was complaining to Kitty and some other girls about the wares for sale from the traders.

"Nothing worth buying," Sam heard her say.

"I quite liked the copper bangles," Kitty ventured.

"Oh, please. I had the lowest of expectations, and I'm still disappointed."

"What I don't understand," said Jessie, "is how would they even have known where to find that overhang at Devil's Peak? It wasn't signposted and there were a bunch of those faint paths leading off in all directions. They wouldn't have known which one to take. How could they possibly have found it?"

"It would have to have been an inside job," said Nomusa, with a sigh. "No-one could find that cave without the help of one of the official guides."

"Unless…" said Sam softly. Thoughts were racing through her mind, making connections, making sense. "Unless they had been there before … and locked the coordinates into a GPS. Then it would be dead easy to find!"

"What are you talking about?" asked Jessie.

"Of course!" said Sam, smacking a hand against her forehead. "Lascaux Caves in France, Alice Springs in Australia, Morocco!"

"Do you know what she's talking about?" Jessie asked Nomusa, who shook her head in reply.

"Those people – on the hike, remember? The Americans – Mitch and whatshername – parrot-woman!"

"Are you talking about that Texan fellow in the safari suit and his wife? What about them?"

"They said they had visited those places. And, according to Bongi's map in there," Sam pointed a thumb

127

back at the display hall, "those also just happen to be the places where rock art thefts have happened recently. Just a coincidence? I think not."

"Are you trying to say that you think those two were …"

"Part of an international rock art theft gang? You bet I am," said Sam firmly, looking from Jessie to Nomusa with an excited gleam in her eye.

"Do you really think so?" said Nomusa, raising her eyebrows.

"They didn't look much like art thieves to me, Sam." Like Nomusa, Jessie looked very doubtful.

"But maybe that was the point! Maybe they were disguising who they really were. Think about it: they were wearing such inappropriate clothes – her with all those colours and him in that brand new, ridiculous safari suit and cowboy hat. And that moustache! I'll bet it was a fake. It's almost as if they were wearing costumes, like fancy dress. It's as if they were deliberately trying to distract us from their real intention."

"Which was … what?" asked Jessie.

"To capture the latitude and longitude coordinates into that GPS! I saw him do it, only I didn't realise what I was seeing at the time. I thought it was an old phone because it was so big and it had an aerial, but what do I know about phones? Now I'm betting that it was a satellite phone, and those numbers on the screen – I knew I saw numbers! – were the coordinates of that cave. He was marking the spot so they could find it again in order to steal the rock art! Why are you looking at me like that and shaking your heads? It makes perfect sense," said Sam.

"I don't know, Sam. I mean, I didn't see the phone or anything, but he just didn't seem like some robber-bandit, big-time art thief to me, just some dumb tourist. The German looked more like a crook to me," said Jessie. Even Nomusa looked sceptical.

"They mentioned the actual names of those places – how do you explain that?"

"I don't remember hearing that," said Nomusa.

"You weren't there," said Sam, who was beginning to feel cross. "It was when I was handing her back the litter she dropped. That's when he was fiddling with the phone and she was drawling on about their travels."

"Did you ask him what he was doing?"

"Yes. He said they just liked to keep a track of the places they visited, to take photos for slide shows back home."

"Well, there you are then," said Jessie. "Maybe that's all it was."

The teachers now stood up, and told all the girls to dispose of their rubbish and go back to the bus. It was time to head back to school.

"I tell you, there was something not right about them, something that didn't fit," said Sam, as they made their way to the bus. She was trying to remember everything about those two people on the hike, trying to picture the scene in detail in her mind's eye.

"What was it?" asked Nomusa.

"I can't remember. It was something … something about … Oh, this is so frustrating!" Sam threw herself into one of the bus seats. "It's like it's on the tip of my tongue and I just can't get it."

"Everybody got everything? Nothing left behind or lost?" Ms Zenobia asked from the front of the bus.

Sam looked down at her hands and then quickly stood up and walked up the aisle.

"Sorry, ma'am. I took this file by mistake, I just need to return it."

"And I forgot my jersey, ma'am," said Uvani Moodley from behind Sam.

"Well, be quick, please, you two."

Uvani hurried around the back of the rock art centre towards the restaurant while Sam ran back inside the display hall and hastened over to the far end, where Bongi was now sitting on a step beside the display table, tying the laces of her hiking boots.

"Sorry, I almost forgot," Sam said, waving the file at Bongi, and replacing it on the table.

"No problem, I'm just glad you remembered in time." Bongi smiled and walked with Sam to the exit.

"Going for a walk?" asked Sam, pointing at Bongi's feet.

"Yes, I'm hiking up to Rainbow Gorge. It's beautiful, but steep. It calls for some comfy footwear."

"Oh!" said Sam, thunderstruck. Bongi looked at her curiously.

"I just realised something! Well, bye Bongi – enjoy your hike," Sam called as she jogged over to the bus, whose engine was already running. She made her way back down the aisle, holding onto the seats to keep her balance as the bus pulled off with a lurch, and stepping over Cindy's protruding feet, before flopping into her seat with a wide smile on her face.

"Boots!" she announced to Jessie and Nomusa.

"Ey?" said Jessie.

"It was their boots – the Texans', I mean."

"What about them?" asked Nomusa.

"Their boots didn't fit with the rest of what they were wearing at all. They were good quality, comfortable, well-worn – very sensible footwear. The sort you would expect to find on the feet of real hikers – not on some caricature of a Texan tourist and his parakeet of a wife! And that's because they probably *are* real hikers – I bet they have to do many tough walks and climbs to get to rock art sites. And now that I think of it, they weren't at all out of breath when they got to the top of the climb. They're fit and experienced. They knew what they were doing, because they've done this before. And, unless someone stops them," Sam said to Jessie and Nomusa's disbelieving faces, "they'll do it again!"

16

Worst enemy

After the visit to the rock art centre, Jessie was even more inspired to master the art of rock paintings. Every afternoon, she disappeared into the cupboard at the back of their dorm room with her paints, brushes and the palette she used for mixing her pigments. Sam and Nomusa were relieved to see that Jessie had apparently abandoned the attempts to paint with egg, butter and her own blood. They kept asking to see the work, but Jessie would only say, "When it's finished!"

Finally one Friday afternoon, Jessie declared her masterpiece "finished – more or less" and invited Sam and Nomusa into the cupboard. They crawled in on hands and knees, fumbling their way between Jessie's shoes and painting materials which lay scattered across the floor of the small, low-ceilinged space. At Jessie's instruction, they sat against the back wall of the cupboard in the pitch dark.

Then Jessie switched on the lights with a flourish and a triumphant, "Ta-da!"

Sam goggled at the array of images which were painted in a row from left to right on the wall in front of her. They were unquestionably very good. They were also undeniably strange. It looked like Jessie had begun her paintings in the style of the work they had seen at the cave and the rock art centre. There were the familiar buck, giraffes, hunters and even an aardvark in the muted hues of ochre, white, black and deep red (was that really Jessie's blood?). Then, in the middle of the wall, there were therianthropes – human figures with elongated limbs and the heads of jackals and buck. It was after these images that the work became bizarre.

Next to the rock art style therianthropes was a peculiar painting of a creature with the body of a tall giraffe, complete with patterned hide and black hooves, but atop the long neck was a bright yellow, and very modern-looking, smiley face. Perhaps Jessie had become bored with the traditional forms because she had painted many more of these mutants in brilliant colours: the recognisable head of Marilyn Monroe on top of a bunny rabbit's body, actor Robert Pattinson's face against the stylised outlines of a black bat, a cellphone on the back of a pigeon and, right at the far end of the panel, a leatherback turtle with, unmistakably, Sam's face painted on the front.

"What do you think?" asked Jessie eagerly.

"Uhm," said Nomusa, staring at the paintings wide-eyed.

"They're very finely done, Jessie, and quite … extraordinary!" said Sam.

"They are, aren't they?" Jessie looked expectantly at Nomusa. Nomusa was still staring at the wall, looking from painting to painting.

"Uhm …" she said again.

"Your technique is really excellent," said Sam.

"But do you get it – what they mean?" asked Jessie, her eyes gleaming with excitement.

"Uhm," said Nomusa, "not really." She was tilting her head from side to side, and scanning the panel from left to right and back again as if this might reveal the meaning of the surreal images. In a minute she might stand on her head to see if the work made more sense viewed upside-down.

"Why don't you tell us in your own words," encouraged Sam, who could feel a giggle bubbling up inside of her and was biting her lip to try and keep it from spilling over.

"They're modern therry-whatsits, see!"

"Therianthropes?" asked Sam, looking back at the vivid images.

"That's it. The San painted images of their spiritual beings, but these days, we're fans of these things, see?" She pointed to the movie stars and the phone. "They're like our modern gods."

"I'm like a god?" said Sam, bemused.

"Well, OK, not you, I was getting a bit carried away by then. But style evolves, you know. I'm going to call this piece *The evolution of the artist*."

Sam was fairly sure that the term evolution implied improvement over time, but she didn't want to hurt Jessie's feelings, so she contented herself with asking, "Why have you put the faces on the different sorts of bodies?"

"Oh, you caught that, hey?" said Jessie happily. "You too, I'll bet," she nudged Nomusa, who replied with a doubtful, "well …", which was a step up from "uhm", Sam supposed. Nomusa was still gazing at the pictures, as if hypnotised by them.

"I chose the bodies to reveal something of their nature, what they are and who they've become to modern society. Robbie P has become just a vampire to millions of fan-girls around the world. Marilyn Monroe was like a fluffy little bunny – all soft and cute and cuddly, but ultimately kind of useless – and she didn't come to a good end. And the cellphone is like our modern pigeon."

"Huh?" said Nomusa.

"We don't use pigeons to send messages anymore, we use text messages."

"And me on a turtle?" asked Sam.

"That's partly because of the work you did with turtles last year, but also because you are – all teens are, really – like a hatchling, making your own journey between the egg and the sea, crossing the beach of life with all its challenges and dangers, to the open ocean of adulthood."

"Oh," said Sam. "Wow!" She was quite impressed.

"And the smiley face on the giraffe?" asked Nomusa faintly.

"That didn't really mean anything. I was just painting the giraffe like San rock art and then inspiration struck and I found myself doing the smiley face. And look where it lead!" Jessie gestured happily to the rest of the paintings. "That's what it's like being an artist, you know. Sometimes you just have to go where impulse leads you."

"That explains it, then," said Nomusa.

"It's a fascinating project, Jessie. Ms Zenobia would be really interested to see it. It's a pity you can't show this to her."

"Yes, I know." Jessie looked disappointed. Then a sudden smile lit her face. "Wait!" She crawled out of the cupboard, cursing as a stiletto heel stuck her in one knee, and was back seconds later with her cellphone.

She snapped off a rapid series of photographs, and then dashed off immediately to go show the art teacher.

Sam and Nomusa exchanged a glance, and then edged out of the cupboard giggling.

"It's nice to see you laughing for a change, Sam," said Nomusa. "We need to get Jessie to do this more often. Maybe she could do a painting of Delmonico's head on a devil's body."

It was true that the situation with Delmonico had been sapping Sam's happiness. None of her other teachers had the same effect on her, even though they were all working the girls hard. She had done well, Sam thought, with her Afrikaans prepared speech in the previous week. Most of the girls had written their speeches about crimes which had in some way touched them and their families directly. Sam had spoken about an armed robbery which had happened at the Pietermaritzburg branch of the bank where her father worked, in which a security guard had been shot and killed. Poppy had spoken about the burglary at their house, while Cindy had described an incident in which she and her mother had been yanked out of their car by a gang of armed hijackers. Her voice choked up a bit as she spoke and the hands holding the speech cards shook a little, when she told of how her father had jetted out overseas that night on a scheduled business trip, leaving her and her mother alone in the house. He had said people should not allow criminals to scare them, and that they should carry on with their lives as usual.

Cindy spoke as though this attitude was something to be proud of, but Sam thought that Mr Atkins's behaviour had been uncaring – even callous. She could not imagine her own father abandoning her on the night of such a traumatic event, and she felt a bit sorry for Cindy. Perhaps Cindy read the doubt and compassion in some of the glances sent her way, or heard Mr De Wet's sympathetic tisking, because she abruptly jutted her chin in the air and, switching to English, said rather defensively, "My father says that what doesn't kill you, makes you stronger."

"Oh my gonna gawie!" Mr De Wet had exclaimed. "I never knew so many of you had been victims!"

English and History classes were better now that Mrs Pillay had better control of the class, although Sam was not enjoying their new set work, Olive Schreiner's *Story of an African Farm*. She had no real problems in her other subjects: Life Orientation, Geography, Biology (Nomusa's favourite subject), Business Studies, Art and Physical Training – though, judging from her complete lack of ability in these last two fields, she could scratch *artist* and *athlete* off the list of possible future careers for herself. Sam had even, finally, mastered the mysteries of Accountancy. She had discovered that the secret was not to overthink the subject, she just needed to follow the instructions to the letter. Although no longer confused, she was now mightily bored and could hardly wait until the end of the year to drop the subject.

It was just her classes with the poison dwarf, as Sam now thought of Delmonico, that were a major headache. All of the hours spent working through the textbooks and doing past papers did not appear to be helping her performance in the classroom and in tests.

"I don't get it," she confessed now to Nomusa, as she huddled again over the books on her bed.

Outside, the wind was buffeting drifts of unseasonable icy rain against the window, but inside the dorm room it was snug and cosy. Jessie was not yet back from her mission to show Ms Zenobia the photographs of "the evolution of the artist"; probably she was off texting Dan somewhere. Her bag lay unopened on her bed, below a sign Jessie had taped to the wall: *Homework won't kill you … but why take the chance?* On the windowsill beside Jessie's bed was her Biology project – the bean plants lay shrivelled and dying on a bed of dry cotton wool.

"I understand the work when I work through it like this and I can do the exercises and past papers, but the minute I'm in his classroom, or writing one of his tests, it all leaks out of my head, like water through a sieve. I go blank and can't remember anything. I just don't get how that happens." As she spoke, Sam's fingers were pulling threads from the bedspread, and laying them out in neat lines along the diamond pattern of the fabric.

"That's because the work isn't your real problem," said Nomusa, who was cleaning two pairs of running shoes. She would be leaving very early the next morning because it was a journey of some 200 km to the Moses Mabhida Stadium in Durban where the KwaZulu-Natal provincial athletic trials were being held.

"What do you mean? Of course I have a problem with the work – have you seen my marks lately?"

"Uh-uh. Your real problem, Sam, is with yourself."

"With me? Don't you mean with the demon poison dwarf?"

"Nope. Look, I know he's foul–"

"And petty. And sadistic, and just plain creepy," Sam said, yanking a recalcitrant thread from the bedspread and then frowning down at the stretch of puckered fabric it left in its wake.

138

"Yes, he's all of those things," said Nomusa, smiling and nodding. "But," she continued, now threading a new pair of laces into the first pair of shoes, "he's not your real problem here, Sam. At least, he's not a problem you can change or fix or do anything about."

"I'm with you there." Sam smoothed out the bedspread and began to rearrange the disturbed threads, one by one.

"Fact is, it's you who is getting in your way. You're your own worst enemy."

"In what way?" Sam looked at Nomusa. Her friend was putting something into words that Sam had only glimpsed at the corner of her mind, in brief moments of calm between waves of rising panic.

"You're worried all the time, anxious all the time, trying to be perfect and giving yourself a hard time because you're not. The reason you go blank and can't remember your work is not because you don't know it, it's because your mind is somewhere else.

"But I could fail! I could do really badly and get into trouble and lose the scholarship – Cindy is already nipping at my heels – and then I'd have to leave Clifford!"

"That's not going to happen," said Nomusa firmly, threading the last length of shoelace through the eyelets. "But you can't focus on what you need to do and to remember, if your mind is constantly worried about what might happen in the future. It's like your brain is tuned into a radio station that plays a constant stream of *what-if's*."

Yes, that's exactly how it is. It's like my brain is tuned to a radio station that plays a constant stream of what-if's, thought Sam.

"But how…? What…?" she began, not even sure what she was asking.

139

"You could go see the school counsellor – I'm sure she could help, it's her job," suggested Nomusa.

"Uh-uh, no way! If it gets out that I'm not coping, Grieve might take the scholarship away. I'm sure you lose points for being crazy."

"Isn't what you tell a counsellor confidential?"

"It's supposed to be. But what if Grieve finds out anyway, or even just sees me going in or out? No, I have to do this myself."

"Then here's what I suggest," said Nomusa gently. "Step 1: just *breathe*. Step 2: relax. Shake your shoulders. Step 3: focus. That means focus on the here and now, Sam, not on the future! And step 4: when the starting pistol goes off – *run!*" Nomusa grinned. "That's what works for me before a race – maybe it would work for you."

"OK, I'll try," said Sam, unconvinced that her problems could be overcome so simply.

"As Obi-Wan Kenobi said to Luke Skywalker: 'Either do or do not – there is no *try*!'," said Nomusa, and she ducked to avoid the pillow that Sam threw at her.

"Are you confident for the trials tomorrow?" Sam asked.

"I'm trying not to think about it. How are *you* feeling about the double-date in town tomorrow? Are we expecting mucho lip-locking on both sides of the table?" Nomusa teased.

"It's *not* a double-date," Sam protested. "Jessie has a date with Dan, and Apples and I are just going, you know, along with them."

"If you say so."

"I do. And I also say it wouldn't be half as awkward if you were coming along too."

"No thanks – I have no desire to play fifth wheel, even if I didn't have the tryouts tomorrow. You can tell me all the dirty details tomorrow night. Where are you meeting up?"

"The coffee shop – where else? It's not like Izintaba is a hive of hot dating spots."

"Well, have fun. It'll be good for you to get away from the books for a few hours anyway."

And, in Izintaba with Jessie the next morning, it did feel good to be having a break.

17

Double-date

It was warm and cosy inside the coffee shop where Sam and Jessie waited, and the air smelled of cinnamon pancakes and coffee and hot toast. When Dan and Apples entered, shaking the rain off their hair, they came straight over to the corner table where the girls were seated and plonked themselves down on the spare chairs, complaining about the cold outside.

"So," said Dan, who was scanning a menu, "what are we going to do today, Jessie?"

"I don't know – what do you feel like, Sam?" Jessie asked.

"Oh, they aren't going to be hanging out with us. You have to go off with Apples today, Sam."

"Why?" asked Sam, indignant at this high-handed treatment.

"Because I lost you to him in a poker game. Soooo, what are we drinking?"

"What!"

"Yes, what?" said Dan. "I fancy some hot chocolate – with mini-marshmallows on top. Jessie, you're more of a coffee girl, if I remember right?"

"I meant what about the poker game, Dan!"

"Oh, that," said Dan dismissively. "Well, Apples and

I were playing a game of poker last week, and I ran out of money, so I bet you, Sam."

"What the–"

"Unfortunately, I lost. So now you officially belong to him"

Sam looked at Apples, aghast. He nodded his confirmation, saying laconically, "True story. I won you fair and square."

"But you can't bet me – I'm not a thing! I don't belong to you." Beside Sam, Jessie had started to laugh. Sam glared at her.

"You're my little sister – that's got to give me some rights."

"Not the right to gamble me away in a poker game!"

"Now be reasonable, Sam. There are some countries in the world where I could sell you. Or maybe trade you for a few camels." Dan waved, trying to get a waiter's attention.

"But not in South Africa!"

"Tell you what, Sam," said Apples. "I'll settle for a day of your company, rather than a lifetime of servitude."

Sam merely sputtered at this.

"Don't you want to spend the day with Apples?" said Jessie craftily, casting her friend a meaningful look and then kicking her under the table. Apples looked at Sam appealingly, dimples threatening at the corners of his mouth.

"Yeah. What she said," said Dan, inclining his head to Jessie.

Samantha was torn. She wanted to teach Dan a lesson for his impudence – sexist git of a brother that he

143

was. But, if she was honest with herself, she also did rather want to spend the day in Apples's company.

"What if I throw in a visit to the bookshop, Sam?" said Apples. She liked the way he said her name, curling it on a soft and gentle smile.

"Oh all right!" said Sam with exasperation. "But not because you *lost* me in a game of cards!" She poked Dan hard in the chest as she got up to go with Apples. "We're still going to have a long, hard chat about this, Daniel Steadman."

"Sure, sure," said Dan, but Sam did not think he took her very seriously because, as she turned back to get her jacket off the chair, she saw him and Apples bumping elbows conspiratorially.

Sam and Apples headed out into the cold winter weather and walked around the corner to the nearby bookshop where they browsed around for a while, before making their way to the town's only museum. The official at the ticket desk was dozing with his head on his arms, and seemed most surprised that someone would want to tour the facility. After wandering around for a bit, Samantha could understand his attitude.

It was a sad excuse for a place that was supposed to preserve and display the country's heritage, and it was doing a pitiful job of educating visitors on the natural and cultural legacy of the land. The display hall smelt of both mildew and dust, and there was little to see. There were a few dusty papier-mâché models of dinosaurs looking lost and forlorn against a backdrop of under-sized plastic palm trees, some unlabelled fossils under a glass case and, at the back of the stuffy room, a display of Anglo-Boer War memorabilia more than a century old. There were parts of old British regimental uniforms and some weaponry, but items were missing from the velvet-lined cases. From the shape of the indented spaces left behind, Sam guessed that they had once housed bullets and bayonets. There was a single display of a Zulu shield, assegai and fighting stick, or knobkerrie, but otherwise no record of the bloody territory wars that had been fought between the indigenous tribes and the invading British and Cape colonials. No-one would have guessed, from this dull and limited exhibition that the ferocious battles of Rourke's Drift and Isandlwana had been fought close nearby.

Perhaps it was a good thing that the museum was so boring, though, thought Sam, because she and Apples wound up talking about themselves – and that *was* interesting. Apples's family sounded fascinating.

"We're a real hodgepodge, I guess," he said, as he lead her into one of the town's only two restaurants, a pizzeria called Luigi's Grotto. They ordered pizzas and drinks and then Sam asked him more about his family.

"My mom's a doctor, a dermatologist. She has a private practice, but also lectures at the varsity – that's where she met Dad, though they were both only students at the time."

"Is he also a doctor?" asked Sam. She was glad that the small table meant that they had to face each other. Her eyes moved over his face as his spoke, from the thick black hair, to the deep teal-blue eyes; from the scar near his lip, to the dimples when he smiled.

"Nope, he's a lecturer in philosophy. So we tend to have strange conversations at dinner time when we're all home. Debates about the ethics of medical experimentation, and Western versus African approaches to medicine over the macaroni cheese – you can just imagine! Also, we're a mixed bag of colour. Mom's white, dad's black – like my little sister, and, as you see, I am–"

145

Gorgeous! Sam wanted to say, but restrained herself.

"–pink all over. My sister and I are both adopted, she's just six years old."

Sam was fascinated. Her own family seemed quite boring by comparison, but Apples seemed interested when she told him about James and her father. He listened without interruption as she told him about her mother's death years before and how she missed her, especially now.

"Why especially now?" Apples asked. He looked down at her hands and Sam saw that her fingers were fiddling with the sugar sachets. She had lined them up, each with their labels upwards, so that their patterns were perfectly aligned. Embarrassed at being caught out in one of her peculiar behaviours, Sam pulled her hands away and sat on them.

"I guess because I could really use my mom's advice right now. I'm having a real problem with this psycho teacher at school – we call him the poison dwarf."

Apples laughed. A waitress brought their food and they each ate a slice of pizza, Samantha trying hard not let strands of melted cheese stick on her chin, before Apples said, "Tell me about him – the poison dwarf."

So, between bites of her Margarita, Sam told him all about her struggle with Delmonico. Parts of the story were horrible, but other bits now seemed kind of funny. Apples listened to all of it, occasionally casting glances at her hands which had somehow escaped and were now occupied with making straight, even lines of sugar granules from a sachet which had spilt its contents onto the red and white checked tablecloth. When she finished telling him the whole sorry story, her hands continued their agitated fiddling.

146

Apples leaned forward, and cupped his hands over hers, stilling them. His hands were very warm against hers. His eyes – the colour of blue on a peacock's feather – seemed to hold a promise as he looked deeply into her own, and said very slowly in his deep, gentle voice, "It's going to be OK, Sam. It's all going to turn out fine. You're smart and strong, you'll figure it out somehow. He's just a bully and you're not going to let him win."

Sam said nothing. She felt like she was falling into his eyes. Then Apples leaned forward over the table and, very softly, kissed the tip of her nose.

Back at school and still somewhat in a daze, Sam saw Nomusa racing up to meet them, her face glowing and split by a wide grin.

"I got in! I made the team! And I came in first on the cross-country event."

"I told you so!" said Jessie.

"Well done you!" Sam gave Nomusa a big hug and they shared high fives all around as Nomusa told them about her day.

"It's going to mean a lot of training and competitions – especially now that cross-country season is coming up," she finished.

"Just make sure you don't skip those survivor games in the hols!" said Jessie. "You got us into them."

"Oh, and have I got a bit of juicy news for you!" said Nomusa. "I bumped into my cousin in Durban today – the one I told you about who went to Academy Girls High in Johannesburg, remember? She's at varsity now, doing teaching, but her younger sister, who's in grade 11, was there trying out for the team – high jump. Shame, she didn't get in even though she's great. And tall – she's even taller than–"

147

"What's the news?" asked Jessie impatiently.

"Oh, right. Well, the official story is that Delmonico left to take up a promotion here. But, actually, it's not a promotion, is it? He was Head of Department at Academy Girls High and now he's just a teacher here, and not even of the senior grades."

"Was there an unofficial story?" asked Sam.

"She said that there was nothing definite, just a lot of rumours and a lot of dissatisfaction because all the girls were doing so badly. And there were complaints about his teaching."

"Imagine that!" said Sam sarcastically.

"What were the rumours about?" asked Jessie.

"She said people were asking questions about why he only ever taught at girls' schools – he was at one before Academy Girls, too."

"You don't mean …?" Jessie was pulling a revolted face.

"No, nothing like that, just that there was a feeling that he was a real bully, and that he could get away with that with girls. If he tried it at a boys' school, particularly with seniors twice his size, he'd probably get decked."

"I'd like to deck him," said Jessie.

"Apples also said Delmonico sounded like a bully," said Sam.

"Oh he did, did he?" said Nomusa, smiling now at Sam and Jessie. "And what else did Apples say? And Dan? Or was there more eye-gazing than chatting going on? C'mon, I want to hear the details. All of them," she said and dragged her two friends off in the direction of the dining room, though Sam suspected that it was she and Jessie, rather than their dinner, that were in for a grilling.

18

Cyber sleuth

It was the third-last week of term before Samantha got a chance to do some investigating into rock art theft. Most of the grade 9 teachers were away on some course that Wednesday, and at breakfast that morning Mrs Grieve advised the girls to spend the free day preparing for their end-of-term examinations, which were only two weeks off.

"Yeah, right," said Jessie, slurping the last of her coffee while paging through a thick fashion magazine. "I'll leave that sort of freaky behaviour to nerdy nuts like you, Sam. I suppose you plan on studying the day away? Hey, where are you going?"

"To the library."

Sam picked up the pad of paper and pencil case she had brought with her to breakfast and then paused, nibbling on a fingernail while she wondered if she would need anything else.

"Why?"

"I want to get going on that rock art research. Oh man!" Sam was examining the tips of her fingers. "I've bitten them all off again."

"You know," said Jessie, rolling up her magazine and leaning forward to whisper confidentially to Sam, "there's a secret to not biting your nails."

"What?" asked Sam eagerly.

"Keep your fingers out of your mouth!" yelled Jessie, walloping Sam about the head and shoulders with the magazine.

"Oh very funny," said Sam, who did not think it was. Jessie and Nomusa and even Poppy, who was sitting nearby, hooted with laughter. Sam squinted her eyes menacingly at Jessie and then headed out the door with a "see you later".

The library at Clifford House was one of the oldest parts of the school buildings, and one of Sam's favourite places. She loved to wander between the high shelves, looking through the rows and rows of books, or to sit at one of the wooden tables beside the sash windows and gaze out at the grounds. Right now, weak sunshine was streaming through the glass panes from the pale, winter-bleached sky outside. It would be lovely to sit at one of those chairs, with the sun warming her back, and read a novel until, lazy with sleep, she dozed off, but Sam had a different mission on her mind today. Branching off from the main library was the media centre – a smaller, more modern room, filled with several computers, printers and photocopiers – and it was to this room that Sam now headed.

She chose a computer at the back of the room and switched it on. Sam did not have a computer at home and was no expert at doing research on the internet, but they had learned some skills in media studies classes and Jessie, who had two computers of her own and who was, in her own words, "a pro" when it came to tracking down things in cyberspace, had given Sam a few more tips.

"Mind you, most of my practice comes from tracking down things like Manolo Bhlaniks and Jimmy Choo's–"

"Jimmy Who's?"

"They make shoes," said Jessie. "Nice ones. But anyway, how different can the research skills be?"

So once Sam had booted up the PC, she loaded the search engine and typed "rock art for sale" into the text box and clicked to search. A total of 118 million results came up. Obviously, she would need to narrow her search somehow – but she clicked on a couple of the first links anyway. She quickly saw that many of the results were for art related to rock music, and others were for books on art. She refined the search by excluding the term "rock and roll" and the search returned 90 000 results – better, but there was still no way she would be able to search them all.

She scanned down the list and clicked on the links that she thought would take her to sites selling art painted on rocks. Most of them were for sites selling rock art souvenirs – prints of cave paintings on posters, T-shirts, key rings and, bizarrely, mini rock art panels inside snow globes. Many of the links were for sites selling replica rock art. There were several artists who painted onto real or fake fiberglass "rocks" and would, for a fee, come paint in the style of ancient artists on "your own rock features or cave walls". You could buy plain chunks of rock mounted on wooden bases, or framed in glass boxes. Then there were scores of artists who painted in modern styles on pieces of rock. Sam thought these paintings – of cougars and woodpeckers and wolves – were ugly, and ruined the natural beauty of the stone. One man was even selling "outhouse art"

– drawings of toilets scratched onto bits of rocks. Who on earth would want to buy this stuff?

She got excited when she saw a result that promised "authentic Aboriginal art" for sale. Perhaps this was one of the pieces of rock art stolen from a site in Australia. When she accessed the site, however, Sam discovered that it was a vendor selling "authentic-*style*" rock art fridge magnets and ashtrays. This was getting her nowhere fast.

By searching for "rock art theft", she found a number of newspaper articles of the sort that had been in Bongi's file, but most of the reports were a dead end because the thieves had never been caught. Sam carefully examined and compared the accounts where there had been arrests, but she could find no common connection or linking pattern.

She paused for a moment to rethink her approach. If she really thought about it, how likely were international art thieves to advertise their wares openly? Not very likely at all. And if they were still operating, it made sense that the thieves she was searching for had not yet been caught. This cyber sleuthing, Sam realised, was going to take a lot longer than she had thought. She cleared her screen of the old results and entered a new search: "authentic rock art". In an attempt to exclude the amateurs and obvious vendors, she added the more technical terms: "petroglyphs and pictographs". There were still over 4000 results, but Sam supposed that was a more manageable number than one hundred and eighteen million. She began reading.

Several hours later, she felt as if her head was full to overflowing with facts and figures about rock art from all corners of the world. She had also learned quite a bit

152

more about the trade in illegal antiquities, but was no closer to tracking down the gang of thieves she believed must be behind the theft and trade in ancient rock art. Her eyes were sore from staring at the screen, and there was a crick in her neck. She now felt a bit silly. She had been naïve to believe that she would be able to find what, presumably, specialised international police units had not been able to. Obviously, illegal operations would have to be covert. She would never find them by searching the net!

At least, she consoled herself, it had been an interesting day's work. Several of the sites she had visited gave her enormous insight into rock art and the ancient cultures in which it had flourished. Many of the sites were quite academic and technical, but Sam enjoyed ploughing through the articles, looking up words she did not understand, and trying to grasp the concepts and theories described. The page that she was currently reading was on one such site. The layout of the website was quite boring and uninspiring: grey block menus and white text against a plain black background. It made for hard reading. Really, thought Sam in exasperation, it was as if they did not *want* to encourage visitors.

The home page contained an introduction to rock art – nothing new there – but there was a *Further Readings* page which listed the topics and brief descriptions of academic papers, research results, dissertations and theses which had been written on the subject. Some of these sounded quite interesting (Sam was quite tempted to read the gruesomely titled "Anthropomorphs and Aztecs: a clue to ancient death rituals and human sacrifices"), but many sounded deadly dull ("Cost-effective rock-art recording within a non-specialist environment") or just too difficult ("Written in stone: etymological underpinnings of language in rock art cryptograms, a postmodernist interpretation").

Sam scrolled through all the article titles until she got to the end of the list. Right in the bottom right-hand corner of the web page, in tiny purple font, was written *Further Readings*. When she held the cursor over the phrase, she saw that it was a link. She clicked on it, wondering why the readings had not merely been listed on the current page, or why the designer had not set up a list of numbered pages so that a reader could easily move through them. The page which appeared was much like the previous one with articles that sounded even more boring, obscure and difficult.

Even though this site must have one of the most comprehensive listings of articles and studies on rock art on the entire internet, Sam noticed that none of the articles seemed to deal with rock art theft. This struck her as a little odd. She examined the menu options at the top and the bottom of the screen and discovered that here was also no way of searching the site for a particular topic – a strange omission, surely, on a site geared for academic research?

Again, the phrase *Further Readings* was tucked into the bottom of the screen. Six more times Sam clicked on the link and six more times it took her to a new page of articles. You would have to be a very dedicated scholar, she thought, to wade through all this detailed information to find the facts you needed. On the bottom of the seventh page, she saw no link and supposed that she had finally come to the end of the material archived on the site.

She was just about to exit the site when she noticed

some small disturbance of the colour on the page in the bottom left-hand corner. She drew her mouse over it and was just able to make out the words *Further Discussion*. They were in black text and, against the black background of the screen, they were almost indiscernible. Almost, thought Sam again, as if they did not want to encourage visitors. In fact, exactly as if they wanted to keep all but certain people out. Excitement rising, she positioned her mouse directly over the writing, and clicked.

19

Chat room

The page which popped up appeared, at first glance, to be a simple chat room where people interested in rock art exchanged messages with each other online. It was titled *Further Discussion Forum* and a quick glance told Sam that there were four discussion threads – one on the best ways of photographing rock art, another on capturing the exact locations of rock art sites with GPS devices, one which offered advice on how best to protect rock art from damage caused by weather and human contact, and one titled "Intact and accessible rock art sites". They were hardly incriminating – none of the titles indicated any illegal activities – and yet Sam thought them suspicious. These would be exactly the sorts of things you would want to know if you were planning to hack out a valuable chunk of rock from some protected place.

Out of habit, she checked the bottom corners of the page and, sure enough, there on the left was a link in tiny purple font: *Taking it Further*. Again there was the use of the word "further" – was it some code, Sam wondered? She clicked on the link, but instead of being taken into a discussion, she was taken to a sign-on screen which wanted a user name and password. Stumped for the moment, she went back to the main chat room page and found a button in the banner which promised to register her as a new user. She hesitated a moment, then typed in her name as Cyber Sam, her age as 44 years, and supplied a false e-mail address. Once she was registered, she returned to the *Taking it Further* page and signed in.

She found herself dropped immediately into a discussion between several users, none of whom seemed to be using real names. She scrolled down to the start of the day's posted comments and began to read carefully upwards from the oldest to the most recent.

RockRaker:	U there, Digger?
Digger_Bill:	I'm here. You haven't posted in weeks. News?
RockRaker:	Been touring the countryside, man. Lots to see, lots to do.
Digger_Bill:	Anything profitable?
RockRaker:	Some. Mostly keeping it small & mobile. Getting harder to get it out & then in here without attracting attention.
Digger_Bill:	Feds are tightening up.

Ha! thought Sam. This was more like it. Then there was a comment from a new person.

Marché_del'art:	Bonjour!
RockRaker:	Hey, glad 2CU Art!
Marché_del'art:	Are you all in good health?
LoneStarGal:	Just peachy, thank you.
Digger_Bill:	Why hi, Star. Didn't expect you today. Thought you might be on an African adventure or something.
LoneStarGal:	It's a small planet, Digger. I'm never more than a 3G connection away ☺. Should we get down to business?

Hang on, thought Sam. *Lone Star*. That rang a bell. Wasn't Texas called the Lone Star State?

RockRaker: Only 1 buyer online 2night. Hardly seems
               worth it.
Marché_del'art: What have you available? Star – you first.

Sam was reading rapidly now. The fingers on her left hand were scrolling up the page, while with her right hand, she was scrawling notes on a piece of paper beside the keyboard: *LoneStarGal, Marché_del'art* and the address of the site. Finally, (finally!) it seemed she had struck gold and found a site where people might actually be trading in rock art.

LoneStarGal: Some fabulous panels, painted, from the
               same area as last time.
Marché_del'art: Size? Quality?
LoneStarGal: I always offer only the best to you, Art,
               you know that, but these are real beauties,
               IMHO. Perfectly preserved, excellent de-
               tail. They were in a very sheltered spot and
               the color is as vivid as the day they were
               painted. As to size, one is about 3ft by 2ft,
               the other two are about 2ft 2" square each.

Sam noticed the spelling of the word "color" and the use of feet and inches; LoneStarGal was definitely American.

Marché_del'art: A little disappointing, Star. A little small.
RockRaker: I've got some merchandise that will inter-
               est U, Art.
LoneStarGal: Shuddup, RockRaker and wait your turn.
               Art, bigger ain't always better! But if it's
               size you want, I've got something really
               special coming up soon. July. A cowboy op-
               eration – it's going to be huge – the biggest
               we've sourced yet.
Marché_del'art: From where?
LoneStarGal: The citadel where the big one lives, in the
               ancient mother.

Marché_del'art:	You're not planning on harvesting the main caves!
RockRaker:	U gotta be kidding!
Digger_Bill:	Impossible! It can't be done, not without destroying the whole thing. Those panels are metres wide!
RockRaker:	No way. LMFAO!

Sam scribbled a few more phrases down: *citadel where the big one lives, ancient mother, main caves, big panels.*

LoneStarGal:	You got to think big, boys! Hey – looks like we've got us a peeping tom!
RockRaker:	Cyber Sam? Don't know U.

With a start, Sam realised that she had read all the way through the conversation and had caught up with posts in real time. They had noticed that she was online and were addressing her directly. What now? She thought quickly, then typed her response.

Cyber_Sam:	Hi Art, Digger, RockRaker & Star. I'm glad I got U all online, I have some gr8 stock I'd like to offer.
Marché_del'art:	Has this user been checked, Star? I don't know him. I'm logging off. We can chat to-morrow at the scheduled time.
RockRaker:	TLK2UL8R

Marché_del'art and RockRaker's icons disappeared from the screen, but Digger and Star seemed curious.

Digger-Bill:	What stock? Taken from where? And why have I never heard of you?
Cyber_Sam:	Pictographs, from the Golden Gate area in the Free State, South Africa.

There was no response from Digger. His icon merely disappeared from the chat room conversation thread.

LoneStarGal:	You're breaking the rules, Sam. Here we never mention exactly what or where – you should know that.
Cyber_Sam:	I'm new to this, OK? Cut me some slack.
LoneStarGal:	You wouldn't be a federal snoop, now would you, Sam? Looking 4 something to investigate?
Cyber_Sam:	Hand on my heart, Star. I've got no more experience investigating than a little girl has. I'm just looking 4 a place to sell some gr8 pieces.

There was a long pause. Sam wondered if Star had left the discussion, even though her icon was still blinking steadily. Then a new comment appeared.

| LoneStarGal: | Have we met, Cyber Sam? |
| Cyber_Sam: | Do you know, I think we just may have. Tell me, how's Mitch these days? |

No sooner had Sam entered the words than LoneStarGal's icon disappeared. Seconds later the screen went blank, except for a message which read: *This site has encountered a problem and will be shut down.* Sam was still debating whether she should try restarting the PC when the processor made a terrible whining noise.

"Uh-oh, that can't be good," said Sam to herself. It was not good. Moments later the screen turned a strange green colour. A black message box in the centre of the screen read: *This computer has encountered a fatal error. Please contact support.*

Sam swore. She had been so close to getting somewhere, she knew it, but now she had almost nothing. On top of which, it looked like she may just have killed a school computer.

20

Never trust a teacher

Sam wasted no time in hurrying off to tell Nomusa and Jessie about what she had found out online, but even as she spoke, she realised how very little she had discovered.

"What's the matter?" asked Nomusa, looking at the face Sam was pulling.

"It's just that I got no real facts," said Sam. "They were being so careful about what they said, that I got no real names or dates or exact places. In fact, I got diddly-squat."

"Maybe not," said Jessie. "There might be a way to track them down from the website. Every computer in the world has a unique address when it uses the internet – maybe some computer geek could trace where the comments were coming from. I think we should log on to that site again."

"OK, but let's take Ms Zenobia so she can see, too. Maybe she knows who it should be reported to."

So the three girls went with Ms Zenobia to the media centre, with Sam explaining to the teacher what she had found on the way. She felt a pang of guilt when she saw a handwritten sign stating "Out of order – computer virus!" stuck on the computer she had used earlier. She tried to avoid making eye contact with the teacher who ran the media centre, but could still feel her accusing glare. Sam sat down at another computer and Ms Zenobia, Jessie and Nomusa clustered behind her while she tracked down the website and accessed the *Further Readings* page.

"It's just after this, you have to keep clicking here," said Sam, clicking through the pages of readings. When she got to the final page, however, there was no *"Further Discussion"* link. She leaned close up to the screen and examined the page closely, moving her mouse all around to check for more of the concealed black-on-black writing.

"It's gone! They've taken away the link."

"You can't find it?"

"It's not here. They've taken down the chat room, or the link to it. That just proves they're up to something!"

"Unfortunately, it proves nothing," said Ms Zenobia, pulling up a chair next to Sam and sitting down.

"What do you mean?" asked Jessie. "Sam told you what they were talking about. They're planning a big theft."

"We've got to do something to stop them," said Sam.

"Girls," said Ms Zenobia, looking at their upset faces, "in truth, they could have been talking about anything or nothing. We have no proof. Imagine me going to the police and trying to get them to investigate something which might be committed somewhere by someone. Where would they even start? I'm sorry, Sam, but you got no real information – there's no evidence that that chat room ever existed."

"I know, it's my fault. I was stupid to mention the name Mitch. But I was so sure it was that Texan woman, Dorothy. At the time, I thought maybe that if I showed I knew their names, then she would think perhaps she

162

knew me. But that was just dumb. The names are obviously aliases, and all I managed to do was warn her that I had met them in their disguise. She knew immediately and so she logged off, closed the chat room and sent a virus to my computer to try to shut me down."

"What about those codes, though?" asked Nomusa.

"What codes?" Ms Zenobia asked.

"Their names, for a start. Digger and RockRaker – those sound like people who would do the excavating. Lone Star refers, I think, to an American from Texas. And this one here, I think it's French."

Jessie leaned over and read the name. "Marché_del' art – that means 'the art market'!"

"Any other codes?"

"They didn't mention exact places, but they – she – was planning a theft in July. She called it a cowboy operation – maybe because they're rounding up stray works of art. 'At the citadel where the big one lives' she said."

"What's a citadel, anyway?" asked Jessie.

"It's like a fortress, or a stronghold. And then she said something about the 'ancient mother'. I figured those were codes of some kind. The others seemed to know exactly what, or where, she meant. It was at a cave."

"Well," said Ms Zenobia with an indulgent smile as she stood up to leave, "if you crack the code, let me know and I'll try to send a warning. I applaud your efforts, girls, but perhaps you should spend less time researching this and more time preparing for your exams – they're only two weeks away."

"Why is it," asked Jessie, staring reproachfully at Ms Zenobia's departing back, "that adults never take us seriously?"

As they arrived back at their dorm room, Sam saw that there was a note pinned to the door. It was addressed to her. She opened it and read the few sentences inside with a sinking heart, then looked up at Nomusa and Jessie.

"What is it?" said Nomusa.

"Mrs Grieve wants to see me."

They all looked at each other for a few moments, saying nothing.

"It's about my Maths and Science, I know it is."

Sam checked that her uniform was in order and brushed her hair into a neater ponytail before heading down to the administration block, her friends' wishes of good luck hanging in the air behind her.

The secretary stationed outside Mrs Grieve's office told her to go straight in, but Sam paused for a moment to take a deep breath before she knocked and entered. The room looked as it had on the only other occasion when Sam, along with Jessie and Nomusa, had been summoned to Mrs Grieve to have a strip torn off them for their prank with the room. This time, Mrs Grieve looked in no better a mood. She told Sam to take a seat on the other side of her massive, polished wood desk on top of which rested a beige file. Even reading upside-down, Sam could clearly see the label: Steadman, S.

"I called you in, Samantha, because I felt it was high time we discussed your performance in Mathematics and Science."

Even though she had been expecting it, Sam still felt the cold, lead weight settle back in her stomach.

"Yes, ma'am."

"I was shocked to see that your marks in these two subjects have declined alarmingly. Mr Delmonico was kind enough to draw my attention to the matter."

Interfering, trouble-making git, thought Sam, but she said only, "Yes, ma'am."

"We can't have the recipient of our academic scholarship underperforming academically, now can we, Samantha?"

There it was – the threat that hung over her constantly, that drove her days and disturbed her nights, the ultimate power that they had over her.

"No, ma'am."

"What seems to be the problem, Samantha?" Mrs Grieve opened the file and studied the printing on a piece of paper which had been lying on top of the filed notes inside. "You appear to be maintaining your marks in other subjects quite satisfactorily."

"It's Mr Delmonico, ma'am. I can't seem to get the work right according to what he wants. And how he wants it." Sam tried to be careful in how she phrased the words.

"He has, I know, exacting standards. But we do want Clifford girls to meet such standards."

"It's not so much that his standards are exacting, ma'am, as that they are petty." Now she'd done it. Mrs Grieve raised an eyebrow, but said nothing, so Sam plunged on.

"He has all these ridiculous rules about exactly where the date and heading have to be, and how many times you should underline them, and exactly how many lines you should leave before you rule off. None of that is relevant to the study of maths or science, surely? And he takes marks off if you do those things differently to how he wants them, even if your actual work is right. And he takes marks off if your spelling is wrong. It's not fair. Surely he should only take marks off for incorrect work and answers?"

165

Mrs Grieve looked a little taken aback. "Have you tried discussing this with him?" she asked.

"Yes. He merely says getting the *exact details* right is important for the hard sciences."

"He has a point."

"Ma'am, – none of the other teachers take marks off for spelling mistakes, apart from English and Afrikaans, obviously. And I suppose French. And so many marks – I got minus 2 out of 20 for my last file mark, even though all the work was there. Surely there should be a limit as to how may marks can be deducted for spelling and presentation?"

"Of course there is. You need to check the rubric."

"He won't give us a mark breakdown, and when I asked him about maximum marks lost for presentation, he said I was being insolent and that he was the one who would decide how to allocate marks. He's completely unreasonable."

Encouraged by the fact that Mrs Grieve was listening attentively and was not rushing to Mr Delmonico's defence, Sam continued.

"He picks on me."

"What do you mean?" Mrs Grieve looked sternly concerned.

"Well, he's tough on everyone, but he seems to have it in for me in particular. It's like he doesn't want me to do well, like it's personal. He seems pleased when I do badly – as if he enjoys it that the person who was at the top isn't anymore. And," the words were tumbling out of her mouth now, like a stream that had been held back but was now able to run freely, "he doesn't ever actually teach – not really. I mean, he doesn't explain properly. He just assigns readings in the textbooks and does one or two examples. And if you ask a question because you don't understand, he accuses you of not listening, or of wasting his time. And he's sexist, ma'am, he says girls aren't fitted for doing maths and science."

"I think you are going a bit far, now, Samantha. Mr Delmonico is a fine teacher with excellent credentials. He has brought prestige to this school by accepting the position here, we are very fortunate to have him. I am sure he wants only the best for his students. And as for him being sexist, that's just ludicrous. Why on earth would he teach at a girls' school if he thought girls were incapable of doing his subjects?"

"He–" began Sam, wanting to tell Mrs Grieve that there had been similar complaints against Delmonico at his previous school, but Mrs Grieve held up a hand while she continued speaking.

"If he seems particularly tough on you, it will be because he knows you are capable of more, take it from me. I will have a word with Mr Delmonico and we will then decide how best to deal with this matter. I suggest, however, that you knuckle down to some serious studying in these subjects – Miss Atkins is currently performing better than you in both. And you know that the scholarship is re-awarded each year to the top candidate. Do your absolute best in the upcoming examinations. You may go."

"Yes, ma'am," said Sam.

She felt slightly more optimistic after her session with Mrs Grieve. She thought perhaps Mrs Grieve had been surprised by some of the things that Sam had told her and that she might talk Mr Delmonico into being more reasonable. Sam hoped that things would get better in his classes. Instead, they got much worse – a turn of events which Jessie predicted when Sam recounted what Mrs Grieve had said.

167

"Big mistake, Sam, huge. You should never have said that stuff about him being unreasonable and picking on you. You mark my words, she'll run straight to him and tell him everything you said, and he'll go ballistic."

"You can't know that she'll blab," said Nomusa.

"Oh can't I? Never trust a teacher. They stick together like packs of crows."

"Flocks," corrected Sam automatically.

"Whatever. And principals are the worst of the lot. They say one thing to your face and another behind your back. A princi is not your pal."

And, judging from the next lesson with Mr Delmonico, it seemed Jessie was right. At the beginning of the lesson, once the whole class had taken their seats and were silent, Mr Delmonico looked at Sam and said, "Mrs Grieve has spoken to me of your difficulties in my classes, Miss Steadman, of your struggles to meet my standards and of what rests on your ability to achieve higher marks in my subjects."

"Uh-oh," breathed Jessie, who was sitting on the stool next to Sam. "Here it comes."

Mr Delmonico stood, straightened his computer so that it sat in the perfect centre of his desk, and walked to stand in front of the class. He looked around at all of them, then fixed his eyes on Sam again.

"She explained that you judge my requirements to be *petty* and *unreasonable*, even *ridiculous*."

Sam felt her ears grow hot. She could not believe that Mrs Grieve had told him her exact words! She could almost feel the "I told you so" coming in waves off Jessie beside her. She looked down at her hands, her fingers were itching to tap, but the poison dwarf would surely read that as impatience. She snatched them under the desk where they began unravelling a loose thread from the hem of her skirt.

"Mrs Grieve and I have discussed the importance of accuracy and rigorous standards in my subjects, and she agrees that there should be no adjustment to my requirements for neat presentation or to my methods of assessment. So that's that."

Samantha looked up, hardly daring to believe that he could have finished. He had not. Speaking in a soft and dangerous voice, he continued.

"However, there are two other issues bothering you, apparently, that I feel compelled to address as they cause me great concern."

He did not look concerned in the slightest. He looked incensed. His nostrils were pinched, a thin blue vein pulsed under the pale skin at his temple, and his brown eyes glittered with barely suppressed anger.

"If I understand correctly, Miss Steadman, you believe me to be a poor teacher who does not explain properly and, moreover, you consider me to be personally biased against you, that I have something against you because you are the top student. And it is these factors to which you attribute your abysmal performance in Maths and Science. IS THAT RIGHT?" His voice rose to a shout on the last words. Sam could only stare at him in shocked silence, the dismay of Grieve's betrayal bitter in her mouth.

"I would like to know," said Delmonico, addressing the whole class now, his eyes glaring a challenge, "I would like to establish by a show of hands if anyone else in this class has complaints about me."

On the stool beside Sam, Jessie shuffled. Her hand began to rise and she started to speak, "We-ell..."

"No!" hissed Sam, pushing Jessie's arm down with one of her own. She herself was already deep in the *dwang*, but there was no need for Jessie to join her. Jessie scowled at Sam, but kept silent. Nobody else in the class said a word or moved a muscle.

"Right. That would seem to indicate that the problem is limited to you, Miss Steadman. Therefore, so too must the solution be. In an attempt to demonstrate that I have nothing *personal* against you," he said with bitter sarcasm, "to show that I only want you to achieve at the level which others appear to believe you capable of, and in an attempt to convince you that I am, most definitely, capable of *explaining* and *teaching* even those whose innate ability is questionable, I will be taking you for a one-on-one extra lesson this Saturday. Be here at 7:30 a.m. sharp. Eight hours ought to do the trick."

Sam slumped in her stool as he turned away and walked over to the desk. He picked up the textbook, opened it to the marked page and said, "Turn to page 261, we begin with exercise 7.2.1." Then he looked at Sam and spoke in a falsely kind voice. "Miss Steadman, if it's not too much trouble, please would you also open your book to page 261, along with the others. I don't for a moment want you to feel that I'm *picking* on you, but I would hate you to fall even further behind."

Sam opened her book and looked down, unseeing, at the page, shielding her face with the open hand on which she rested her forehead. Swallowing hard, she brushed a drop of moisture off the paper.

21

Poison dwarf

The rest of that day and the next flew by in a blur of revision for the coming exams and a mounting dread of the extra lesson with Delmonico on Saturday. Every time Sam thought of either event, she felt physically sick. Her taps and fidgets, her checking and what-iffing had reached an all-time high.

"You need to take a chill-pill, Sam. No offence, but you're going nuts," said Jessie, and she was not the only one who had noticed.

"You're a freaking headcase, Steadman," said Cindy when she caught Sam entering the Afrikaans classroom, then backing out, tapping an equal number of times on each side of the doorframe, and then re-entering. "Any day now the men in white coats will come to haul you off to the loony-bin."

On Friday afternoon, as the temperature outside plummeted, everyone had some different last-minute advice for how best to handle the next day's session with the poison dwarf

Mercy Tshabalala, who had also suffered in Delmonico's class, told Sam softly that she would pray for her.

"Thanks," said Sam, "I'll take all the help I can get."

Jessie's advice was tempting, but not very practical: "I reckon you have to avoid the whole thing altogether, because if you go, you'll wind up killing him. I know I would. A whole day – a Saturday – with the poison dwarf! No ways! I think you ought to run away for the weekend – it's still not too late. Call your dad and tell him you're having a nervous breakdown. I mean, you kind of are," she added, casting a glance at Sam who, in an attempt not to bite her nails right down to the quick again, was now feverishly popping the bubbles on a piece of bubble wrap she had found in the art room supplies cupboard.

"Tell him to come fetch you, today still. Or else – wait, this is a good idea! – fake you're sick and check into the sick room tonight, groaning and stuff. Maybe if you start eating a lot of prunes now, you could give yourself real stomach cramps and diarrhoea. Matron would protect you – I'd like to see that sick midget get by her. She could take him any day."

"There's no point. He'll only reschedule it. I advise tissues, very soft two-ply's," said Nomusa, and she handed Sam a wodge of them.

"What…?"

"He's going to make you frustrated. Well, he always frustrates you, but I reckon he's really going to go for it this time. And you know how you are – when you get angry, and you can't let it out, then you cry."

Sam stuffed the tissues in the pocket of her blazer, which hung in the wardrobe ready for the next day's ordeal, and sighed. Then she grabbed her phone and crept into the cupboard at the end of the room; it was a favourite spot from which she and Jessie enjoyed making their private calls to Apples and Dan. The green glow from the old phone's screen reflected dimly on the happy-faced giraffe. It seemed to be mocking her. Sam turned her back on it to listen to Apples's encouragement. He spoke so kindly and gently that Sam felt tears welling up in her eyes; apparently her tear glands were also activated by tenderness.

"He's going to try to crack you, Sam," Apples predicted. "He's going to press all your buttons and try to get you to say or do something that will land you in even more trouble, put you even more under his power. Sounds to me like he's got a thing against girls and especially top students. Maybe he always came second to a girl back in the Middle Ages when he was at school. You just need to hang in there, stay steady."

"How?" asked Sam. It was all she could get out past the constriction in her throat.

"Just don't respond to anything he says or does. Don't rise to the bait. Nod and agree and do the work he gives you, but don't argue or try to convince him. Don't lash out. You need to sit there like a stone, a rock. I'll call you after, OK?"

"OK," said Sam in a little voice.

Later, in the chilly corridor on her way down to go bath and brush her teeth, she realised that news of her date with Demonico must have spread to the other grade 9 classes. Cindy Atkins, coming out of the bathroom, blocked Sam's way, smiled widely and said, "Enjoy tomorrow, Steadman, hope you have loads of fun. And don't worry so much – next year all the pressure will be off."

"What's that supposed to mean?" Sam could not help asking.

"See, if you don't have the scholarship, no-one will care what marks you get." Cindy made a point of bashing against Sam's shoulder as she pushed past, laughing.

It was still dark the next morning when Sam woke up from her restless sleep, and dressed in her uniform

173

(as Delmonico had specified) as quietly as possible so as not to wake Jessie and Nomusa who were still buried beneath their thick duvets. She wound a school scarf around her neck, zipped up the regulation navy-blue windbreaker and pulled the hood up before stepping outside. The late June morning was bitterly cold as she made her way across the grounds to the dining hall. She figured that she needed to eat something before she started, but she managed to force down only a few spoons of porridge before pushing the bowl away. She grabbed a banana and an apple, stowed them in her bag and headed down the dark and deserted corridors to Delmonico's classroom. Heavy grey clouds hung threateningly low in the sky, and the world was silent and still except for the icy breeze which whistled down the passages, around the columns and quadrangles, and bit at Sam's face and hands.

Mr Delmonico was already waiting in his classroom, seated behind his desk. He was muffled in a thick jacket and scarf, a heavy rug was tucked snugly around his legs and the twin red bars of a small electric heater were glowing under his desk. When Sam knocked at the door, he looked down at his watch, but she had made sure not to fall into the trap of being late.

"Good morning, Miss Steadman. You may enter and take a seat." He indicated a stool against the wall, just below a large open window. The classroom was freezing – apart, presumably, from the toasty spot where Delmonico sat – but when Sam made to close the window, Delmonico forestalled her.

"Leave that window open, Miss Steadman. A little fresh air will be necessary, I think, to blow the cobwebs from your brain and keep you wide awake for my lesson."

Sam clenched her teeth and tried to remember Apples's advice. She kept her windbreaker and scarf on. She sat down on a stool at the long lab bench, took out her books, pencil case and paper, then looked up expectantly at him. The lesson began.

It seemed like an eternity later that, checking her own watch and seeing that it was only half-past nine, Sam realised she was still not yet even halfway through her day's torment. A pile of used tissues lay crumpled beside her place at the desk.

For all of their time together so far, Delmonico had sat under his blanket, occasionally pouring himself a cup of what smelled like hot chocolate from a large flask on his desk. He instructed Sam from a distance, clicking the odd slide or example onto the smartboard by tapping a finger on his computer. When he needed to check her work, he made her come to his desk, but never for long enough for her to warm her legs at his heater. She disliked being that close to him, anyway. The pale translucence of his skin revolted her and the sweet, spicy smell of his aftershave turned her stomach. When he pointed to a diagram of a formula in the textbook, she noticed that there was an exact even crescent of white at the edge of each of his nails, and that the nails gleamed with a dull sheen. Could it be possible that the man manicured and buffed his nails?

When he stirred himself to explain, Delmonico seemed deliberately to skip steps. When she asked him to clarify, he tisked in mock concern and said things like, "I can see this is very difficult for you to grasp, Miss Steadman. Very well, let me try, *again*, to explain how this works. Try to keep up this time."

Samantha had never felt so stupid in her life. When he made her demonstrate calculations for him, crouch-

175

ing awkwardly over the paper from where she stood next to his desk, he interrupted to criticise the layout of her work, the untidiness of her handwriting, the pressure with which she applied her pen to the paper. He called her careless and sloppy. She became so self-conscious about *how* she was doing the work, that she lost focus on *what* she was doing, and made silly mistakes. She rather thought this had been his intention.

When he said, "Oh dear, Maths and Science seem to defeat you at every turn, Miss Steadman. Perhaps the most sensible option would be for you to give up the subjects at the end of the year, and select a less challenging course of study for matric," Sam clenched her hands into fists so hard that she could feel the little that remained of her nails digging into her palms.

"I will definitely be taking both Maths and Science for matric, sir."

"I see," said Delmonico and a small smile curved his lips, showing the sharp little teeth beneath. "But perhaps not here."

"Sir?"

"It's my understanding, Miss Steadman, and please correct me if I'm wrong, that your attending Clifford House is made possible only by the academic scholarship which you hold. Or *currently* hold, I should say – it's always important to be precise, to be absolutely accurate, isn't it? One must get the details right. If you lose your top position in the academic standings, then you lose the financial assistance. Which may mean you might need to leave the school, since it seems your family is hardly, shall we say, rolling in the dough. Dear me, that would be a tragedy. How we would miss you." The smile had reached his eyes now. The tears had reached hers.

Samantha said nothing. *Steady, steady, steady* she repeated to herself in her mind, and she tried to make her face as blank as the unresponsive rock Apples had described, but Delmonico's next words made it impossible.

"You mother *would* be disappointed. Perhaps it is better that she is not here to witness your underperformance."

"I beg your pardon?" said Sam loudly, standing up so suddenly that her stool was knocked backwards onto the floor. She ignored it. Her heart was thumping hard in her chest and she felt a tightening of skin creep over her scalp.

"Your mother was a lawyer?"

"To be precise, she was an advocate."

Delmonico gave her a suspicious look, but continued, "Well, she would have valued intelligence and academic achievement rather more highly than dim-wittedness and failure. From what I understand from my reading of your personal file, your mother passed away when you were eleven?"

"No."

"Excuse me?"

"To be accurate, I was ten years old when she died." Sam felt as if hot laser beams were projecting from her eyes now. They seemed to have sizzled up all the tears.

"Are you being insolent, Miss Steadman?"

Sam was delighted to see that the little smile had been wiped off his face.

"Not at all, sir." Sam tried, and failed, to inject a note of false politeness into her voice. The words came out flat and grim. "I'm merely trying to be *absolutely* correct. You have taught me how vitally important that is, sir."

He stared at her for a long moment, then said, "Pick up that stool Miss Steadman, and continue with your work. You have many more hours still to go."

Sam bent over to pick up the stool, noticing as she did so that her hands were shaking with rage. She banged it loudly back onto its feet and sat down, yanking her work towards her. Her hands no longer felt the urge to tap or fiddle, they longed to wring his scrawny, pale neck. Through the haze of anger which pulsed through her, she became aware of excited cries coming from outside. Looking out the window, she was shocked to see that the grass and the bushes and trees of the gardens outside were all covered with a dusting of white. White flakes were drifting down from the low clouds above. It was snowing!

Girls were running through the gardens to one side of the lab, and through the quadrangle beyond the corridor on the other, yelling happily and pointing to the imprints their footsteps left in the snow-covered ground. A few were trying to scoop handfuls of the stuff together to throw at each other. Sam saw Nomusa and Jessie leaping about gleefully in the quadrangle, casting looks at Delmonico's lab to see if they could catch sight of her; she half rose out of her seat, her body leaning towards the door and the noisy joy beyond.

"What exactly are you doing, Miss Steadman?"

"Sir, it's snowing!"

"Indeed. And have you never seen snow before, Miss Steadman."

"No, sir." She wanted to add, "I live in Africa, you moron," but she did not. Perhaps he would relent, given how exceptional the circumstance of snow was.

"This is the first time you have seen it in your life?"

"Precisely, sir."

178

"You have never seen it overseas?"

"I have never been out of South Africa, sir."

"I see." He fingered his chin with his small, white hands. "Then it seems to me that it would be very cruel to keep you from joining your friends and enjoying this unusual event. Why, it might be the only time you ever get to experience the stuff!"

"Yes, sir. So may I ...?"

But Delmonico's cold smile was back. "Sit down, Miss Steadman, and do your work."

"But, sir!"

"I said, sit!"

She knew it would be hopeless to protest and she refused to beg – it would only give him more of the twisted satisfaction that already lit his eyes. She sat down and stared again at her books. The anger which, minutes before, had strengthened and buoyed her, had drained away. She was stuck here. Even when Jessie and Nomusa knocked on Delmonico's door to plead for her to be released from the lesson so she could see the snow, Sam's spirits did not rise.

"No," said Delmonico baldly.

"But, sir, don't you think it's important for the true scientist to experience different phenomena first-hand?" asked Jessie.

"Unless you wish to experience first-hand the phenomenon of joining Miss Steadman in her extra lesson, Miss Delaney, I suggest that you take yourself away at once."

Jessie looked a question at Sam, who merely shook her head glumly. A little while later, a small, tightly-packed ball of icy snow flew in through the open window above Sam's head, sailed over the empty desks and stools, and landed with a splat on Delmonico's desk. It was an excellent shot – Nomusa must have been the one to throw it – and it gave Sam the only glimmer of satisfaction she had had all day.

Delmonico betrayed his annoyance only with a slight tightening of the mouth. He swept the icy pulp off his desk to the floor, where it soon melted into a small puddle. Then he stood up, pulled on a pair of black leather gloves and announced to Sam that he was off to investigate the snow for himself; she was to remain behind and continue with her work. A good half-hour later, he returned, holding a handful of snow in his gloved hands.

"Fascinating stuff, snow," he said. "A quite remarkable substance. Each snowflake is actually a crystalline structure – that's why you can pack them together, like this," he squeezed the snow into a ball. "Each flake has a unique shape, determined by the temperature and humidity at which it is formed." He examined the icy crystals from every angle.

"You wouldn't guess it from the racket those girls are making out there – my, they *are* enjoying themselves, aren't they? – but fresh snow actually absorbs sound. The air trapped between the snowflakes minimises vibration. It also absorbs short-wave radiation from the sun. All these scientific details are interesting and yet, the overall impression which stays with one, is that snow is *fun*! Hm!"

He looked at Sam and gave a little shiver of delight. Then he tossed the snowball out the classroom, closed the door and returned to his desk.

"Let's see, where were we?"

The rest of the day ground on in a torment of malice and nit-picking instruction from his side, and silent

180

misery from hers. When, eventually, she was released from the lesson, the sun was low in a sky clear of all but a few wisps of cloud. Sad puddles on the stone floor of the quadrangle, and a few thin traces of white along the shady edges of the now muddy grass were the only evidence that remained of the snow. It had snowed for the first, and possibly the only time in her life, and Sam had missed it. Because of him.

She loathed him with every fibre of her being and, as she kicked the door of their dorm room open, banging it against the wall and startling Jessie and Nomusa inside, she vowed, "I am going to get even with him, if it's the last thing I do."

22

Revenge

The chance to get even with Delmonico presented itself sooner than Sam could have hoped – in Monday's Science lesson with him, just two days after the Saturday extra lesson. It was a double period before second break and seemed to stretch on for hours. Sam seethed quietly in her usual seat, avoiding eye contact with the poison dwarf and consoling herself with fantasies of revenge.

Five minutes before the bell for break was due to ring, Mr Delmonico's cellphone rang and he stepped outside the classroom to take the call. Just as he walked back into the room a few minutes later and placed his phone on the desk, the intercom buzzed. It was Mrs Grieve requesting Mr Delmonico to come to her office for an important matter. He assured her he was on his way, retrieved his jacket from a hook near the door and slipped it on, then ran a hand over his hair to smooth it down.

"No-one is to leave this classroom before the bell rings. Last one out closes the door. Understood?"

"Yes, sir," they all chanted, but muttered some less polite words to him once he had left the room.

"Wish she'd called him out at the start of the lesson," said Charné Roos, a pretty girl with short brown hair.

"Maybe it's a parent, come to complain," said Skye MacAdam.

"Perhaps it's the police, come to arrest him for cruelty to children," said Nomusa hopefully.

"With our luck, she's calling him in to promote him to deputy principal," said Jessie. Everyone was already packing away their stuff, and putting on their blazers and windbreakers so as to be able to leave the moment the bell rang.

Sam said nothing. She was staring at the front of the classroom with glazed eyes. When the bell rang half a minute later, and everyone scrambled for the door, she remained seated. Jessie waved a hand in front of her eyes.

"Hullo? Anybody in there?"

As if in a dream, Sam stood up and walked over to Mr Delmonico's desk. She reached out a hand and picked up his cellphone, then said, very calmly, "Nomusa, please would you stand at the door and keep watch? There's something I want to do, and I don't want to get interrupted. Or caught."

"Sam, are you sure?" said Nomusa, looking worriedly from Sam's face to the phone in her hand. Sam's fingers were already swiping across the touch-screen, switching it on.

"Oh, yes," said Sam. "I'm perfectly sure. And look – no password protection – how *careless and sloppy* of him not to take care of that *detail*."

Nomusa shrugged and headed to the door where she positioned herself just inside the doorway, occasionally peeping out to make sure the corridor was clear. Sam's fingers flew over the keyboard.

"What are you doing?" asked a stunned-looking Jessie, who had walked up to Sam.

183

"I'm changing one digit in every telephone number of the contacts in his favourite people list," said Sam. "So that when he tries to call them, he'll get the wrong number. It's so important, I've been told, to get every last *detail* right."

"Awesome!" cackled Jessie, who was now looking delighted. "Epic!" She rubbed her hands together and looked around as if in search of something she could do to get back at Delmonico, too.

"There," said Sam, placing the phone back on the desk a few minutes later. "Done."

"Not so fast. I want a go at Mr Moontan, too," said Jessie. She snatched up the phone, rested her butt up against Delmonico's desk, and began typing.

"Coast still clear, Nomusa?" asked Sam.

"Yes."

Sam sat down in the chair behind Delmonico's desk, paused for a moment as she scanned its surface, and then fished a metal nail file out of a blazer pocket. She pulled the small grey laptop computer from its spot in the precise centre of his desk, closer to herself. Using the nail file she prised buttons of the letter-keys off the keyboard, switched them around with others, and then clicked them back. When she had finished, the entire alphabet and number pad was muddled and out of sequence.

"Time to go, Jessie. We're done here," said Sam.

"No ways, I'm on a roll here," said Jessie.

Sam stood and peered over Jessie's shoulder. It seemed that Jessie was giving Delmonico's friends, family and colleagues new names. The list of names under his Contacts now included King Kong, Elvis Presley, Mr D. Etail, Attila the Hun, Madame Curie, He-who-must-not-be-named and the Gingerbread Man.

Sam gasped with laughter, but said, "Enough! Let's go."

"Just two more minutes!"

"Hurry!" whispered Nomusa urgently.

Sam looked around, then pulled a few of the identical black files off the shelf where they were so neatly ordered. Working quickly, she extracted pages at random and filed them back in different places, under the wrong dividers; she even put a few into the wrong files. She was just placing the files carefully back into their correct places on the shelf when Nomusa whispered, "Chips! Teachers!"

Jessie tossed the phone back onto the desk, and she and Sam scuttled over to Nomusa, squeezing themselves behind the open door. They squashed up against the wall – Sam had to put one foot in the dustbin to prevent toppling over – and tried to stand as quietly and as still as they could, all the while fighting the hysterical giggles which threatened to spill over. Jessie actually clapped a hand over her mouth, though Sam could still hear muffled hiccupping noises. When the voices and footsteps coming up the corridor got closer, Sam could tell that it was Mr De Wet and Miss Abeille, the French teacher.

"We could go out for dinner, but I only know steak-houses, no fancy places. I know you people from France like to eat frogs' legs and drink red wine," they heard Mr De Wet's voice coming from up the corridor.

"Not every night, Mistair De Veet, and never together!" Miss Abeille gave a light laugh.

"No?"

"Ah, no. It is white meat, you know – les cuisses de grenouille."

"Le who de what?"

185

Sam was relieved that Mr De Wet's infatuation with Miss Abeille made him so engrossed in her that he did not even glance at the classroom, or wonder why its door was open even though it was practice for every teacher to close their doors at break.

"Ze frog's legs. Therefore, it matches ill with red wine. A light white would be better, perhaps a Chardonnay."

"A Chardonnay, ja, for sure!" Their voices were fading now, they had passed the classroom.

"We're pushing our luck," said Nomusa. "Let's get out of here now."

"But I still wanted to read his text messages," protested Jessie.

"No," said Sam, "that would be wrong." Both Jessie and Nomusa gave her baffled looks. Sam could not have explained why she thought that invading his privacy was worse than jumbling his numbers and keyboard, but she did.

So they grabbed their bags, crept to the door and peeped out. There was no-one in the corridor, and only a few girls at the back of the quad beyond. They slipped out of the room, pulling the door closed behind, and walked away quickly. They had got a mere thirty paces away when they burst out laughing in a mixture of shock, fear and absolute joyous delight.

For one glorious day, it seemed that they would get away with their prank. They had taken a vow between themselves not to tell another living soul – "and that includes Dan, Jessie!" – and Sam hoped that Delmonico might not want to share his embarrassment with anyone else either.

"Maybe his pride won't let him report it. Maybe he'll just act like nothing happened."

Her hopes were misplaced, however. On Wednesday morning, their class was told to remain behind in the school hall after the morning assembly. Mr Delmonico and Mrs Grieve stood in front of them, their expressions severe, waiting while the other girls filed out of the hall.

"Someone," said Mrs Grieve to the silent class, "some ill-disciplined and very unwise young lady in this class has played a prank on Mr Delmonico by swopping around the keys on his computer and by changing the names of his contacts in his cellphone to names which are patently false, including: Henny Penny, Chicken Little and Justin Bieber!"

Sam burst out laughing with the rest of the class, but the smiles were immediately wiped off their faces by the glare which Mrs Grieve shot them. Mr Delmonico looked like he would rather not have had the details of the prank made known. His usually pale face had flushed a deep red, and his lips were pinched white. He stared from one girl to the next with deep malevolence etched on his features.

"There is nothing amusing about behaving in a way that causes others upset and trouble, grade 9's," said Mrs Grieve. No, there isn't, thought Sam, not even when it's a teacher doing it to a pupil. She looked straight back at Delmonico, whose floating brown irises had now settled on her. She kept her own face expressionless while, inside, she was rejoicing that Delmonico had apparently not yet discovered the disorganised state of his files. That particular treat still lay in store for him.

"I would like the individual, or individuals, responsible for this prank to step forward and confess right now. I am giving you precisely one minute," said Mrs Grieve.

No-one moved – except to glance around to check if anyone was going to take the blame. Sam, Jessie and Nomusa exchanged brief looks, but otherwise stayed still and said nothing.

"Woe betide the culprits when I catch them, as I will. If anyone has any information for us, we will remain here after you leave and that person can come tell us in complete confidentiality."

Jessie snorted derisively at this.

"In the meantime – you leave me no choice – I will be punishing the entire class. You will all have detention every afternoon this week and on Saturday and Sunday afternoon as well. You will not be permitted to attend extramural activities. Those of you who had made arrangements to go home this weekend will cancel your plans. You will all report to Mr Delmonico's classroom immediately after school today."

A chorus of groans and protests met this announcement, but Mrs Grieve merely declared them dismissed and turned to talk quietly with Mr Delmonico.

"It's so unfair," complained Pat Mbalula, in a whiney voice.

"I'll tell you what's unfair," snapped Jessie as they all walked down the corridor to their next lesson, "it's unfair that he can treat us like he wants and no one stops or punishes *him*. What's a little inconvenience compared to what he's done to us?"

"Yes, but now we all have detentions – every day. *And* this weekend," said Pat.

"I don't mind at all," said Uvani Moodley. "I say cheers to whoever did it. We all hate him, he's been awful to each of us. Whoever pulled that prank did it for all of us. I don't mind a few detentions – we have to

188

stay in and study for the exams next week anyway. I just wish I knew what other names were in that phone. It's hilarious!" she laughed.

Most of the class seemed to take the same view as Uvani, but Sam was no longer listening. Her shoes, like her heart, felt as though they were filled with lead. She had made a mess of Delmonico's things to get back at him for his meanness to her, but now everyone was suspected, everyone was in trouble. She stopped walking. Nomusa and Jessie were a few steps ahead before they noticed that she was not with them.

"What's wrong, Sam?" asked Nomusa, turning around to face her.

"She's right. It *is* unfair."

"Oh ignore Pat. She's always whinging on about something. It's about time she learned that life isn't fair. You'd have thought she would have learned that already from being in the poison dwarf's class," said Jessie dismissively.

"It's not right," said Sam.

Jessie walked around behind Sam and gave her a little push in the base of her spine. "C'mon Sam, let's go" she urged.

But Sam stayed where she was.

"Sam?" said Nomusa.

"I'm tired," said Sam.

"Too tired to walk to Biology class? It's not far," said Jessie.

"I'm so very tired – sick and tired – of feeling afraid."

"Well then, don't feel it anymore. They're not going to catch us."

No, thought Sam to herself, they probably wouldn't. But she would always fear they might. Like she always feared doing something wrong, feared disappointing others, getting into trouble, losing the scholarship, getting expelled. She needed to make a decision, and it felt like a big one – bigger than this mere issue of the prank. Either she had to live the rest of her life like this – in endless fear and heavy dread and joy-sapping anxiety – or she had to confront the thing that terrified her head on.

"Hey! Where are you going? We've got Biology now," said Jessie as Sam spun around on her heels and headed rapidly back down the corridor.

"I'll be there in a few minutes – I just forgot something," Sam called back, and she walked back to the hall where Grieve and Delmonico waited.

23

Worst fear

Sam's certainty that she was doing the right thing grew as she strode back to the hall; she only doubted *whether* she would be able to do the thing she so feared. Her whole body felt as if it was trembling, and she was battling to take a deep breath. She knew she stood to lose the scholarship, but she knew, too, that if she did not stand up to Delmonico and to Grieve, that she stood to lose even more: her dignity, her self-respect and sense of worth. Was she always going to knuckle under to the threat of losing the scholarship, always going to back down and not defend her friends against unfair teachers because she might "get into trouble"? Was she going to allow bullies like Delmonico to get away with ill-treating everyone, herself included, because she was too cowardly to take a stand against him?

She took a deep breath and then stepped into the dim light of the hall.

"I did it, it was me," she said.

The words sounded loud in the empty space. Grieve and Delmonico both looked up from their conversation. Her face showed only shock. His was filled with malicious satisfaction.

"You committed the prank on Mr Delmonico's phone and computer, Miss Steadman? *You?*" asked Mrs Grieve.

"Yes."

"Who else?" asked Delmonico, walking closer and studying her carefully. "Who helped you, who else had a hand in the mischief? Was it Miss Delaney?"

"I am solely responsible," said Sam. "No-one else is to blame. I'm here to own up and take my punishment."

"You realise, Miss Steadman, that we will need to re-evaluate your scholarship in the light of this?" asked Mrs Grieve.

Sam swallowed hard, but said, "I understand."

"Things might go easier for you, your punishment might be less severe, if you come clean and tell us the names of all the perpetrators. Are you still sure you want to take all the blame?" said Delmonico.

"Yes," said Sam firmly. Then, looking squarely at Mrs Grieve, she continued, "I thought Clifford House prized the development of good character in its girls. If I didn't own up to this and take what is coming, then I would be placing cowardice and fearfulness ahead of honesty and courage."

Mrs Grieve blinked at this. After a moment's silence, she said, "I will need to consult with my management team, Miss Steadman, and decide what needs to be done about this. They may decide that a period of suspension from school is in order, and they may advocate that the scholarship be reallocated to a better-behaved pupil. In the meantime, I will be contacting your father, to let him know of your behaviour and you will, of course, be attending those detentions as scheduled."

"What about the rest of the class, ma'am?"

"I suppose they need no longer attend," said Mrs Grieve, though it looked like it pained her to say the words.

"Yes, ma'am. May I go now?"

Mrs Grieve nodded and, with a last steady look at Delmonico, Sam turned and left. As she walked, her spirits surged. Her chest felt light and open, her feet wanted to run, and a giggle bubbled out of her mouth. She wanted to punch the air and shout, "I did it! I *did* it!" but all along the corridors, teachers were starting the next lesson. Luckily, Miss Stymen was handing out dissecting equipment in her room and had not yet started the lesson when Sam entered and headed over to her desk with a smile which stretched from ear to ear.

"What's up?" asked Nomusa, smiling back in response to Sam's infectious grin.

"I went back and owned up – to Grieve and Delmonico."

"What!" said Nomusa and Jessie together. Jessie, who had been drawing another caricature of Delmonico, got such a fright that her pencil slid, giving the sketched demon a tail which stretched right off the end of the paper.

"You didn't! You're not serious?" said Jessie. She looked horrified. Sam nodded happily.

"But Sam!" said Nomusa. It looked to Sam that all the worry that had just left her was now tightening Nomusa's face.

"Don't worry – I didn't tell them about you two."

"That's *not* what we're worried about," said Nomusa.

"Why did you do it?" said Jessie in the voice of someone who has just watched a lottery winner tear up his ticket.

"It wasn't right that everyone should suffer when I was responsible."

"I also did it, heck I probably did more than you," said Jessie glumly.

"I was responsible," repeated Sam. "I started it and I could have ended it anytime. Besides, it's more than that. It's personal. I had to stand up to them, to him. I was in danger of becoming a total wimp. And I've got to say, I feel *great*!"

"She's not well in the head," said Jessie in an undertone to Nomusa. "And just for the record, I called it the first day I ever met her."

"I feel light and happy and ... and *free* – for the first time in ages! I've done the thing I was most afraid of. Let them do their worst – it doesn't scare me anymore. I have nothing left to lose. I feel like I could do anything, achieve anything now. The pressure's off!"

And, although Jessie turned her finger in circles at her temple and whistled a crazy tune, Sam was right. She sailed through the week's remaining classes with a warm glow of pride inside, and a degree of concentration and focus that had been markedly absent in the previous months. Even in Delmonico's classes, she merely got on with the work. Only once, when he looked up from rifling furiously through his disorganised files to catch her watching him, did she make direct eye contact with him. The smile which curved her lips seemed to drive him crazy. Apples would have been proud, she thought.

On her way out of the last lesson that day, she passed Cindy and Kitty in the corridor and was surprised when Cindy called her by her first name.

"Hey Sam?"

"Yes?" said Sam. Nomusa and Jessie stood beside her, and they all three watched Cindy warily.

"I hear you played a serious prank on Delmonico."

"Yes," said Sam slowly, waiting for Cindy to add some snide comment. But Cindy merely stared at her with an unreadable expression on her face, then gave a small nod, before turning and walking off down the corridor.

"Wow!" said Sam. "Did that just happen?"

"Nah, couldn't have. We just imagined it," said Jessie.

"You'd better hurry, Sam, or you'll be late for your detention," said Nomusa, because Sam was still standing still, gaping after Cindy.

Sam actually enjoyed the daily detentions. They gave her an opportunity to study in peace and quiet for the next week's exams – away from the noise and distractions of Austen House. The exams themselves were not too difficult. Sam was well-prepared, knew her work inside and out, and did not go blank or panic in any of them. She suspected that she may even have cracked A's in Delmonico's subjects.

"OK?" checked Nomusa, after their last Maths paper.

"Fine," said Sam.

"That makes one of us," muttered Jessie.

"No freaking out?" asked Nomusa.

"No freaking out. I think I got my mojo back." Sam smiled. "Now, let's go pack for the Survivor Games. You realise we leave tomorrow at 5:00 a.m.?"

And, arm-in-arm, they walked back to their dorm room, their minds already on the adventure which lay ahead.

24
Brats and baboons

A sudden bouncing bump jostled Sam's head against the window, waking her up. She yawned, rubbed her eyes and stared out of the window of the bus. Morning had broken over the countryside outside. The high, winter-dry grass was bathed in the golden glow of the sun's early rays. The mountains beyond, still in shadow, hulked tall and impressive, their peaks a jagged barrier of spears – as the name uKhahlamba suggested. The road to Giant's Castle was rutted with potholes and the bus driver wound his way between them at speed, missing most.

On the seat beside Sam, Nomusa was sleeping quietly, her head resting on Sam's shoulder. Most of the girls on the bus, as well as the teachers who were sitting up front, were dozing, although a couple were texting on their phones. Jessie, who was sitting next to Poppy on the seat across the aisle from Sam and Nomusa, was sketching with thin sticks of charcoal on a large sketch pad. Catching Sam's eye, Jessie held up the pad for Sam's inspection. There were several practice sketches of the goats and Nguni cattle to be seen in the passing countryside, though in the bottom right-hand corner of the paper was a drawing of a pair of eyes that looked very familiar to Sam. Below them were half a dozen variations of a signature: "J. Steadman". Sam grinned and made a thumbs-up gesture, then went back to gazing out the window, watching the sun light up the land.

As they reached the small settlements which dotted the hills, they passed villagers alongside the road – a small girl in a short pink dress swinging a broken umbrella, boys with sticks herding their scrawny cattle over the veld, groups of women walking in single file alongside the road, balancing heavy water containers or long bundles of firewood branches on the tops of their heads. Men in overalls and gumboots, carrying knobkerries, walked the long roads from their homes, while some of the smaller children raced along on the road beside them, pushing bent wire toy cars with elongated steering wheels. The occasional lone soul, walking nowhere near anywhere, as far as Samantha could see, would lift a pointed finger at the sound of their approach, mistaking them for one of the rusted, dented minibus taxis that drove dementedly on roads pitted by potholes and dongas.

They drove past a muddy soccer pitch where two teams, dressed in red and in blue shirts, jogged fiercely on the spot and dribbled balls, warming up for the early match to come. To the side of the pitch was a spaza shop which Samantha knew would sell everything from paraffin stoves to cellphones. Alongside was a field where half a dozen bony-hipped cows grazed, the bright white plumage of a few foraging herons contrasting with their dusty blacks and russet browns.

Driving on, they passed clusters of houses – thatch-topped mud rondavels, and more modern square brick houses with corrugated iron roofs. Women with babies swaddled tightly with blankets onto their backs fed

197

chickens and hoed vegetable patches, while outside the doors to the houses sat thin men and women, warming their bodies in the morning sun.

Every few kilometres, it seemed, a large sign pointed down another sand road to another small school. They were just a few minutes past a brand-new, modern building – which Sam was pleased to see was a community library – when the bus drove straight into a deep pothole with the force of a collision, and juddered to sudden standstill. Everybody lurched in their seats – some girls toppled right off and into the aisles. There were a few confused cries and complaints, and then Mrs Grieve had a brief word with the driver before addressing them.

"We appear to have a puncture. Please will you all get off the bus so the driver can change the tyre. Miss Stymen will hand out your packed breakfasts and we'll use this as a chance to eat and stretch our legs, but please do not wander off. Once we get going again, it's not far at all."

They all clambered off the bus, taking a brown paper packet from the crate Miss Stymen held out, and had a look around, stomping their feet and rubbing their hands to stay warm in the chill breeze. They appeared to be in the middle of nowhere. On one side of the road stretched fields of tall wild grass and sharp-smelling khakibos plants. On the other, the grassy embankment dipped sharply down to a river curving its way down from the mountains. A few small children appeared and stared curiously at the gaggle of noisy girls.

"I'm starved. And so thirsty," said Jessie.

She opened the brown paper bag and began rooting around in it. Soon they were all drinking their juice, munching their sandwiches and peeling their naartjies. Jessie stared up at a distant flat-topped mountain while she popped the sweet segments of citrus into her mouth.

"That looks like Table Mountain," she said.

"Yes, Delaney, because we're outside Cape Town. Just over the next rise you'll see the sea," said Cindy sarcastically.

"I didn't say I thought it was Table Mountain, you big bag of butt, just that it looked like it!"

"Come see this," said Nomusa.

She was peering down over the embankment, down to the river, where two men with their backs to the girls were wrestling a green rubber dinghy out of the water. One of the men, who was shouting orders unintelligibly from this distance, was shorter and quite stout, while the other – who seemed to be doing most of the work – was enormous. A white truck with writing on the side was parked on a dirt track near to where they stood.

"Check this out," said Jessie. She pulled her cell-phone out of the pocket of her jeans, turned on the camera feature, and zoomed in on the truck's branding.

"You can read it, even from this distance, clear as anything. *Wild Water River Rafting – We take you further!* Cool, hey?"

"Very," said Sam.

"You can even see what's in the boat. Here, look." She passed the phone to Sam, who focused on the in-side of the dinghy. It felt like spying, but she could not see much. Whatever was in the bottom of the boat was covered by a dark green tarpaulin. Apart from that she could only see a water bottle, a hat, and a coil of rope.

"They really ought to be wearing life-vests, if they're white-water rafting," said Nomusa, who was also using

199

her phone's camera feature to examine the scene. "It's not safe otherwise."

"But *are* they white-water rafting, though?" said Sam. There was something about the scene that bothered her. "It's hardly the season for it – the rivers must be at their lowest. Surely it would be a better sport in summer?"

"Maybe it's just a tourist willing to spend their bucks and take the chance," said Jessie.

"Maybe that's why they're getting the dinghy out the river – there isn't enough water for good rafting at this time of year," said Nomusa.

"Yes, but there's something else. Haven't I … doesn't he–"

"Ooh, look – fire!" yelled Kitty Bennington, and everyone swivelled to look where she was pointing. "They're starting fires!"

A long, thin line of fire blazed horizontally across the nearest foothills. Thick, black plumes of smoke rose up in a dark column against the cloudless blue sky. The figures of men, small when viewed from this distance, could be seen beating at the ground with something.

"This is a good opportunity to teach you something about this environment," said Miss Stymen, calling them together. "Does anyone know what they're doing? Sam?"

"Are they making firebreaks?"

"Exactly," said Miss Stymen, smiling approvingly at Sam. Cindy scowled at this.

"They set deliberate fires so as to burn a broad strip of grass right down to the ground. If you look carefully, you'll see that they beat out the fire with wet sacks as soon as the grass is burned. Then, if a veldfire starts up on the mountain, it can't burn all the way down to the village. Or, conversely, a fire from this side won't burn all the vegetation across the range. It's a way of limiting fire damage to fauna and flora. The grass is tinder-dry at this time of year and fires spread only too easily. Of course, some species like our indigenous proteas, rely on fire for seed dispersal, and the ashes put valuable nitrogen back into the soil. But still, you don't want a fire to get out of hand."

"I think it looks ugly," said Cindy, pulling a face at the black strip which circled the hill like a charcoal necklace. "They shouldn't be allowed to destroy the scenery like that."

Mrs Stymen did not hear this comment because Mrs Grieve was calling them over. The driver, with the help of Miss Gamion, had succeeded in changing the tyre, and they were off. Half an hour after they piled back onto the bus, they were pulling into the car park at Giant's Castle Nature Reserve. They parked in front of a rusted sign which warned them against the local crows – which apparently had a fondness for pecking the rubber off windscreen wipers. The driver must have known about this, because he wrapped strips of shiny tinfoil around the wipers as soon as he got off the bus.

"Will you all please come assemble over here, so I can explain the programme to you. Mercy Tshabalala! Get out of the road – good Lord, girl, do you want to be knocked over and killed? Come over here girls!"

They crowded around where Mrs Grieve stood on top of a small boulder so that they could all see her. Behind her was a sign showing pictures of the activities forbidden in the reserve. Sam tried to figure out what the symbols meant: no hunting, no fishing, no fires, no boating, no littering, no feeding the baboons.

"Right, this is the Giant's Castle Camp," said Mrs Grieve. "Over there is the main building and dining room where you will be having your meals. It is also the assembly spot in case of fire. Back there is the main camp where all the bungalows are. Miss Gamion and Miss Stymen and I all have copies of your room assignments, which have been done according to your teams," she waved a paper in the air. "When I have finished, you may collect your bags from the bus, get your room number from one of us and make your way to your bungalow to unpack and settle in. Please meet at this spot again at precisely 10:30 a.m. for your first challenge. I will be posting the whole programme, as well as regularly putting updated scores for the competition on the noticeboard outside the main building. Today, we will kick off with a nature treasure hunt."

"Ooh," said Sam.

"Whoopee-ai-aye," muttered Cindy sarcastically.

"And after lunch you will all do an obstacle course."

"Uh-oh," said Jessie.

"Tomorrow we will do a full-day orienteering course."

"A what?"

"What's that?" asked a few girls.

"And the day after – our last day – we will make the hike up to the caves where there are magnificent examples of rock art."

"Thrilling. Not. More scribbling of stick figures."

"What's that, Miss Atkins?" asked Mrs Grieve.

"I was just saying how exciting it all sounds, ma'am," said Cindy, with a bright, false smile.

"We will have an awards ceremony for our Survivor Games on our last night here. You know that points will be given to the houses of the three top teams, but there will also be individual prizes. The top team will win the right to choose their own dorm room next year, and each girl in the team will also receive a voucher to spend R500 at the school tuck-shop."

"Cool!" said Uvani Moodley.

"I'm in it to win it!" said Skye MacAdam.

Even Cindy raised her eyebrows and nodded, looking much more enthusiastic now that there was potentially something in it for her.

"For every event, remember: full water-bottles, hats and sunscreen! The sun shines – and burns – even in winter, and we're at high altitude here. You cannot outwit, outplay and outlast if you're burning to a crisp. I don't want to hear any complaints about–"

Just then, a loud shriek startled them all. Pat Mbalula was hopping up and down on the spot, pointing to the empty bus – only, it was not empty. A big, dark shadow was clambering about inside, leaping over seats and swinging on the handrails.

"It's a baboon!" said Mrs Grieve. "In *our* bus!"

She stalked over to the back of the bus, with the two other teachers and the girls following her to get a better look. The enormous baboon was now sitting on the back seat, his feet resting up against the back of the seat in front, his long toes curled around its rail. His fur was a deep gray, his brown eyes intelligent beneath a heavy, ridged brow, and his long fingers were tearing open a packet of biscuits. Standing on tip-toes, Mrs Grieve hammered imperiously on the back window of the bus. The baboon turned around and peered out the window, looking down at them for all the world as if he were the tourist and they the wildlife. It was the first time Sam had seen Mrs Grieve's orders ignored.

"Shoo! Get away!" shouted Mrs Grieve, pounding the window again.

The baboon wrinkled its brow at her as if intrigued by this curiosity and then bared its teeth. They were long and sharp and yellow. His hot breath fogged up a small patch of the window. He bent his head down to examine this, then suddenly licked the window, leaving a smear of thick saliva – "ew!" said several girls – before popping another biscuit into his mouth.

"Miss Stymen – you're the Biology teacher – do something!" ordered Mrs Grieve.

Miss Stymen immediately trotted off to the main building to summon help. Meanwhile, the girls watched as the baboon finished the biscuits with evident enjoyment. Miss Stymen emerged a few minutes later with two khaki-uniformed park rangers. One carried a thick stick and a metal dustbin lid, while the other held a large and colourful plastic gun, shaped like an automatic weapon. They strolled unhurriedly around the back of the bus, where the first man made an enormous racket by banging the stick against the metal lid, and the second pulled himself up onto the wheel brace, aimed the water pistol through the window and deluged the baboon with a strong stream of water. Chattering angrily, the baboon scrambled over the seats to the exit and swung down the stairs onto the tarmac.

"Hey! That's my bag!" shouted Jessie.

The baboon loped off, swinging Jessie's handbag at his side, through the path that the girls rapidly cleared for him. The rangers gave chase, yelling and whistling, banging and squirting. A few metres further on, the creature stopped, sniffed inside the bag, took something out and then scampered off, tossing the bag casually aside. Jessie ran to retrieve it.

"He stole my mints and my chewing gum!" she complained loudly, but Sam and Nomusa could only laugh.

"He'll have the freshest breath in the Berg, Jess," said Nomusa.

"Speaking of baboons," said Mrs Grieve with a sniff, drawing their attention back to herself. "I am obliged to tell you that some grade 11 boys from Clifford Heights will also be at this camp over the next few days. They are attending a leadership camp here."

There was a lot of excited whispering and elbowing amongst the girls at this announcement. Cindy looked positively eager now.

"However, our paths should not cross at all – except in the dining room at mealtimes, when I expect you to keep to separate tables. There will be *no fraternizing*. Do I make myself clear? There is to be no contact with the boys. This is not an occasion for socialising and we will be keeping an eye on each and every one of you."

"Jeez! Wildfires, mutant crows, kleptomaniac baboons – and we haven't even left the car park yet," said Jessie. "Plus – no contact with the boys. I hope it doesn't get worse than this."

25

Obstacles

Jessie's eyes were closed and her head, which had been drooping lower and lower, finally dropped all the way down onto her chest. She swayed a little in her chair. Samantha, afraid that Jessie might slump forward and land head-first in the bowl of lukewarm chicken noodle soup, gently pushed her back so that she rested against the back of the chair. It was supper time in the dining room at Giant's Castle and all the girls were exhausted and filthy after their day's challenges.

Things had started off well, thought Sam as she reviewed the day's events. The thatch-roofed bungalow to which they had been assigned was in a very pretty part of the camp's gardens. It was clean, comfortable, perfectly round and had its own small bathroom. Unfortunately, it only had two beds so Sam suggested that they play the rock-paper-scissors game to see who would have to sleep on the sofa.

"I don't know why I'm bothering – you'll win for sure. You always do," Jessie grumbled.

Sure enough, Sam did win. She was relieved: as the tallest of the three girls, she had not much fancied the idea of sleeping on the short whicker-work sofa. Nomusa won the next play-off and opted for the other bed, so it fell to Jessie to bed down on the couch.

"Charming," said Jessie. "But I have dibs on the shelf in the bathroom."

The girls were given only a few minutes to unpack before they had to assemble to get their instructions for the treasure hunt challenge, which was taking place in and around the camp. They would be heading out into the mountains on the following day. Each team was handed a sheet with a list of items to find and bring back: those who discovered the most items in the shortest time would get the most points. Sam consulted the list.

"OK, so we have to find the following things: a piece of red ochre rock; a piece of yellow ochre rock; a feather – ooh, there are bonus points if we can identify the bird that it comes from; the husk of an old protea flower; a stalk from each of three different species of wild grass; a dead twig with some lichen on it and a water-eroded pebble. There's a warning in big capital letters that we're absolutely not allowed to pick any living flowers or plants – apart from the three stalks of grass – because this is a protected reserve. And there are some theory questions – Biology and Geography, it looks like. Well this should be fairly easy – let's go."

The challenge was relatively painless for the team. Sam knew all the answers to the theory questions and so they filled those in immediately. She also regularly went on hikes into the mountains with her father and brothers, so she knew the plants, birds and animals well, and lead her team straight to the spots where they would be most likely to find what they needed. Nomusa's sharp eyes spotted the last item they needed to find: a feather. It was dark grey and long – longer than a ruler.

"Let's take a chance and say it's a tail feather from a lammergeyer. I think it is," said Sam, filling the name onto the sheet.

"A lamma-what?" asked Nomusa.

"A lammergeyer. It's a type of vulture found in this area: huge, flies incredibly well and drops its prey from great heights onto rocks to kill it and break its bones. It likes to eat the bone marrow."

"Just add it to the list of bizarre and dangerous creatures found here," said Jessie.

They headed over to the teachers' table to have their list checked and were delighted to discover that although Cindy's team had returned first, their own team had more items correct. That, plus the bonus points for the feather – "You're quite right, girls, it is from a lammergeyer, well done!" – meant that Miss Stymen awarded them maximum points. Cindy, who had stuck a delicate red flower behind one ear, looked very put out at this, but Jessie smiled brightly and said, in a voice dripping with sweetness, "Better luck next time, girls." This show of apparent good sportsmanship earned an approving nod from Miss Gamion.

Jessie's glee did not last long, however. As they were walking over to the dining room for lunch, Sam noticed something small and black on the back of one of Jessie's hands.

"What's that on your hand?" she asked, pointing to it.

Jessie looked down at her hand and immediately began flapping it around, trying to fling the speck off.

"Ugh – it's a gogga." She stopped shaking her arm but saw that the insect was still there. "Why won't it come off?"

"Maybe it's a tick." Sam took Jessie's hand and had a closer look. "Yes, it's a tick for sure. Oh dear. If it's stuck on, that means it's already biting you."

Jessie went wild at this pronouncement – hopping about and flapping both arms madly in the air.

"Get it off me! It's freaking me out!"

"Trying to fly, Delaney?" said Cindy, who was walking past. "Let me point you in the direction of a cliff where you can practise."

Jessie stopped her hopping and flapping and made to pick the insect off.

"No – don't!" said Nomusa.

"Wait, wait, wait!" said Sam. "You mustn't try to pull it off – you'll leave the mouthparts still attached and maybe get an infection. Don't you know that?"

"I'm a city-girl, OK? They don't have ticks in hotels and spas. So, how am I supposed to get it off then?"

"We-ell," said Sam slowly. She knew Jessie would not like what she had to say. "You make it let go by … by burning it off. With a match."

"You're going to burn me?" Jessie now looked more nervous than revolted.

"No, not you. You hold a hot match to the tick and it lets go. But you'll have to stand *very* still."

"Hang on a sec. We learned an easier way on the first aid course," said Nomusa. "Sam, do you have any Vaseline on you?"

"No, but I've got a tub of lip balm – will that do?"

"Perfect," said Nomusa. She took the small tub from Sam, scooped out a large blob and slathered it thickly over the tick and the surrounding area of skin.

"And now?" said Jessie, holding her hand out in front of her as if the goop-buried tick on it was a bomb that needed defusing.

"It should suffocate and drop off by itself in the next half-hour or so."

As Nomusa had predicted, by the end of lunch, the tick detached and Jessie wiped her hand clean with a paper serviette before they set off for the next challenge. Jessie grumbled that she would far rather spend the afternoon by a cosy fire, painting her toenails or perhaps taking a nap. By the end of the afternoon, Sam wished they all had done precisely that – the morning's activity may have been fun, but the afternoon's was much more challenging.

For the afternoon's activity, an obstacle course had been laid out near the camp, starting in a grassy field, stretching over a small gorge, crossing a mountain stream and ending back at the field. Each team would be timed separately from when they set off at five-minute intervals and all members had to complete each obstacle in order to finish the course. Sam's team was the fourth to start. Cindy's team would be right behind them. Mrs Grieve explained that teachers and guides would be stationed at the different obstacles and would be "observing and making notes on your performance and progress".

To negotiate the first obstacle, which was under the eagle-eye of Mrs Grieve, they had to leopard-crawl on the ground under a big net nailed to a low wooden frame. Nomusa, who was lithe and limber, had soon scrambled under and out the other side. Sam was not too far behind her, but had no sooner crawled out from under the net than she heard a wail from behind her. Jessie's curly hair had somehow become entangled in one of the nails pinning the net to the frame, and she was stuck beneath it, flailing her arms and legs, unable either to move forward or to retreat.

"Hang on–"

"I'm hardly going anywhere," said Jessie sourly.

"I'm coming to get you."

Sam slunk back along the ground until she got to Jessie. It took a few minutes of careful fiddling to free the hair from where it had snarled on the nail, during which time Cindy, her friend Kitty and the third member of their team – a short and very freckled girl called Julie Clayton – had leopard-crawled past.

"Hang in there, Delaney! And I mean that literally," snickered Cindy, and she, Kitty and Julie laughed as they ran off ahead.

The next obstacle looked like a giant ladder lying horizontally on a frame about three metres up in the air, straddling a small gorge. The girls had to clamber up the side, which was a wall made of split wooden poles, using a thick-knotted rope for help, while all the while getting a long plank to the top of a structure. Then they had to use the plank to get across the ladder, whose rungs were spaced too widely apart to allow them to take them in steps. Once they had all crossed the ladder, they had to climb down the other side, which was a vertical wall of net, dropping the plank back at the start. The challenge took a great deal of manoeuvring and some careful planning when it came to the use and moving of the plank.

"What if we drop the plank?" Sam asked Miss Stymen, who was overseeing this obstacle.

"Then you get down and start again, or else forfeit the points."

"What if we get stuck up there?"

"Then we shoot you with tranquilizer darts and when you fall asleep, you fall down," said Miss Stymen, but then added reassuringly, "Only joking. Don't worry

Sam, no-one's gotten stuck yet – though I haven't ruled out this team yet."

Sam's team managed fairly well and were able to figure out how to use and move the plank so that they could all cross. Nomusa ran across the plank nimbly, Sam walked in a sort of low crouch, feeling a lot like a baboon, while Jessie crawled across on hands and knees. Sam was beginning to feel that they were really letting Nomusa down, and said so.

"I'm sorry – you would have been better off with some more athletic girls."

"Don't be silly," Nomusa laughed. "It's just a game. I'll save the need to win for real races, OK?"

Next up was a very high climbing wall. Jessie clapped one eye on this structure and let out a feeble whimper.

"That must be all of seven metres!" said Nomusa enthusiastically, craning her neck to look up the wall which was studded with hand- and footholds that looked, to Sam, way too small to provide anything like a proper grip.

"What if we slip and fall?" asked Sam.

In answer, Miss Gamion and one of the camp guides helped each girl into a safety harness to which they attached nylon ropes. Looking up, Sam saw that the ropes were tied through large metal rings at the top of the wall.

"Right girls," said Miss Gamion cheerfully when they were all three strapped in. "You need to climb up to the top and then rappel down the other side. You know – bounce down with your feet against the wall while letting the rope slide *slowly* through your hands." Seeing their blank looks, she added, "Just get up and get down in one piece, OK?"

Predictably, Nomusa climbed quickly and agilely to the top, where she waited for them, sitting with her legs straddling the wall and yelling down encouragements. Looking at Jessie's pale face, Sam rather thought that she might need more help than this, so she climbed up slowly alongside her friend, saying things like, "That's right, one step at a time," and "c'mon, not far now, you can do it" and, over and over, "don't look down". Once Jessic's foot missed a hold and she slipped, but the rope kept her from falling. She groaned something that sounded like "mweremmnnh" while she dangled and looked like she might refuse to move, but Sam guided her foot back to the hold and urged her up with the entirely false promise that they were almost at the top. Once at the top, Jessie looked down, turned a shade of pale green and said past clenched teeth, "Think I'll just stay here – send the boys from the fire brigade with a ladder."

By dint of a combination of hearty encouragements, bribes, promises and sheer force, Nomusa and Sam were able to get her to the ground. Sam, who was not particularly fond of heights herself, realised when her feet touched the ground, that she had been so busy helping Jessie that she had not given a thought to her own fear. Her hands were stinging from rope burn and her upper arms were aching, but she felt rather proud of herself. They ran across a narrow bridge which spanned the river, and then caught up with Cindy's team at the second-last obstacle.

"It's a foofie-slide!" said Sam.

Jessie looked at the slanted, sloping zip-line in the air above the river. It stretched from a high platform on their side of the riverbank to a lower platform on the other, where Cindy stood tapping her foot. Kitty Bennington stood on the high platform, clutching a metal bar in the shape of an upside-down T attached to a grooved wheel-like device mounted on top of the thick metal cable.

"What exactly is that?" said Jessie, her voice deep with foreboding. "Just how are we supposed to..." A look of stark horror crept over her face as she watched Kitty step off the platform and zip down the line, dangling from the metal bar.

"No way. No way!"

"Oh come on, it's fun! Even I can do this," said Sam, grabbing Jessie by the arm and dragging her to the platform.

"And it only takes a few seconds," said Nomusa, joining them. "The trick is not to think about it, you must just do it."

The guide on the platform pulled on a rope tied to the T-bar, hauling it back up the line to the platform, and fitted Julie Clayton, the third member of Cindy's team, into a safety harness linked to the hand bar.

"Is it even legal – to make us do this? I mean, where's the net?"

"You wear a safety harness, Jess," Nomusa pointed out.

"I think it's child abuse! Reckless endangerment! I think we should take a stand against–"

"Get a move on, Julie. Just GO!" Cindy shouted from the other side of the stream.

"I'm scared," Julie called back in a faint voice.

"She looks it, too," said Jessie, who seemed heartened that someone else was apparently as afraid of heights as she was.

214

Julie Clayton was gripping the T-bar so tightly that her knuckles stood out like a ridge of white pebbles on her fists. Her eyes were wide and round in her pale face and a sheen of sweat beaded her top lip. It was not far to the other side, but from up here, thought Sam, it did look like a long way down to the cold and rock-strewn water below.

"Go!" shouted Cindy again. "You're wasting time. GO!"

"I can't," said Julie. She was frozen in place and looked as if she might be sick at any moment.

"If you know what's good for you, Julie Clayton, you'll go right this minute. I am *not* going to lose because you're too much of a baby to do this. You better do it right NOW!"

Julie looked from the foofie slide to Cindy's incensed face. Apparently deciding that the zip-line held less of a threat, she stepped off the platform and zoomed down the line, crashing into Cindy and Kitty below, who both fell backwards onto their bottoms.

With no fuss, Nomusa allowed herself to be strapped in, then leapt off the platform, landing with a graceful swing of her legs on the other side. Jessie was still laughing at Cindy and Kitty, who were marching off back to the field, dusting the seats of their jeans, when she looked down and saw that she had been strapped into the harness.

"Now wait just a mo-" she began, but Sam, who had anticipated resistance and devised a plan, shoved the T-bar into Jessie's hands, spun her around with a command to hang on tight and then shoved her off the platform, yelling "Bungee!" loudly after her. Before Jessie had a chance to protest, she was on the other side and Nomusa was unstrapping her from the lines.

215

Jessie looked dumbstruck for a moment, then yelled an exultant, "Yeeha!" into the air. A few minutes later, Sam was by her side, agreeing with Jessie that she had been awfully brave.

The last obstacle looked deceptively simple. Two rows of old tyres had been laid out side by side across the field, leading up to the finishing line. The girls had to run through the course, putting their feet down in the centre of a different tyre with each step. It was neither scary nor difficult, but Sam was so tired by this point that she tripped and went sprawling twice – which was two less times than Jessie. Cindy and Kitty, who had already completed the course, stood nearby, passing rude comments and screeching with laughter every time Sam or Jessie tripped.

"Never again. NEVER!" gasped Jessie as she and Sam staggered over the finishing line.

"Water!" croaked Sam, heading to a large tin bath in which bottles of water floated between large chunks of ice.

"We didn't do too badly," said Nomusa, who was standing at the teachers' table comparing the results of all the teams. "We're still in with a chance."

Now, sitting at the dinner table and staring exhaustedly at their evening meal, Sam could not find one fibre of her being which cared whether they won or lost. All she wanted was a hot bath, a warm bed and a long sleep. It seemed like an enormous effort even to lift the peas on her fork to her mouth. Jessie, who had been dozing with her head on her chest, started awake when the boys from Clifford Heights clattered noisily into the dining room, jostling each other and calling greetings to the girls. Their teacher chivvied them to tables on the other side of the room, however, and they had to be

216

content to make eyes at the girls from across the way. Sam saw that both Dan and Apples were amongst the boys, smiled and waved at them tiredly.

While they were having their dessert, Dan suddenly popped up at their table, having apparently slunk from table to table until he reached theirs. He snatched the Clifford House windbreaker from off the back of Jessie's chair and slipped it on.

"Stealth mode activated," he whispered, pulling the hood up to hide his face.

Jessie perked up considerably at Dan's arrival and soon they were chatting away happily. Sam looked over at Apples. He jerked his head to the door, then got up and walked out the room. Sam waited a minute and then grabbed her own windbreaker and followed. She found him in the garden outside the building. It was a still, clear night, with no breeze; her breath misted in the cold air. She could hear a loud chorus of frogs above the rushing water of the nearby stream. Overhead, stars glittered like chips of diamond against the deep blackness of the sky and the remote cloudlike smudges of the Milky Way. A full moon hung low in the sky.

Apples took her by the hand and lead her over to a low garden wall. His hand was big and very warm. She sat down next to him on the cold stone, and they spoke softly for a while, catching up on each other's news. Sam's eyes were drawn again to the crescent-shaped scar at the corner of his mouth.

"How did you get this?" she asked, tracing the thin line lightly with a finger.

"It's an exciting and gruesome story."

"Oh, yes?"

"Oh, yes. You know I'm a werewolf, right?"

"I'd forgotten."

"And werewolves and vampires are mortal enemies, right?"

"Ye-es," said Sam uncertainly.

"Well, this one night, a vampire was trying to attack and suck the blood out of a bunch of poor defenceless kids at this orphanage, and I got into a fight to the death with it, and one of its fangs ripped into here," he touched his lip, "and here," he pushed back the sleeve of his sweater and pointed to a long silver line on his forearm, "and a few other places, too, and left me with these scars. The vampire, it hardly needs saying, came off much, much worse."

Sam laughed softly and looked meaningfully up into the sky.

"I see it's a full moon tonight. Shouldn't you be transformed?"

"I do feel an irresistible urge coming over me," said Apples, moving closer, leaning his head towards hers. Sam stopped breathing. Her own face tilted up towards his. Their lips had just touched when a shout made them jump apart.

"Samantha! What *are* you doing? Get back to the dining room at once."

Luckily, it was Miss Gamion, rather than Mrs Grieve. But Sam did not feel grateful. If only the dratted woman had come out a minute later!

"Good night, Apples," she called sadly as she followed after the teacher.

A soft, wolfish howl from behind her returned the smile to her face.

26

Lost

"Good morning, girls. I hope you all had a good breakfast – you're going to be doing lots of exercise today!
I'm glad to see everyone is wearing sunhats, but please
be sure you've all packed a warm jacket – the weather
looks sunny and fine now, but it can turn very suddenly here. You should each also have been issued with
a packed lunch and three bottles of water as you left the
dining room, yes? Even though the water in the streams
is apparently quite safe to drink. Each team should also
have been issued with one orienteering pack – please
open that now."

Mrs Grieve was standing on her rock in the car park
area again, giving them instructions for that day's orienteering challenge. It was very strange, Sam thought, to
see their headmistress dressed in jeans and a sweater.
Somehow, it looked all wrong.

"Miss Gamion, will you please explain how the challenge works."

Miss Gamion stepped onto the rock and held two
sheets of paper and something that looked like a pocket
watch up in the air.

"Each team has been given a navigational map, a clue
sheet, and a compass. If you look carefully at your map,
you will see that a triangle marks the start of the course

– here, where we are standing now – and a double circle indicates the finish point."

Sam looked down at the map Jessie was holding and pointed out the start and finish points. A meandering purple line connected the two.

"The four red circles marked on the purple hike route are the four control points which each team needs to visit. You navigate to the control point using the compass and the clue sheet – which gives you your directions to and descriptions of the site. You'll know when you hit a control point because each one has a flag marking it." Miss Gamion waved a rectangular flag with a white triangle on the top and an orange triangle on the bottom.

"Each control point will have a packet tied to its flag. Inside the packet you will find a stamp. You must stamp your clue sheet at each control point to prove you were there. Please be sure to replace the stamp in the packet. You will set off at 10 minute intervals, and no team has exactly the same control points in the same order, so you won't be able to follow one another. The control points are sites of interest on the lower slopes of the mountains, the kloofs and around the valley, and spots down at the river – do not try to swim, girls, the water's icy! Please don't be tempted to go visit the caves – the area is locked and we'll be going on a guided tour there tomorrow, anyway. Any questions?"

"How does the scoring work?" asked Cindy.

"The team to visit all their sites in the shortest time will get the most points. This is not a quick challenge, though – we're expecting it will take you the better part of the day. More points will be deducted for sites not found, than for a slower time."

"Can we eat lunch any time?" asked Mercy.

"Yes, but don't guzzle it all too early, or you'll be hungry later on. Oh, and remember not to eat your lunches at the control points – we don't want to attract baboons to those sites. If you should meet baboons on the walk, steer clear and don't interact with them."

"I hope someone's telling the baboons to steer clear of *us*," said Jessie.

"What if we get lost?" asked Sam.

"I think that's unlikely, Sam, the maps are very clear. But if you don't return, we'll send out a search party to the sites you were due to visit."

"How does a compass work?" asked Poppy.

"Right, choose one member of your team to be the compass reader, and then those individuals come over here and I'll give you a quick lesson."

"Who wants to …?" asked Nomusa.

"Not me," said Jessie, "I'll be the map navigator person. I'm determined that we won't walk a step more than necessary – I'm still sore from yesterday!"

"Do you want to?" Sam asked Nomusa, speaking around the elastic band between her teeth. She was plaiting her hair to keep the tendrils out of her face.

"Sure," said Nomusa, taking the compass and walking over to where a group of girls was clustered around Miss Gamion.

Sam looked down at the clue sheet and saw that they had to visit four control points: Cleft Rock, Durnford's Camp, Bannerman's Bridge and then the pleasant-sounding Champagne Pools. On the back of the map was some interesting information about the area and the sites they were going to visit.

"It looks like the first three are on the mountainside of the camp – that way, but Champagne Pools is way on the other side. Probably we can do that after lunch. I think Miss Gamion's right – this is going to take hours and hours. I wonder what the teachers will be doing all day?"

"Probably drinking coffee beside the fire and comparing notes on all of us," said Jessie.

They stowed their lunch packs and water bottles into their backpacks and put them on over their shoulders. Soon Nomusa joined them, with assurances that she knew what she was doing with the compass, and when Miss Gamion gave their team the go-ahead, they set off in the direction of Cleft Rock, with Nomusa in the lead. Shouts and noise from the field to the side of the camp suggested that the boys would be spending their morning on the obstacle course.

The first part of the path was paved with concrete, but soon it became a dirt path, eroded in places to show ochreish red and yellow patches, which dipped into small gullies and rose on gentle climbing stretches. The veld around them was a blend of dry hay-coloured grass and dull olive vegetation, studded with the blazing reds and oranges of flowering aloes.

"That one's called a *red hot poker*," said Sam, pointing to one of the flowering succulents with tall spikes of scarlet flowers.

"And there, next to the bottle-brushes, are proteas, but they flower mostly in the summer." The protea bushes and trees were a dry brown; a few desiccated old buds still clung to the branches.

"And what are those?" asked Jessie in a voice of deep disgust, pointing to a few piles of shiny, fly-topped black masses on the paths.

"Baboon poop. Don't step in it," said Sam.

"Charming," said Jessie.

222

"Look, there's smoke over on that side – must be a fire," said Nomusa. On the other side of the river rose a distant plume of grey smoke.

"Good thing it's not on this side," said Sam and after consulting Jessie's map and Nomusa's compass, they continued walking in the direction of the mountain closest to the camp. It rose steeply up with grassy sides, a band of thick forest and precipitous basalt cliffs on the top. There were big grey shapes on its slopes that might be eland or, more probably, just rocks.

"That's where the caves are, we'll be climbing that tomorrow," said Jessie. She did not sound enthusiastic.

"Good thing for you we're not climbing to the actual Giant's Castle, Jess," Nomusa said over her shoulder.

Beyond the mountain with the caves was a further ridge of peaks. While they had waited for the last teams to finish the obstacle course the day before, a field ranger had pointed out the 3314-metre-high mountain, with its various peaks that looked like a giant, lying on his back, arms folded across his chest, belt buckle jutting into the air, with a flattish ridge for his legs, ending in a last peak which were his feet. Today the top of the distant ridge was covered in low clouds of mist, like a fluffy, white pillow lying on top of the giant's head, instead of underneath it. A smattering of snow frosted the high rocky outcrops and lay like strings of pearls in thin drifts on the mountain ledges.

"I think we need to head east, here," said Jessie. She was turning the map around and looking at it from different directions in a way that did not fill Sam with confidence. "There should be a path heading to the right somewhere along here."

"We passed one a little way back," said Sam.

223

"Oh, did we? I didn't see it – must have been looking at the map."

They turned around and headed back down the sandy path, this time with Jessie in the lead. The gradient fell away steeply to their left now, dropping down to the river in the bottom of the valley. Massive granite boulders lay here and there on the grassy slope, like marbles strewn by a giant.

"Um, Jessie, it's here – you walked past it again," said Sam pointing to a smaller path which branched off down the slope.

"This place could use some better signage," Jessie grumbled, cutting across the grass to join up behind Sam and Nomusa on the new path.

"That must be it, there," said Nomusa. Ahead of them, on the lower side of the path, were two towering granite rocks, with a narrow cleft between them.

"Wow," said Jessie. "Those are actually beautiful."

"I wish I'd thought to bring a camera," said Nomusa.

"Wait, I've got my phone – we can use that," said Jessie, rummaging in her backpack.

"You brought a cellphone – on a hike?"

"I never go anywhere without my phone," said Jessie.

"I brought mine, too," said Sam, a little sheepishly. "I mean, what if we have an emergency and need to call? But now it seems a bit silly – I don't reckon there's reception out here away from the main camp, anyway."

Jessie took out her cellphone and took a few photos of Nomusa and Sam posing in the cleft, as well as some close-up shots of the delicate pink and pale grey lichens growing on the rock's pitted surface. Sam circled the base of the rocks until she found the orange and white flag. She carefully stamped their clue sheet with the stamp, returned it to its packet looped around the flag, and then looked at the others.

"Next is Durnford's Camp – ready to go?"

"Can't we have a break for a bit? We just got here." Jessie slumped down in the shade of the rocks, hauled out a bottle of water and drank deeply. Sam had only a few sips of her water, she knew they had a long walk ahead of them and she was afraid of running out while they were nowhere near the river. Sam gave Jessie five more minutes to rest, but when Jessie tilted her hat over her face as if settling down for a nap, Sam kicked her feet.

"Let's go," Sam said. "Which way, Nomusa?"

After taking a reading on the compass and studying the map, Nomusa set off back up the path they had come by, with Jessie shouting directions from behind Sam. As they walked around one of the giant boulders, they almost bumped into Poppy, Mercy and Angela, who were walking quickly down the path towards the cleft rock.

"Hi!" they all said at once.

"Cleft Rock?" asked Poppy.

"Down that way, you can't miss it," said Sam. "Where are you headed after this – Durnford's Camp?"

"No, somewhere called Mushroom Rock."

"That's not one of our sites. But maybe we'll see you round. Good luck!"

"You too," said Poppy and she and her team continued down the path.

The route to Durnford's Camp had seemed straightforward to Sam when she had looked at the map, but it seemed to be taking an awfully long time to get there. When they passed a familiar-looking and very distinctive stump of tree growing sideways against an enormous rock, Sam wondered if they had walked in a circle.

"Are you sure this is the right way, Jessie?" she said tentatively.

"Of course!" said Jessie, sounding wounded. "Don't you trust me? It's definitely this way. Keep heading west, Nomusa."

"If you say so," said Nomusa, but Sam thought she detected a trace of doubt in Nomusa's voice, too.

Twenty minutes later, they were passing the rock with the tree again.

"Jessie, we've passed this tree before. We're going in circles."

"No we haven't, it's not the same tree at all," Jessie insisted.

"Are you sure we're going in the right direction?"

"Yes. I think so."

"You think so?"

"I know so. Definitely."

"Don't you want me to take a look at the map?" Sam said. She said it gently, keen not to hurt Jessie's feelings, or to come across as being bossy.

"No, Sam! I know what I'm doing, OK?"

But when they passed the tree yet again, Sam was through being diplomatic.

"Stop!" she said loudly and all three of them came to a halt on the pathway.

"Tree on rock," Sam said pointing at the landmark.

"Lost," she said, gesturing at the three of them.

"Map!" she said, holding out her hand to Jessie.

"OK, OK," said Jessie, handing it over. "I really thought I'd got it straight that time, I still can't figure out why we haven't seen Durnford and his blessed camp. But I think we might be a little ..."

"Lost?" suggested Nomusa, sighing in frustration.

Sam studied the map, then the compass, then the clue sheet, while Nomusa and Jessie drank water and studied the impressive view from the high spot where they stood.

"Right, I think I've found the problem," said Sam. "We've being climbing up when we should have been going down. Durnford's Camp must be somewhere down there, near the river. Not up here, near the freaking clouds!"

"Sorry – my bad," said Jessie.

"From now on, I do the navigating. Any objections?"

Jessie shook her head and Nomusa looked relieved. They set off, retracing their steps until they found a path that forked down the hill in the direction of the river.

Sam, now in the lead, was scanning the view ahead of them, trying to match landmarks to the map in her hands, when she noticed something odd.

"Is that those rafters again, down there, at the bottom of the mountain?" she asked, without breaking stride.

Nomusa and Jessie squinted down into the valley. Where the river curved around a patch of reeds as it coursed through the bottom of the valley, they could clearly see an inflatable dinghy on the river. Its bold green stood out against the muted khakis and browns of the surrounding vegetation. Two men, one very tall and broad, and the other shorter, stouter and wearing a hat, were on the bank of the river, next to the boat.

"It looks like the same crowd," said Jessie, tripping over a small rock in the path and only just stopping herself from going sprawling by clutching onto Nomusa.

"I'm sure it's them," said Sam, alternating looking at the river with glances down at the path and the map. "But what's weird is why they're out here. For one thing, the river's not deep enough for white-water rafting. Watch out – poop in the path! And for another, boating's not allowed in the reserve – the sign at the entrance said so. They wouldn't have been able to bring the boat into Giant's Castle on a trailer – they would have been stopped at the main gate."

"Then how did they get it in?" asked Jessie.

"They could have brought it in flat and only inflated it down at the river, once they were out of sight, I suppose," said Nomusa.

"Or they could have dragged it upriver from outside the reserve all the way to this spot," said Sam. "But how desperate would you have to be to do that, when the river's so low?"

"It is strange," said Nomusa.

"What was that?" said Jessie suddenly, jumping sideways.

"What?"

"There was a rustle, in the grass, beside the path," said Jessie, sounding breathless and frightened.

"Probably just a snake," said Sam. They were low enough down the path now that they could no longer see the river bank where the men were, but Sam was still puzzling over their presence there.

"A snake!" yelped Jessie. "They have snakes here? Why did nobody tell me?"

"Jessie, we're in the middle of the veld. In a nature reserve. In Africa. Of course there are snakes. But I wouldn't worry about it," said Sam.

"That's rich – coming from you!"

"They're more afraid of you than you are of them. And most of them are harmless."

"Most of them?"

"Well, the info on the back of the clue sheet says there are rinkhals, puff adder and berg adder in this area, but that they're almost never seen. Apparently they're quite shy."

"Pick up the pace there, Nomusa. I have a sneaky suspicion that shy snakes are just as poisonous as confident ones," snapped Jessie, walking faster and looking nervously over her shoulder.

"And speaking of snakes ..." said Sam, slowing to a stop.

Nomusa peered over Sam's shoulder to the path ahead of them. "Oh, no," she groaned.

"What is it? Is it a snake? A berg puffer?" asked Jessie worriedly from behind.

"Nope, but just as poisonous," muttered Sam.

27

Found!

Walking towards them up the path were Cindy, Kitty and Julie; they were all wearing matching neon pink windbreakers. Cindy wore an elegant, wide-brimmed straw hat – more suited to a day at the races than a hike in the Berg – on her head and a smug smile on her face.

"Oh, look. It's the champions of the obstacle course," Cindy snickered. "We've just ticked off our third control point. Are you still trying to find your first, Steadman?"

"No, we're looking for our second, Durnford's Camp – probably where you just came from."

"No it's not. We've just come from Bannerman's Bridge down at the river. Durnford's Camp is way back up there – you must have missed the turnoff. You really are clueless. Well, toodleloo, got to hurry to our last site."

With a wave of her fingers, Cindy and her two friends strode quickly off in a southerly direction, down a little-used path.

"Don't tell me we're lost again," groaned Jessie.

"I won't, because we're not. She's lying. I'm sure the control point is just down there," said Sam and she set off down the path again, in the direction of a copse of scrubby trees and bushes.

"I'll bet that's not all she's lying about," said No-musa. "No ways could they already have done three control points. I'd put money on it that they've only done two. They're just trying to psych us out and make us uncertain and discouraged."

Jessie mumbled something which sounded like "it's working", but she trailed along after Nomusa and Sam.

"There you are!" said Sam triumphantly.

Ahead of them was a cluster of large boulders and some small trees and bushes. An orange and white flag was stuck below a tree growing in the cleft of a lichen-encrusted rock. A rusted sign stuck in the ground read "Rock 75".

"This is it? This is Durnford's Camp? I was expecting more – some tents, or canvas chairs, or … something," said Jessie, sounding unimpressed.

"It says here," said Sam, reading off an informa-tion board, "that this is where soldiers from the Eng-lish Army, the 75th Regiment under Colonel Durnford, stayed in 1874. This was during the rebellion of the local Zulu chief, Langalibalele, who refused to pay taxes to the colonial British government."

"Good for him," said Nomusa.

"They camped here for about four months and the regimental cook carved '75' into one of the rocks, to show they had occupied this spot."

"Here it is," said Jessie, running her fingers over the numbers which had been engraved into one granite boulder. "Vandal! He should have stuck to cooking."

"I wonder at what point does graffiti become his-tory?" asked Sam. "I mean, you could argue that those San artists were tagging their spots same as the cook, here."

231

"Sam!" said Jessie, sounding outraged. "You can't compare the two. San rock art is just that – art. It's beautifully done, and the symbolism tells us of their culture, their spiritual and physical world. This," said Jessie, flicking her fingers dismissively at the engraving, "is just a number."

"I suppose so, but what if–"

"I can't find the stamp – it's not here," interrupted Nomusa. She was holding up the packet from the flag; it was clearly empty.

"I wonder... Do you think maybe Cindy hid it? To try and slow other teams down?" said Sam.

"I wouldn't put it past her," said Jessie. "Maybe she even took it off away with them."

"She wouldn't dare," said Sam, but she was not at all certain.

They began searching the camp. Nomusa scrambled to the top of the rocks, while Jessie searched at their base and Sam peered under the branches of the low bushes. She found nothing but an empty chips packet and a cola can, which she stuffed into a packet tied onto the outside of her backpack.

"You're collecting litter now?" asked Jessie, eyeing Sam curiously.

"Yeah, my family usually brings a rubbish bag on our hikes. You know, to leave the world a little better than when you found it?"

"Found it!" called Nomusa. The stamp had been wedged into the cleft in the rock of the flag tree. It would have been very difficult to find, unless you were searching thoroughly, but it was conveniently close to the packet so that its position could have been ex-plained away as accidental.

"Honestly, she is such a bad sport!" said Sam.

"Can we eat now? I'm starved," said Jessie.

"We're not supposed to eat at the sites," said No-musa. "But we can eat while we walk. Let's not waste any more time here."

"Yes, heaven forbid we should actually have a rest. It's not like we're tired or hungry or anything," said Jessie, biting into a sandwich as soon as they were on the path leading out of the cluster of rocks and down towards the river.

They heard the river long before they saw it. The terrain around them had changed from shoulder-high, dry grass to a dense, marshy patch of tall reeds, which were higher even than their heads. The muddy ground squished beneath their feet and they had to step care-fully so as not to slip. A cool breeze had picked up, and the reeds rustled against each other, seeming to whisper a message to Sam. The sun dimmed as a cloud passed over it.

"It's a bit like a horror movie – I wouldn't like to get lost in here," said Jessie.

Bulging nests of yellow weavers hung from the reeds and the bird calls sounded shrilly above the background rush and murmur of the river. Suddenly, the reeds opened out and they were at the river. It was more of a stream – about eight metres wide – and despite the strong flow which surged around the bigger boulders in its path, it did not look very deep. The water was crystal clear and, when they felt it, bone-chillingly icy.

"It looks like we have to cross here," said Sam, check-ing the map and then looking at the river.

"But of course," said Jessie.

A series of large, relatively flat rocks were spaced out in a crooked row across the water. Holding hands, they stepped carefully on the slippery, moss-covered rocks,

233

wobbling on the odd loose stone. Sam stopped in the middle, where the water ran clearest, to fill the one water bottle she had used, and urged Nomusa and Jessie to fill their empties, too.

"You're neurotic about running out of water, Sam, you do know that?" said Jessie but she filled her bottle anyway.

Dry and in one piece, they made it to the other side where the path picked up again, but it looped back to the river after just a few minutes' walk. Sam thought they must be very near to the spot where the men with the dinghy had been. There was no sign of them now, though.

"We have to cross back again," said Sam.

"What the heck was that for, then?" said Jessie.

"If I understand this map right, then there was a deep gorge along the other side of the river and so we couldn't just walk along the bank on that side."

"At least there's a bridge, this time," said Jessie, nodding her head in the direction of the narrow wooden structure spanning the river.

She was less pleased once she stepped onto it, however. It was a suspension bridge, which dipped and swayed as they walked across it. Nomusa terrified Jessie and Sam by running to the other end of the bridge and then bouncing up and down so that the whole thing rippled under their feet, but stopped when their protests turned to screams. Sam crossed as rapidly as she dared, being careful to step over the gaps where planks were missing, but Jessie moved slowly, clinging for dear life to the rusty chains and steel cable from which the bridge hung and swung, and muttering objections and imprecations all the way across.

"It's too much. I don't know how they can expect us to do this stuff. Snakes, and swing bridges, and raging rivers and baboon poo! I can't, I tell you. I won't! It's too much. What's next, huh? That's what I'd like to know? Lost in the wilderness, most like. Trapped by a raging veldfire or attacked by a rampaging troop of baboons. Or kicked in the head by an eland!" Then she froze and let out a most unladylike word as one of the planks gave a sharp crack between her feet.

"Chill, Jessie, you're almost there," encouraged Nomusa loudly, but she whispered to Sam, "Somebody forgot to put on their big-girl panties this morning."

"Do you want me to come fetch you, Jessie?" called Sam, fighting giggles.

"Not unless you come in a helicopter," muttered Jessie.

She started walking again, a bit more quickly this time, as if afraid the wood might give way beneath her feet if she took too long. She tottered off the bridge and staggered several paces along the path before sinking onto the ground and declaring herself in need of resuscitation. With trembling hands, she pulled a chocolate bar out of her backpack and began to eat it steadily, pausing only to take a long drink from her water bottle.

Nomusa and Sam carefully avoided each other's gaze, but studied the map and the compass instead. The path divided into three right at the point where Jessie sat. When she leaned forward to retrieve her bottle of water from the knapsack lying on the ground in front of her, Sam spied a small, rusted signpost nestling in the grass behind where Jessie sat. It had three arrows pointing in different directions. The one pointing at the path curving back into the reeds read "Bannerman's Bridge",

235

while the arrow pointing to the middle path read "Main Camp". Sam had to kneel beside the signpost and push away a clump of grass to read the writing on the arrow pointing up the steep path which looked like it lead directly up the back of the mountain. It read: "Main Caves Exit. Strictly NO Entry."

"Remember how Mrs Grieve said the caves were kept locked and you could only go with a guide? I reckon you go in the other side and do the cave tour with the guide, then come down the mountain this side, and head back to the camp down that path," said Sam.

"I think you're right," said Nomusa. "So, it's obviously this way – let's go." She turned to take the left-hand path.

"Hang on a sec." Sam was bending over, reaching for something on the ground near the sign.

"Honestly! Is there no place where people won't drop their filthy litter? And who wants to smoke a cigar out here anyway?" Using a tissue, she picked up a fat, brown cigar butt and made to drop it into the litter bag on her knapsack, but then, suddenly, she snapped her head up to look at the path climbing the mountain. She stretched out a hand to touch some low, broken branches on the bushes to either side of the path.

"Sam?" asked Nomusa.

Sam mouthed two of the words written on the upwards-pointing arrow: *Main Caves…*"

"What is it? What's wrong?" asked Jessie, hastily getting to her feet and looking about, as if for snakes or baboons. Sam was looking from the path, to the cigar butt, to the river. She smacked a hand against her forehead.

"Of course – Giant's Castle! I've been so stupid!" She

clamped her hat onto her head and strode past Jessie and Nomusa to the path that lead up the back of the mountain.

"Sam! You're going the wrong way," called Nomusa. "That's not the right way to Bannerman's Bridge."

"I know," said Sam grimly, marching on. "But it *is* the right way to the Giant's Castle Main Caves!"

28

Climbing the Castle

"Sam – wait!" Jessie called.

"Where are you going? Stop!" said Nomusa.

"It's them," said Sam, urgently. "It's the art thieves, the same crowd. I *knew* there was something familiar about him when I saw that dinghy at the river. They're here to steal the panels at the main caves."

"How do you figure that out?" asked Jessie.

"It's a bunch of things, they just all clicked into place. That man, down by the dinghy at the river – the fat one with the hat? – that's Mitch, the Texan with the Stetson, from our hike to Devil's Peak. He *was* locking in coordinates of rock art sites that day. They come back later to steal them. They probably use the dinghy to bring equipment in and out, and to carry off the rock art. The big guy is helping them. Do you remember what was painted on the side of the van near the dinghy at the river?"

"Something like 'We take you further'?" said Nomusa; she looked like she was thinking hard.

"Yes, and that's just like that website – *Taking It Further*. This," she waved the cigar butt at them, "is his. He was smoking a cigar before that hike, too, and the guide made him put it out, don't you remember? And that hat – it's a cowboy hat. When I was online in that chat room, Lone Star Gal said they were planning a *cowboy operation*. That probably meant it was an operation under Mitch."

Seeing their unconvinced faces, Sam rushed on, "It is! It *is* them. In that chat room, they spoke about doing a big heist in July – now, in other words – at the *Main Caves*. That's what these are called." Sam jabbed a finger up to the basalt cliffs high on the mountain above them.

"But Sam," said Nomusa, "many places must have sites called 'main caves', it's probably not just here."

"I know that, but they also said 'at the citadel where the big one lives'. And what's another name for a citadel? A castle!"

"I thought you said it was a fortress," said Jessie.

"Same thing! And the 'big one' is obviously a giant – *Giant's Castle!* And they said it was in the 'ancient mother' and that must mean–"

"Africa," said Nomusa.

"Exactly. And this grass is flattened and the bush branches are all broken because they've dragged something big and heavy, something wider than this path, up the hill. Maybe it's their equipment, or something to carry the paintings back down in before they haul them off on the boat, until they're safely downstream and can transfer it to their van. I'll bet that's what they were doing the day before yesterday, when we saw them at the river. They're probably up there right now."

They all looked up the slope. From where they stood, they could not see the actual cave, only a massive, mist-circled rock face perched like a basalt crown above a band of deep mountain forest.

"We've got to stop them, and we've got to hurry!"

"We don't know for sure that they're even there," said Jessie.

"Then we need to check!"

"You realise," said Nomusa slowly, "that if we go up to the cave, we'll be throwing away any chance of winning the competition."

"This is more important," said Sam, earnestly.

"And," Nomusa continued, "we'll be breaking Grieve's explicit rule not to go to the caves."

"Do you think I care about that now?" said Sam, irritated. Couldn't they see that all this standing about and debating was just wasting time?

"I'm going. You can decide for yourselves what you want to do," said Sam and, without a backwards look, she began climbing.

The path up the northern face of the slope was intended to be used only to descend the mountain. It was very steep, zigzagging up the incline at sharp angles. Soon Sam was puffing and panting; from behind her, she could hear Nomusa's easy breathing and Jessie's wheezy gasps over the stamp of their feet on the path. She was grateful now for the chill breeze which cooled her face.

After about fifteen minutes of steady climbing, a misty veil of cloud descended from the peak and enveloped them in a thick, white silence. They could see only a few feet ahead of them through the mist. It was growing colder. They paused briefly to catch their breath and to get out their jackets and windbreakers and slip them on, and then, as rapidly as it had appeared, the mist dissolved away. Sam saw that they were standing at the top of the foothill. Ahead of them, the path disappeared into the shade of the mountain forest above which the caves stood. Behind them, the sheer slope stretched down to the river where three figures were walking along the path; even from this distance, the bright pink of their jackets was clearly visible.

"I think we should try to get a message to them," said Sam. "I would feel better if someone knew where we were. I just wish it wasn't..."

"Cindy. Yeah," said Jessie. "Just our luck."

"Stop them! Try and get their attention," said Sam.

Jessie took a deep breath, apparently preparing to holler, but Sam clapped a hand over her mouth to shush her.

"Shh! We don't know where these guys are, we don't want to alert them," said Sam.

"If they even exist," grumbled Jessie.

"Let's just try and get Cindy's attention as quietly as we can, OK?" said Nomusa.

They all three jumped up and down, waving their arms about frantically, but the girls on the path below were not looking up. Nomusa bent over, picked up a small rock and hurled it with unerring aim down at them. It hit a bush just in front of where the girls were walking and they jumped backwards in fright before looking up and seeing Sam, Nomusa, and Jessie.

"Pity you didn't get her hat," said Jessie, while Sam waved with both arms and then indicated "wait" by holding her hands up, palms-out. The other two imitated her. The three girls below were now standing still, gazing up the hill.

"Jessie, did you by any chance bring a sketchpad and a pencil?" asked Sam.

"There's a pad of paper and some charcoals in my backpack."

241

Moments later, Sam was writing a note on a piece of paper. The stick of charcoal kept breaking in her fingers, but she was soon finished.

"Why are you writing it in Afrikaans?" Nomusa asked, peering over Sam's shoulder.

"Just in case the thieves somehow get hold of it, they won't be able to understand a word."

"Will Cindy?"

"Of course she will – she's in my Afrikaans class."

"What's it say?"

"We are at the Main Caves. There are thieves trying to steal the paintings. Send help! From Nomusa, Jessie, and Sam," Sam translated.

"How are we going to get it down to them?" asked Jessie. "Should we make a paper aeroplane?"

Sam shook her head. "No, I think that would be too light to carry all the way down."

She picked up a rock about the size of her fist and crumpled the paper around it. Then she pulled the elastic from the bottom of her plaited hair and secured the note to the rock, before handing it to Nomusa. Nomusa took careful aim, pulled her arm back and threw hard. The girls below ducked, but the rock overshot its mark and landed several metres away in a clump of bushes on the grassy slope. The three figures looked towards where it had landed, but made no move to fetch it.

Jessie had taken out her cellphone and was using the camera function to focus in on Cindy, while giving Sam and Nomusa a running commentary.

"She's having a drink of water ... Oh, come on, go get it already! OK, now she's looking up at us ..."

"Does it look like she understands? Is she nodding?" asked Sam.

"No, she's shaking her head. And smiling – kind of evilly," said Jessie. Then she gasped.

"What?" said Sam and Nomusa together.

"She's making an L-sign with her fingers and sticking it up against her forehead! And now she's–"

But Sam could figure out this part well enough for herself. All three girls now had their hands up against their faces and Sam could just hear the faint cries of "Losers! Losers!" carried up on the wind. Cindy gave a big wave, and then she and Kitty and Julie carried on down the path. Sam, Jessie and Nomusa looked at each other.

"I guess we're on our own now," said Nomusa.

"You don't think we should go back to the camp and get help, alert the police or something and let them come here?" suggested Jessie.

"And tell them what? That we saw some broken branches and a cigar? No – they'd just think we were talking rubbish and dismiss us – like Zenobia did before. What we need is evidence. And even if we could get the authorities to take us seriously and come check, these guys will probably have cleared out – and taken the San paintings with them. At any moment, they could destroy it all!"

"Okay," said Jessie, with a resigned sigh.

"But maybe you two should go down and get help. I'll go up and try to stop them somehow."

"No ways, we're not leaving you!" said Jessie.

"We're in this together, Sam," said Nomusa.

"Right. Thanks," said Sam, swallowing a sudden lump in her throat. "OK, then. Let's go," and they all three turned and entered the deep shade of the forest.

29

Discovery

The forest was cool and dark. Trees stretched up over their heads, blotting out the sun. Thick vines curled up their trunks and draped down to the floor below. Ferns and cycads grew in dense clumps to the sides of the path, and thick, green moss blurred the edges of rocks and branches. It was still and quiet, their footfalls were soft on the spongy ground beneath their feet, where a layer of dead leaves, bark and soggy twigs lay in a deep cushion of mulch that absorbed the sound. The cooing of turtle doves and rock pigeons had faded, though Sam could hear the distant *tik-tik-tik* of what she thought might be a woodpecker. Wild fig trees grew sideways into the tangles of undergrowth, but their gnarled and twisted roots clung to the path. Sam, Nomusa and Jessie stepped carefully over the protruding roots and slippery leaves, and clambered over a few trees which had fallen across the path. The logs lay rotting – a home for termites, trailing strands of black moss, weirdly shaped mushrooms and vividly coloured fungi.

"How much further?" said Jessie, and her voice sounded strangely loud in the stillness. A small, mottled-brown toad jumped onto her left sneaker. She cursed and kicked a panicked foot out sideways, but managed not to scream.

"It can't be far now – it's starting to lighten, see?" Sam pointed at patches in the undergrowth where sunshine dappled the shade.

A few minutes later, the path ended at closed gate set into a tall wire fence which stretched on in both directions as far as they could see. A heavy chain and large brass padlock held the gate locked.

"This is the exit from the caves," said Sam.

"It looks undisturbed to me, Sam," said Jessie. "It doesn't look like anyone's come through here."

"Oh yes it does," said Sam. She pointed out the trail of broken twigs and flattened plants that lead off away from the path, along the left-hand stretch of fence.

"This way."

About fifty metres further, Sam found what she was looking for. The diamond pattern of the wire fence had been cut through from the very bottom, all the way up to the top, and the fence had been peeled back to provide an opening about the width of five men.

"I told you," Sam could not resist saying. "OK, quietly now, and eyes and ears open," she whispered.

Moving slowly and carefully, and looking around them, they all walked through the opening. There was a dense patch of dry, scrubby bushes and then they emerged into a clearing. Sam and Nomusa looked around to check whether anyone else was there, but saw no one. Jessie just gasped, "It's beautiful!" and headed, as though in a trance, to the rock cliff which lay before them.

On the peachy sandstone was painted, in black and white and ochre, a magical display of forms and figures: springbuck, eland, baboons and elephants; strangely distorted human figures with the heads of eland and lines of red drops seeming to spray out of their heads; a series of hunters leaping and running across the rock.

"It is magnificent, but we're not here to admire the art, Jessie. Let's search this place," said Nomusa.

"Oh, just a few quick photos," said Jessie, fumbling her cellphone from her backpack.

"I'll check out this side, Sam," said Nomusa, heading off to the left.

Sam set off in the opposite direction, keeping to a path that was obviously laid out for the guided tours. A tumble of fallen boulders and shards of rocks hemmed the sandstone cliff which rose up on her left, and the forest slid away to her right. Years and years of graffiti – names, hearts, dates, initials – had been carved into and spray-painted onto this section of rock. It was ugly, unimaginative and so unnecessary, Sam thought crossly. These futile little attempts at immortality had become only permanent monuments to stupidity.

The climbing, rocky path followed a curve to the left and Sam found herself standing on a wooden boardwalk in front of an enormous rock overhang, which shaded sandstone walls decorated with even more art. A large sign pinned to a wooden viewing platform read:

> Notice: All rock art and archaeological sites in South Africa are protected by law. Anyone found guilty of damaging sites can be fined or imprisoned. Report anyone who damages the art to the police immediately.

She craned her neck to look up at the ancient basalt roof. Untidy nests of swifts were wedged into crevices in the rock overhang, and small piles of tiny black droppings on the dusty floor indicated that rock dassies now inhabited the shelter which had housed tribes for hundreds, perhaps even thousands of years.

Feeling a little guilty, Sam climbed down off the

wooden structure and walked into the cave-like space beneath the rock overhang. At the front, a small diorama was laid out, showing a typical scene from the life of the ancient cave dwellers. On the ground, around the ashy remains of a fire, sat two life-size sculpted figures. A San man fiddled with an arrow, perhaps putting poison on its tip, while a San woman knelt on her knees, threading an ostrich-shell necklace. Between them lay a few examples of Stone Age tools – a small hand-axe, a thumb-scraper and a digging stick.

Sam walked past the little scene, across the clear floor to the back of the cave to examine the art there. On the wide rock faces at the back of the cave were painted yellow and red eland, writhing snakes, a leopard, bushbuck and rhebuck; more of the unearthly therianthropes with multiple heads and tails, and rows of tiny people – some with bows and arrows, others with digging sticks, some seeming to dance wildly. On the underside of a nearby boulder, Sam could plainly see the images of two hunters and some rabbits. The figures were done in varying styles – delicately painted by different hands at different times – and many were superimposed on each other which, Sam knew from her readings on the subject, the artists had thought would make the power of the spiritual images more potent.

She shook herself out of her reverie and forced herself to turn her back on the panels. Nomusa was right – they were not here to appreciate the art. At once, she noticed several things.

There were some bright yellow stars and arrows sketched on the edges of the rock, and alongside the crevices in the overhang. These looked modern and out of place to Sam. She walked right up to one star, leaned up close and studied it carefully, then she blew on it.

247

Coloured dust flew back into her face. Reaching out a finger, she rubbed at one of the arrows.

"Chalk," she said to herself. The arrows and stars had been drawn recently to mark these spots for some purpose.

Against a side wall of the cave rested three large inflatable mattresses pumped full of air, a pile of thick, grey, woollen blankets, some sleeping bags, coils of blue and white nylon rope, a big hiker's backpack, a primus stove with some tin mugs and plates alongside, a gas bottle with lamp attachment, some torches and an array of tools. Stepping closer, Sam saw that these included a sturdy pair of long-handled wire-cutters, plus chisels, crowbars and several hammers – some of which had pointed heads. A plain black plastic box, about the size of three shoeboxes, lay alongside. Sam lifted the lid. Lying inside were several plastic-wrapped packages of a brown, putty-like substance, and rows and rows of what looked like thumb-sized, red firecrackers. Sam replaced the lid gingerly; she doubted they were fireworks.

Not wanting to shout for her friends, she scrambled up onto the wooden walkway and raced back down the path to fetch them. When she came back to the cave, with Jessie and Nomusa in tow, she was immediately struck by the sight of something else; she wondered why she had not noticed it before. An enormous, rectangular crate, made of wooden slats, sat nestled up against the vegetation at the far end of the cave.

"Jeez, check this all out!" said Jessie, and Sam was pleased to see that she was not looking at the paintings again. "I'll get some photos of this equipment – we can use it as evidence against them."

"You were right, Sam. They're definitely up to no good here," said Nomusa.

"What's that?" asked Jessie, pointing her phone's camera at the big, wooden crate but then shaking it and muttering, "Oh no! I think I'm out of battery power."

She sat down on a small rock in the centre of the cave and began fiddling with the phone, taking it apart and reassembling it, apparently in the hopes that it would restore itself to working order. Nomusa walked over to her.

"Can I help?" she asked, looking down at the useless phone in Jessie's hands.

Sam walked over to the crate to investigate. The sides of it were higher than her shoulder, branded with *fragile* and *this side up*↑ stamps, and it was twice as long as it was wide. Standing on her toes, she peered over the edge: it was empty, save for two large rolls of bubble wrap lying in the bottom. Walking around the giant box, she found that two smaller crates sat to the side of it. One of these had been nailed securely shut, but the other was still open, its wooden lid resting tilted against the side of the box.

Sam got down on her haunches and looked inside the open crate. She saw that it was half-filled with a few bubble-wrapped packages and her heart sank. Pushing aside the protective plastic, she saw that the packages contained flat chunks of rock with paintings on one side, obviously recently chipped and chiselled away from a nearby rock face.

"Useless, rotten phone!" Still seated on the rock in the centre of the cave, Jessie shook her phone in annoyance.

"Sam, I know yours doesn't have a camera, but double-check that it doesn't have reception. Maybe it will allow emergency calls if you've still got battery life."

Sam took hers out, switched it on and examined the old screen. "Sorry, no. I've still got a full battery, but no reception at all."

"Let me see, Jess," said Nomusa holding out her hand for the phone, but at that moment, a short, stout man wearing a large Stetson hat entered the clearing of the cave, closely followed by a giant of man wearing dusty black overalls.

"Well lookee here!" the man called Mitch said loudly, and from a leather holster on the belt of his jeans, he pulled out a gun and pointed it at Jessie and Nomusa. "Stand up and turn around, you."

From where she crouched to the side of the large crate, Sam saw Jessie open her hand and drop the phone onto the sandy floor. Using the toe of one sneaker, Nomusa pushed the phone under the curve of the rock and, as Jessie slowly stood up and turned around, she swept sand over the phone with the side of her foot, hiding it from view.

Sam ducked behind the tall crate – Mitch had not spotted her yet, and she was keen to keep it that way. She needed to find a way to get away and get help. Her heart was beating in her chest as if it, too, wanted to escape and her mouth was suddenly as dry as the floor of the cave. What should she do?

Just then, a loud whistle-blast pierced the air. Peeping around the corner of the crate, Sam saw Mitch tucking a whistle into a pocket of his shirt, then he waved his gun at Jessie and Nomusa, gesturing them to the back wall of the cave. His back was to Sam – it was now or never! A sudden idea flashed into her head and, without hesitating, she acted on it.

A moment later, Sam was creeping along the edge of the clearing, where the vegetation began, heading for

250

the spot beyond which was the gap in the fence. She dared not enter the brush until the last moment, when she could run for it, because she knew that the twigs and branches would make a loud noise when she moved through them. Over at the back of the cave, she could hear Jessie arguing loudly with Mitch. Sam knew that Jessie and Nomusa who, unlike Mitch and his crony, faced the cave opening, would be able to see her and figured that Jessie was trying to keep the man's attention solidly on her, giving Sam the best chance of escape.

"I see you've lost your moustache, Mitchy. Can't say it's an improvement," Jessie goaded him.

"Shut your mouth and keep your hands where I can see them."

"You can't do this to us – this is kidnapping! We won't stand for it."

"And what do you plan to do about it?" Sam heard Mitch say derisively. "Two little girls all alone?"

"Little girls?" Jessie sounded irate.

As quietly as she could, Sam crawled along the line of bushes and rocks. She estimated that she must be very near to where the gap in the fence lay. She pulled herself into a crouch, and was just about to leap up and run forward into the brush like a sprinter from the starting block, when an enormous pair of booted feet stepped in front of her. Looking up, she saw a pair of black-clad legs, thick as tree trunks, topped by an enormous body.

30

Harvesting

A pair of thick arms reached down to where Sam crouched in the dirt, and clamped around her shoulders. Next thing, she was being carried through the air, across the cave, to where Mitch stood guarding Jessie and Nomusa.

"Put me down!" yelled Sam, and the giant of a man dropped her so quickly that she went sprawling into the dust.

"Thank you, Moby, now finish laying those charges," said Mitch.

The big man lumbered off towards the box with the explosives inside. Mitch trained the gun on Sam, Jessie and Nomusa. Sam could see now that it was an automatic weapon, an ugly, heavy-looking steel thing with a diamond-patterned black grip. It gave her a cold feeling in her stomach and she thought that the image of that weapon would be burned on her memory for as long as she lived – which might not be very long, given how things stood. A strident woman's voice shouted from the other side of the cave.

"What is it now Mitch? You keep interrupting my work – I almost had that three-headed therianthrope out when I heard the whistle.

"Come over back here, darlin', and see what I found," called Mitch.

252

A woman came around the corner of rock and stepped into the cave. Sam saw at once from her long face and horsey jaw that it was the same woman, Dorothy – if that was her real name – from the Devil's Peak hike, though she looked very different today. Gone were the big sunglasses, the styled hair, the bright clothes and the fuchsia lipstick. Now she wore hardy khaki overalls, her hair was pulled back into a plain ponytail and the hands which she was dusting against the seat of her pants had short, unvarnished nails.

"Well, well, well," said the woman, coming to stand beside Mitch and stare at the three captives. "If it isn't the little girls from Devil's Peak!"

"We're not little girls," said Sam.

"Ok, then – *little ladies*. There – happy, now?"

"Not particularly."

"Girls, ah, pardon me, ladies, I'd like you to meet my wife – she's a famous art historian, you know. You can call her Dorothy, and me Mitch. Please don't be offended that we don't trust you with our real names."

"Shut up, 'Mitch'," said the woman. "What are your names?"

The girls exchanged glances and shrugged; there did not seem to be any reason for them to give false names.

"Jessie."

"Nomusa."

"I'm Sam."

"Hang on – not 'Cyber Sam' by any chance?"

"Let me guess," said Sam to Dorothy, "Lone Star Gal."

"Very clever. A little too clever if truth be told." Dorothy grimaced, then asked Mitch, "What are we going to do with them?"

"Just let us go – we won't tell anyone," said Nomusa quickly.

"Yeah, right, sure you won't!"

"Who knows you're here?" said Mitch

"Everyone," said Sam.

"Liar," said Dorothy, with a twisted smile. "You're not supposed to be up here, are you? We saw all the girls running around the valley, but none of them came up here."

"They'll come looking for us," said Nomusa. "They will."

"I sincerely doubt it, sugar. How would they know where to look for you? And dark will be falling soon, no-one searches in the dark," said Mitch.

"Besides which – your emergency services and rescue volunteers are all already occupied. There's a very nasty bush fire raging on the other side of the river and that's keeping them nice and busy," said Dorothy, pulling a plainly false sad face. "Hmmm-mmm – all that loss of flora and fauna, and this a World Heritage Site and all. No, I'm pretty sure the fire will be their first priority."

"You set that fire," Nomusa accused angrily.

"It's always good to have a little distraction over there, while you're busy over here. Moby – come tie these girls up."

The large man shambled over to Sam, Nomusa and Jessie from where he had been packing the brown putty-like substance into cracks and crevices on the rock walls and overhang. He grabbed a few coils of nylon rope from the pile of equipment, dragged the girls to the front of the cave – "Careful there, Muscles!" protested Jessie – then tied each of their hands tightly behind their backs. He made them sit back to back on the sandy floor, a few

254

metres away from the stationary figures of the diorama. Checking to see that Mitch was watching them, he collected their knapsacks and dumped them against the cave wall with the other equipment. Then he returned to his task, packing the stiff brown substance into the places marked by the stars and arrows, and sticking little rectangular objects into them.

The cave was set in the lee of the mountain, and soon the light began to fade to a dull dusk. Dorothy lit the gas lamp and held it up to illuminate the areas where Moby worked. Mitch kept his beady eyes on the girls although, Sam was relieved to see, he had replaced the gun in its holster. She was thinking frantically. They desperately needed to escape – but how would they get free of the ropes?

A shadow flitted across Sam's vision. At first she thought she had imagined it but, looking up, she saw that little black bats were swooping and darting around the cave, preying on insects drawn to the light. Jessie must have spotted them at the same time, because she ducked her head and let out an outraged shriek.

"Bats! First fires, then baboons and snakes and, and … Cindy. And toads! And now – bats! I can't take it anymore!"

Just when Sam thought Jessie might descend into raging hysterics, her friend shouted in a loud, but completely sane, voice: "And I'm hungry over here! And cold."

Mitch, Dorothy and Moby ignored her.

"Listen," whispered Sam as quietly as she could while still being sure that Jessie and Nomusa would hear her. "I've got a plan." She tried not to move her lips as she spoke, explaining her idea. "Every time they're not

255

looking, move back a few inches." She jerked her head backwards in the direction of the diorama. "Little by little – so he doesn't notice."

"Hey, Mitch," Sam said, her tone challenging. "Your wife's an art historian, and you presumably appreciate the artistic worth of this work."

Mitch focused his attention on her and nodded reluctantly.

"So tell me, how do you justify this pillaging of the art?"

"It's not pillaging," he snapped, "it's harvesting."

"Harvesting? That's a funny word for theft! Which ones were you planning to take?"

"We are *going* to take as many of those," he turned and pointed to all the paintings along the back wall, "as we can."

As soon as his back was turned, the three girls scooched backwards several inches on their bottoms, but were sitting still when he turned back again.

"You're a vandal," said Sam.

"I'm a collector," said Mitch, his face growing red with anger. "I collect these pieces and make sure they get to people who will appreciate them and take care of them – *properly*."

"What? They aren't being taken care of properly here?"

"Are you kidding me?" said Mitch scornfully. "Look here and here and here!"

As he pointed out areas where the paintings had been defaced and damaged at human hands, the girls moved backwards several more inches.

"These are priceless artefacts, and they're being treated as just another piece of rock. They're degrading by

256

the day. Here they sit, out in the open, exposed to the elements, and apparently not at all protected from the philistines who are set on making their own primitive mark."

He gestured furiously at a set of initials carved into the rock. Sam, Nomusa and Jessie shoved themselves backwards on their rear ends, pushing with their legs. It felt to Sam like they were playing a childhood game of K-I-N-G, when you had to sneak up on the watcher while his back was turned, and then freeze when he spun around. But Mitch didn't seem to notice their movement, he was so absorbed in his argument.

"Look at this, for Pete's sake. 'DR ♥ GW'. For crying in a bucket of blood!"

He turned around to face them and wagged a reprimanding finger at them.

"Your country is not taking care of its own heritage – a heritage, I might add, that is so important that it belongs to the whole human race. And especially to those who understand its significance and appreciate its value."

"You mean, to those who are willing to pay you for stealing it," said Nomusa.

"We tried to ask nicely, but they wouldn't give it to us for some reason," said Mitch with a bark of laughter.

"Look at the true glory of this," he said, turning to admire the art but, before they could move, he looked back at them. "I'm on the good side here, you know."

"Just how do you figure that?" said Nomusa, who had frozen halfway through pushing herself backwards.

"I collect these treasures and then they're preserved for all eternity. Safe from the elements and the graffiti artists and the incompetent government officials. This art, this rare and precious beauty, will be safe once we get it to it to the collectors who will truly appreciate it and protect it from wear and tear and erosion, in temperature-controlled rooms, safe from wind and sun and rain and greasy fingers. They will protect this legacy of humanity so that it will not be lost." Then he sighed happily, contemplating the art surrounding them.

The girls moved backwards; they were close to the diorama now. Dorothy and Moby were still at the back of the cave.

"It will bring such joy!"

"But only to a privileged few," Sam countered. "Only in private collections that most of us will never get to see! It belongs to everybody and everybody should get to see it."

"So they can carve their worthless initials into it, or splash it with water, or take pot-shots at it? Surely art belongs to those who understand and appreciate it, not to every Tom, Dick and Harry idiot? If your country is unable to protect these gems, then we will save them."

"Loot them, I think you mean," said Sam. "And sell them on for a fat profit!"

"Why shouldn't we make a profit? We do all the work, we take all the risks."

"What about trying to study the art and understand it?" Sam protested. "Once you've removed the paintings from their setting, half the meaning is lost. You destroy the rock art site itself, so that no-one will ever know which paintings were next to each other, or what way they faced. Maybe the view from the location of the painting is part of understanding it, maybe they were painted to be oriented to certain stars for a reason. Once you've ripped them from their environment, we lose all of that. We'll never know what they mean! When you take a section of the rock art, it's like tearing pages from a great mystery novel."

"I'm finished," said Moby from the back of the cave. His voice was rough and deep and strongly accented.

"Hey, Muscle-man!" Jessie shouted at him. "Do you always do as you're told? Don't you think you're big enough to decide for yourself what's right and what's wrong?"

Moby ignored her.

"Have you packed all the plastic explosives?" Mitch asked.

"Yes."

"And set the electronic fuses?"

"Yes."

"I trigger it electronically with my phone," said Mitch, hopping excitedly from one foot to the other while he spoke. "The trigger activates the detonator and that ignites the C4 – that's the plastic explosive – causing the blast which will widen those cracks," he pointed at the crevices, "and bring that down." He gestured with a sweep of the arm to the panels of paintings.

"Lay out the cushions," Dorothy instructed Moby.

"Hey, Moby-man," shouted Jessie. "It seems they make you do all the work, while they just stand around giving orders. If you untie us, we can help you."

"Shut your smart mouth," said Dorothy, cuffing Jessie hard behind the head, then walking over to supervise Moby's work. He had walked over to the side of the cave, grabbed the inflated mattresses and woollen blankets and was now laying them up against the panels and under the overhang. Once the mattresses and blankets were in place, he covered them with double-layers of bubble-wrap.

"For a nice, soft landing – we wouldn't want our treasures to come to harm, now would we?" said Dorothy, watching in satisfaction. "Right – do it, Mitch!"

"Ready?" whispered Sam to Nomusa and Jessie. They nodded. "Now!"

"Bat! Bat!" Jessie screeched loudly and flung herself first sideways into Sam and the backwards into the diorama. "There's a bat in my hair!"

Jessie crashed into one of the San figures, which toppled over and lay immobile on its back, bent knees pointing up at the sky, hands still threading beads. Sam was shoved onto her side in the sand. Her fingers scrabbled around in the dirt and ashes, until they closed over the small hand-axe. She seized it and slipped it into the back pocket of her jeans.

"Oh, for goodness' sake – you are such a ninny!" Dorothy said to Jessie. "Just quit your bellyaching."

Moby came over and pulled Sam and Jessie back upright. Then he dragged all three of them to the edge of the clearing where the vegetation began and where, presumably, they would be out of the way of falling rocks when the explosives were set off. He tied another length of rope around all three of them, so that they were trussed together.

Sam, Nomusa and Jessie watched in horrified fascination as Mitch took a cellphone out of his breast pocket. He, Dorothy and Moby stepped back away from the entrance of the cave.

"Don't do it!" Sam pleaded futilely.

"Three – two – one!" said Mitch and then, very deliberately, he pressed a button on the phone.

31

Escape!

There was one moment of long silence as they waited for the explosion. Sam stared at the overhang, holding her breath. Then ... nothing happened. She sighed in relief.

"What the–?" said Mitch, holding the phone up to see it more clearly.

"Cellphones don't work out here, you moron! There's no reception!" Jessie cackled.

"This damned backwoods of a wretched, uncivilised country!" snarled Mitch. He made as if to hurl his phone at the rock face, but apparently thought better of it, and settled for kicking one of the inflatable mattresses instead.

"Really, Mitch. Y'all might have checked before-hand," said Dorothy disapprovingly. "I guess we'll just have to do it with manual charges: squib explosives and a long fuse wire."

"Too dark," said Moby in his deep, rough voice.

"What's that?" said Dorothy.

"We can't do it now – he'll never find all the points in this dark," said Mitch, slouching over to the sleeping bags. "We can do it tomorrow morning, at first light. I'm going to try and get some sleep."

Moby began working in the area that was visible by the light of the lamp, pulling out the electronic charges and, in their place, sticking the tiny, red sticks of explosives which looked like thumb-sized fire-crackers connected by black fuse wire.

"Hey Moby, don't leave us here," protested Jessie. "There are bugs and snakes in the forest. Hey, Mitch – it's cold and we're freezing! Can't we have a blanket?"

Mitch dragged a blanket off one of the cushioning mattresses and flung it roughly around them, saying, "This isn't even extreme weather. Why, back in Texas–"

"Yeah, yeah, we know," said Jessie. "Everything's bigger and better there. And stupider." Then she shouted, "We're hungry, too! Hey, Dorothy! Mitch! We want something to eat. Hey, Muscles – we're hungry! Don't they teach you manners in Texas?"

"Stop your sassing," said Dorothy, aiming a kick at Jessie's ribs as she walked past. "You won't starve in one night. Besides, that's the least of your worries!"

Under the blanket wrapped around them, Sam started scraping away at the ropes with the hand-axe. It soon became clear, however, that it was going to be a long process to saw through the bindings. The edge of the tool was not very sharp, but it was the only hope they had and so Sam, trying to keep her shoulders still, kept working away at the ropes which bound her own hands.

Dorothy, Mitch and Moby heated a stew of some kind on the primus stove – ignoring Jessie's demands that they share – and then boiled a kettle and made some coffee. The aroma of the food and hot drink made Sam's stomach growl. After a long while, Dorothy and Mitch wrapped themselves tightly into their sleeping bags and lay down on the inflatable mattresses under the overhang. Moby positioned his mattress closer to the girls, where he could keep an eye on them, and then he, too, lay down.

After what seemed like hours of scraping the chunk of rock against the ropes binding her hands, Sam finally felt them give way. She pulled off the pieces and, being careful not to drop the hand-axe, rubbed at her wrists where the rope had bitten into her flesh. It was a relief to allow her shoulders to slump forward and rest for a few moments, and she longed to rub at the aching muscles, but she dared not. Even though Dorothy had turned out the light, and they sat in pitch darkness, Sam could not be sure whether Moby was still awake. The snores sounding against the overhang reassured her that Mitch, at least, was asleep. She kept her hands behind her back and soon started on the next set of ropes.

"I'm going to do Nomusa first," she whispered to them, "in case she gets a chance to run."

The hand-axe was rubbing her fingers raw and she could feel a blister starting in the palm of her hand where the back of the tool rested in her tight grasp. She was so tired – more tired even, than she was hungry. She scraped backwards and forwards, over and over again. Jessie slumped against her, fast asleep. To and fro, Sam scraped. Just a bit more, just a little while longer, almost there. She felt herself slowing down and taking long blinks. If she could just close her eyes for a while, just rest for a few moments…

A nudge from Nomusa woke her up. "Do you want me to do it for a while?"

"No, it's much easier with free hands." Sam yawned widely, trying to get some of the cold mountain air into her fuzzy head. "You can do Jessie when you're free."

She had dropped the tool when she drifted off and now had to feel around in the sand before she found it again. A long while later, Nomusa was finally free. Sam slumped backwards against Jessie's side and allowed

herself to doze. It seemed only minutes later that someone was tugging the blanket off her.

Sam blinked and opened her eyes. She was halfway
to stretching her stiff muscles when the blast of cold
air woke her up fully and cleared her brain. Behind her
back, she could feel that all of their wrists were free. She
grasped Jessie and Nomusa's hands tightly so that they
would not give themselves away by moving their arms.

In the grey light of pre-dawn, Sam could see that
Moby, Mitch and Dorothy were already awake and
moving around the clearing. Their mattresses and sleeping bags were back under the overhang – ready for a
second try at the detonation. Moby was busy sticking
the small explosives into the packed plastic explosive,
while nearby Mitch and Dorothy – with their blanket
wrapped around her shoulders – were stretching and
drinking coffee from green tin mugs. It was time for
them to make their move. Sam wondered how to signal
to Nomusa that she should make a run for it.

"What are you looking at?" asked Dorothy.

"I think we need to *go now* – um, to the toilet, I mean."
She squeezed Nomusa's hands.

"Oh. Yes," said Nomusa. "Excuse me, Dorothy? I
need to go to the toilet. Now"

"Me too," said Jessie.

"We all do, Jessie, but Nomusa needs to go *now*."

"Oh, right," said Jessie, catching on. Then she added,
"She's got bladder problems, you know. If she doesn't
go immediately … big mess. Huge!"

"Thanks very much for that, Jessie," snapped Nomusa.

"Well, go then – who's stopping you?" asked Mitch.
"There's bush right behind you. Moby can loosen that
one rope so y'all can move a little bit."

His words were followed by a loud clamour of protest.

"Go here? In front of you? No ways!" said Nomusa.

"Sis! What kind of a disgusting pig watches while girls go to the toilet?" shouted Jessie.

"You're revolting!" said Sam loudly.

Mitch's face flushed a purplish-red. "I'm not letting you lot out of my sight," he insisted, provoking another round of protests.

"I don't know how they do things in Texas–" began Jessie.

"Oh all right!" said Dorothy, shrugging the blanket from her shoulders and then crouching down to untie the rope which wrapped around the three of them. "I'll take her back a ways. Just shut up, you lot – you're noisier than a flock of roosting chickens!"

Nomusa got to her knees awkwardly, keeping her hands behind her back as if they were still tied, clutching the loose ends of rope tightly inside her fists. Dorothy grabbed her by one elbow and lead her stumbling away from the clearing, a few metres away down the path to the official exit where the locked gate was.

Sam groaned in frustration. Mitch looked at her anxiously, perhaps worrying if she, too, had an uncontrollable bladder. Sam had hoped that Nomusa would be able to get closer to the gap in the fence where she could slip through and run away. Now how would she be able to run back to the hole in the fence without getting recaptured? After only a few moments though, Sam heard a series of sounds – a scuffle, a loud grunt, the rattling of a gate, a shrill yell – and then Dorothy came running back into the camp.

"She knocked me sideways and then climbed up and over that high locked gate like a damned chimpanzee! She's run away down the path, Mitch!"

"Moby! Go get her," commanded Mitch.

"Good luck with that, Muscles," sneered Jessie.

"You'll never catch her," said Sam gleefully. "She's the school's cross-country champ. She's in the provincial athletics team. She's gone, and soon she'll be back with the police!"

Mitch cursed and flung his tin mug across the clearing. It bounced off a boulder with a clang, splashing coffee onto the rock with the rabbit painting.

"Hey!" protested Sam.

Mitch tossed another rope to Moby, who began tying it tightly around Jessie and Sam's feet. Then he replaced the one around their waists, which bound them to each other.

"Make sure you get it nice and tight, Moby. Damned interfering little brats!"

"How much time do you reckon we have?" Mitch asked Dorothy.

"Not enough to get that down and packed," she said, jerking her head back to the overhang and the rock panels. "Probably only enough time to get out of here. Let's cut our losses, and take what we've got so far."

Mitch nodded his agreement. "Moby, pack only what we can get down in one run. Dorothy, let's get those crates sealed and ready."

He strode over to the large crate and tried to reach inside, but even though he hung right over the edge with his feet waving in the air behind him, he could not reach the bottom of the crate where bubble-wrap lay. Once Moby had retrieved it for him, Mitch shoved a long length of the packaging material into the smaller crate and Dorothy nailed the lid shut. Moby, who had already strapped on a heavily-laden backpack, hoisted

266

one crate under each arm and walked off through the bushes to the gap in the fence. Apparently, he was well-practised in making quick getaways. Mitch, wearing a much smaller knapsack, made to follow him, but then stopped and contemplated Sam and Jessie.

"I reckon it's safe to just leave you – you know nothing about our operation, not even our real names. But I sincerely recommend you stay the heck away from poking your noses into other people's business."

"And I sincerely hope you get what you deserve!" said Sam.

"A few hundred more treasures, then," Dorothy taunted. "Though it causes me a pang to leave these beauties, I admit it. It fair breaks my heart to turn my back and walk away from them."

"Oh, honeybuns, don't be too blue about it – we can always come back and harvest them another time. They've stood here for hundreds of years, they ain't going anywhere." Then he guffawed loudly and turned to go, calling over his shoulder, "Well, not without our help, anyway!"

"You'll never get them – never!" Sam shouted to his departing back. "We won't let you!"

"Now, sugar," said Dorothy, but her voice was anything but sweet as she leaned in close to Sam's face. "I've put up with just about as much as I'm prepared to take from you gals. I think…" she nodded and looked over their heads at the dry vegetation behind them, "Yep, I really do think that a nice cosy fire is in order."

"A fire? No!" said Jessie, sounding alarmed.

"Yes!" said Dorothy. "Haven't you been bellyaching all night about being cold? A nice fire will warm you right up." She patted her pockets and brought out a cigarette-lighter in the shape of a small pyramid.

"Shake a leg there, Dorothy," they heard Mitch calling from somewhere down the path.

"You better hurry. You don't want to hang about here – you might get caught," urged Sam, frantic now that she saw Dorothy clicking the lighter open and holding the tall flame to first one, then another, of the bushes near to them.

"A good way not to get caught is to be sure and not leave no incriminating evidence. And I've always found," Dorothy said, now setting fire to a dry clump of grass behind Jessie's back, "that a nice, hot fire is a good way to destroy all evidence behind me."

"But you can't set a fire – it'll destroy the paintings, it might even set off the explosives and they'll collapse and you won't be here to cart them off," said Sam, trying to lean away from the flames which were even now beginning to lick at the dry leaves and twigs of the bush next to her.

Dorothy looked at the expanse of sandy floor between the vegetation and the walls of paintings.

"Oh, I don't think the fire will jump this break, but that's a chance I'm willing to take, sugar. Besides, there are plenty more sites to strip all over the world, even in this country."

"If we die – that'll be murder!"

"Only if they catch us," said Dorothy, laughing at the very idea of it in a slightly mad way. "Well, it's been nice and all, but I've really got to go now. Don't y'all get too hot, y'hear?" And with a last wave to the painted panels, she left.

Behind Sam and Jessie, the grass and bushes were already crackling and popping in the heat of the flames, which grew larger by the moment. Without wasting another second, they freed their arms from the severed ropes. With trembling fingers, Jessie began untying the rope tied around their waists, while Sam leaned over and worked at the knot on the rope around her feet. It took only minutes, but felt like an eternity as the heat emanating from the fire reached their cheeks. Smoke stung their eyes and caught in their throats.

"Stick your face under your top!" Sam urged Jessie. With their noses and mouths tucked under the cotton of their shirts, it was slightly easier to breathe.

As soon as her feet were free, Sam leapt up and ran over to where their three backpacks still rested against the side wall of the cave. One by one she snatched them up, turned them upside-down and shook hard. A jumble of jerseys, lip balm, sunscreen, chocolate bars, charcoals and a sketchpad tumbled out, but in amongst these were the full bottles of water. Jessie had by now managed to loosen, but not completely untie, the rope around her ankles. Hobbling over to Sam like a prisoner in manacles, she grabbed two of the bottles and made to go back to where the fire was licking at the dry leaves of low trees.

"No!" shouted Sam. "Don't waste it! Here, pour it on this instead." She dragged one of the thick woollen blankets off the inflatable mattresses still lying under the overhang, and scattered the water across it. Jessie followed suit. When they had poured out all the water, they dragged the damp and heavy blanket over the fire.

"On the count of three, chuck it on top of the worst flames. One-two-three!"

They swung the blanket up in the air and then brought it down hard on the fire. The whoosh of downward air extinguished some of the flames. Gasping and coughing, Sam hurled herself on top of the blanket, beating it down with her hands and stomping on it with her feet, trying desperately to suffocate the fire beneath. Jessie bunny-hopped on top, tumbled over and rolled around from side to side. Then they climbed off, lifted the thick blanket up again and brought it down on the adjacent burning patch. Over and over they beat at the flames; bit by bit they made headway against the fire. When Sam thought the worst had been smothered, she ran to fetch another blanket and began beating at the smaller flickers of red. One rogue spark, one twig left glowing could easily set off another fire, she knew.

When, at last, all the flames and embers had been put out, she and Jessie clutched each other tightly and then collapsed, exhausted, on the singed and smoking pile of blankets. They looked at each other through faces blackened with soot, hair damp with sweat and eyes red from the smoke.

"We did it," croaked Sam.

Her throat felt raw, there was a taste of blood in her mouth, and when she coughed, she puffed a tiny cloud of soot into the air. She pointed at it and began laughing, while at the same moment, Jessie began crying loudly. After a few minutes, Jessie pointed at Sam's face and, apparently finding it amusing, she switched to laughing hysterically. Sam, meanwhile, was beginning to tremble. The shaking moved up from her knees and her hands up to her face and by the time her lower lip began to wobble, she found that she was now crying. Sam and Jessie sat like that for a long while, hanging on to each other, no longer knowing or caring whether they were laughing or weeping. The tears of relief and shock mingled in the salty rivulets which trickled down their dirty faces.

32

Reception

"Time to head down?" Sam said.

Jessie groaned and buried her face in the blanket. Sam fetched their knapsacks and packed the contents back inside, but put the two chocolate bars in the pocket of her windbreaker. Remembering the hidden phone, she retrieved it from its sandy spot under the rock, and put it into Jessie's knapsack which she handed to her friend. Jessie looked like a wreck: her face was soot-stained, her eyes swollen and reddened, and her hair was a bird's nest of twigs and leaves. Sam thought that she must look just as bad.

"Come on. Up!"

Sam grabbed Jessie by the hand and yanked her to her feet. She slung Nomusa's knapsack over one shoulder and her own over the other and then headed for the place where the fence had been cut open.

"Come on, Jessie!" she urged.

"I can't. I'm tired and dirty and cold and hungry. I can't walk another step."

"There's a cosy bed waiting for you at the camp. And a nice, hot bath. And food: bacon and eggs and buttery toast – and coffee!"

Jessie looked up at the last words, though she still swayed on her feet and shivered violently.

"And, in the meantime, cho-co-late," said Sam. She pulled one of the chocolate bars out of her pocket, opened it and, breaking off a small piece, waved it temptingly in the air.

"Give," said Jessie feebly, holding out a cupped hand.

"Fetch," replied Sam. Then she made the sort of noises she usually made to call her dog over for a treat. "Come and get it," she sang.

Jessie whimpered weakly, but took a few reluctant steps over to where Sam stood. Backing up through the vegetation, holding up the piece of chocolate, Sam lured Jessie into the forest. Jessie walked a little faster to catch up with Sam, snatched the chocolate out of her hand and stuffed it into her mouth. She groaned in pleasure.

"Don't stop – there's more. Come and get it," called Sam, walking ahead into the undergrowth until she found the path that lead down the mountainside.

Jessie stumbled after her. The noisy dawn chorus of birdsong accompanied them from overhead. By tempting Jessie forwards with the chocolate and feeding her the odd piece, Sam was able to get them through the thick forest and out onto the grassy slope of the mountain. Jessie was now awake and walking steadily, so Sam thought it safe to hand over the rest of the chocolate bar. She opened her own and took a big bite. The chocolate was sweet and rich, with a chewy toffee centre. Sam thought it was the most delicious thing she had ever eaten.

They walked carefully down the steep, zigzagging path that lead down the side of the mountain. Dawn was breaking behind stretched strips of cloud low on the horizon, and the sky was a wash of peach and coral and cerise. The hills around them and the valley below were lit with a pink glow. Against the blushing sky, the dark outline of a distant lammergeyer riding the thermals seemed to summon them onwards.

The steady sound of their steps on the path – broken only by the occasional "om-nom-nom" from Jessie walking behind her – lulled Sam into a kind of walking trance. She felt older, somehow, than the girl who had climbed this path less than a day ago. Was it only two days ago that they had arrived here? School seemed a million miles away – small and insignificant and fleeting when set against the ageless, timeless peaks and valleys around her. Delmonico seemed like a petty irritation, a mere mosquito buzzing annoyingly in her life. How could she have been so intimidated, so scared of him? She shook her head in amazement that she had ever worried about whether she had ruled off her work correctly, or written the date on the right side of the page.

She felt like a completely different person to that frantic girl. It was absolutely clear to her now that he was just a nincompoop – an insecure little man who tried to make himself feel more important by bullying those under his power. He was laughable, pitiful even – not powerful. She didn't need a report card to know that she had done very well on her last exams, in spite of his attempts to break her down. And she knew, with a deep certainty that straightened her back and put an added kick in her step, that he would never again get under her skin. In fact, she wondered if she would ever worry about anything as much again.

She now knew the difference between genuine fear in the face of real threat, and useless anxiety. All of her worries, all of her what-if's and future dreads had not prepared her one iota for the actual danger that had collided with their lives. Her habit of perpetual worrying, she now realised, did not help her at all, it did not protect her from future problems, it merely drained her of strength, happiness and confidence in the present. When confronted with kidnapping, guns and fire, she had felt no inclination at all to tap, or count, or check – she hadn't even bitten her nails. She was embarrassed, now, thinking of those silly habits. And she had also not panicked or lost her head – she had merely got on with doing what she needed to do to survive. Surely if she could deal with that, she could deal with anything!

She might never be as laid-back and relaxed as Jessie or Nomusa, she thought, as the sky lightened to a pale blue and they joined the last gentle stretch of path that lead to the main camp, but she was through being a nervous wreck.

"We made it," said Jessie.

Sam looked up. Yelling their names and flying down the path towards them was Nomusa, a smile splitting her face from ear to ear. Close behind her were Dan and Apples; several uniformed fire-fighters and paramedics carrying heavy equipment; a group of men and women carrying ropes and stretchers and wearing jackets with the words *Mountain Rescue* on them; a few park officials standing with two police officers; a white-faced Mrs Grieve, together with Miss Gamion and Miss Stymen; and a loud gaggle of girls bringing up the rear.

Once Nomusa had released Sam from a crushing hug, Dan took her place.

"Good timing, little sis," he said. "We were just about to set off to come find you." He grinned, but his face showed the strain of a sleepless night spent worrying over her.

A moment later, Dan had his phone out and was calling his father and brother to reassure them of Sam's safe return, and Sam found herself in Apples's arms.

"Sam," he said against her ear. "Sam ... Oh, Sam," and seemed incapable of saying more.

Mrs Grieve cleared her throat loudly, separated Sam from Apples, and then moved over to prise Jessie from Dan, who was not only embracing, but also kissing her right in the midst of the noisy crowd of friends and officials who swarmed around them, peppering them with questions. As soon as Mrs Grieve's back was turned, Apples leaned over and gave Sam a quick kiss on the lips. It was soft and warm and over almost before it began, but still, it made Sam blush and Apples smile.

"I am so glad you're safe, girls – so relieved!" said Mrs Grieve. "We spent all of yesterday afternoon searching for you, but we were looking in the wrong place. We thought you'd be at Champagne Pools – your last control point – but you were nowhere to be found. Nobody even suspected you'd gone up the mountain to the caves!"

Sam, Jessie and Nomusa all looked at Cindy, who was standing sour-faced on the outside of the excited throng. Julie Clayton, who was standing next to Cindy, cast her a very nervous look, but Cindy merely stared back at Sam, giving the faintest of shrugs. *Prove it*, her look seemed to challenge.

"And then, of course, the fire-fighters and police and paramedics all got called away because there was a dreadful fire raging on the other side of the river."

"We know," said Sam. "They set it deliberately, as a diversion."

"They set another one up near the caves this morning, too. The woman was crazy, she wanted to burn us to a crisp!" added Jessie.

275

Mrs Grieve shuddered. "When I think of what might have happened. Your parents would have– … But you're safe now, and that's what matters."

"Um, may I just ask," interrupted a worried looking park ranger, "are the paintings in the cave also safe?"

"Yes," said Sam. "They're still there and in one piece, though they chipped away some smaller pieces of rock from one of the sites around the side. But you need to be careful, the whole place is packed with plastic explosive and charges."

"We'll get the bomb disposal unit guys out," said one burly policeman. "I'm Lieutenant Khumalo," he said, stepping forward to shake Sam and Jessie's hands.

"You girls did a great job stopping that gang. We know they've been operating in the Berg for a while now, off and on, but we never even came close to catching them. And from what Nomusa here told us, it sounds like they are one of the big-fish operators."

Sam beamed with pride. Jessie fished her cellphone out of her knapsack. She blew sand and dust off of it and then handed it to Lt Khumalo.

"Here you are. I doubt the phone works any more, but the memory card will still be okay. We took lots of photos of the site, and their equipment and stuff. Maybe you can use them as evidence."

"Excellent," said the petite police woman standing beside Lt Khumalo. "That was also good thinking."

"I think your phone might be stuffed, though," said Lt Khumalo. He was holding the phone upside down, and a trickle of sand was still falling from the keyboard.

"Not a problem," Jessie waved a hand dismissively. "It was time for an upgrade anyway."

"We'll need to get a full statement from you three just now."

"Lieutenant," interrupted Mrs Grieve. "These girls need to rest, and I'm sure they could use a good meal. Surely the formalities can wait until later?"

Jessie nodded eagerly at this, but the police woman shook her head.

"The sooner, the better, ma'am. It's better if we get it while it's still fresh in their heads. We need descriptions of the gang, and any identifying details you can remember that might help us track them down." She looked regretfully from Nomusa to Jessie to Sam. "We were so close! It's just such a pity that they got away."

"We-ell, maybe not," said Sam, and all eyes turned to her. Everyone was listening now.

"There might still be a way to track them down."

"Oh, yes?" asked Lt Khumalo. "How?"

"Yes, how?" asked Nomusa.

"I'd like to hear this too," said Jessie.

From the back of the crowd, Cindy sneered disbelievingly. "They could be halfway to anywhere by now," she said.

"I don't know exactly how it works," Sam continued, ignoring her, "but I know you can track down the location of a cellphone – if you know its number?"

"Yes, it's called triangulation. As long as a cellphone is switched on and has reception, it keeps pinging a signal, looking for transmission towers. And we can locate it using the two nearest towers which it signals," said Lt Khumalo.

"I managed to hide my cellphone in one of the crates that they were packing the stolen rock art in," said Sam.

"You didn't?" exclaimed Jessie.

"But when?" said Nomusa.

"When they walked into the cave, I was still hidden behind that big crate, and I tucked it under some bubble-wrap in the smaller, open crate. I thought – just in case, you know? I reckon it's still there, because they nailed the lid shut."

"You're brilliant!" said Jessie, punching Sam on the arm.

"Genius!" said Nomusa.

"She's my sister, you know," Sam heard Dan bragging to someone.

"And my girlfriend." She looked over her shoulder and smiled back at Apples.

"And it's switched on?" said Lt Khumalo.

"Yes."

"And is the battery still strong, do you think?" asked the policewoman, looking very excited.

"Oh, definitely," said Sam. She looked up and smiled directly at Cindy. "Those big old phones have the absolute best battery life, you know."

33

Rock steady

After the police had taken their statements, Sam, Nomusa and Jessie were escorted by the very grateful manager of the camp to one of the resort's luxury lodges, where they spent the rest of the day sleeping in wide, comfortable beds, soaking in hot baths laced with fragrant bubbles, and eating their fill of the food and snacks brought to them on trays by the restaurant staff.

"Now this is more like it," said Jessie, finishing her third cup of coffee and tucking into a second portion of apple-pie and cream.

"Not bad at all," said Nomusa, toasting her toes in front of the fireplace in the living room of their lodge.

Samantha, who had had enough of fires for one day, sighed happily from her couch on the other side of the room and snuggled deeper into her soft blanket. She felt warm, full, clean and completely content, but her peace was disturbed by a knock at the door. Nobody felt like getting up to open it, apparently, because they all yelled "Come in!" together.

Poppy Katakouzinous walked in, looked around admiringly and said, "Nice for some!"

"Come and join us," invited Sam.

"Can't," said Poppy. "We've got that final dinner – they're announcing the winners of the Survivor Games and stuff. Mrs Grieve sent me to fetch you – she says you have to attend, too."

"Do we?" asked Sam, surprised.

They had been excused from the rest of the day's activities. Unable to do the planned hike to the caves, where the police had cordoned off the crime scene and experts were busy defusing and removing the explosives, the girls had been sent instead on a long hike up to the "vulture restaurant" – a bird hide on top of a cliff where lammergeyers and other birds of prey visited to feast on bones and carcasses laid out for them by park rangers. Jessie had been delighted to skip this activity: "Apart from the fact that vultures feeding on rotting meat and bones is not really my thing, I can't walk another bless-ed step. Honestly, if I never see another mountain hike, it'll be too soon!"

"Yes," said Poppy now. "There are people there who've come especially to see you: Park Board officials, I think, and a bunch of press."

"Hmmm," said Nomusa, unenthusiastically.

Sam knew how she felt. The trio's past encounters with members of the press had not always left them looking very intelligent or well-informed.

"And, I also have a message for you two from Dan and Apples," said Poppy, looking at Jessie and Sam.

"What?" they asked.

"Come. Now," said Poppy simply. She grinned at them, and left.

"I suppose we'd better go," said Sam.

Nomusa sighed and started putting on her sneakers and jacket.

"Aah, the tiresome demands of fame and glory," said Jessie, adjusting her hair in the mirror on the way out the lodge.

The dining room was packed full of the pupils from both Clifford House and Clifford Heights. A long main table had been set at the front of the room, and the teachers, a senior-looking police officer, the park manager and two men in suits were seated there. In chairs along one side of the room sat several reporters, complete with cameras, notebooks, fur-covered microphones and even, on the shoulder of one, a heavy-looking television camera. They paid no attention to the officials at the VIP table, but hungrily eyed the food at the students' tables instead. The meal was followed by a round of speeches.

"First, we need to hand out the award for the winning team in our Survivor Games competition. The prize goes to Cindy Atkins, Kitty Bennington and Julie Clayton. Congratulations, girls!" said Miss Gamion, standing on tiptoes to speak into the microphone standing beside the top table.

The girls from Clifford Heights, the teachers, and one or two of the officials clapped politely. Cindy and Kitty stood up and walked to Miss Gamion, who handed them a certificate and an envelope each. Julie, who had stood up uncertainly, hesitated for a moment, then sat down again. Cindy turned around to face the audience, smiling widely and holding up her certificate, even though the applause had already petered out and Kitty had headed back to her chair.

"What's she waiting for?" asked Nomusa.

"A photo and some publicity," said Jessie.

None of the photographers or reporters seemed interested in the results of a school competition, however. Sam even saw the man with the video camera put it down on his lap and then reach out to snatch a chicken drumstick from a nearby girl's plate. Cindy cleared her throat and it looked, for a moment, like she intended to make a speech, but then Mrs Grieve swept her aside with a firm, "You may go back to your seat, now, Cindy."

"Ha!" said Jessie. "Look at Cindy's sulky face."

"We would also, of course, like to congratulate three more of our Clifford House girls who braved great danger and took a stand against thieves and vandals, ingeniously foiling their heinous plot. Some of our officials," she turned and smiled at the people sitting at the main table, "will soon be thanking the girls personally, and I believe there is a reward on the cards for our girls, but before I turn the microphone over to them, I would like to say: Samantha Steadman, Nomusa Gule, and Jessie Delaney, you have done us proud!"

"Can you spell those names, please?" shouted one of the reporters.

"Can we have a picture of the three girls all together?" shouted another.

They had all perked up and were now pointing cameras at Sam, Nomusa and Jessie, and microphones at Mrs Grieve, while scribbling in their notebooks. One or two of the photographers had crept forward to get a better vantage point. The video camera operator had shoved the chicken drumstick between his teeth and was fiddling with the camera's controls. Mrs Grieve repeated the names, and spelled them.

"Is it true that one of them is only at the school because of a scholarship?"

"Cindy's little tip, no doubt," murmured Sam.

"Samantha Steadman is the current and deserving recipient of the Clifford House Full Scholarship Award for academic excellence. We are delighted that, at Clifford House," Mrs Grieve appeared to be attempting to mention the name of the school as often as possible, "our girls are not only highly intelligent, but also courageous, and they reflect the values so treasured at our school."

"There you are, Sam," said Jessie. "You're in her good books again for bringing fame and glory to the school. Your achievements have gone public. No way they're taking away your scholarship or suspending you after this! Sucks to Delmonico!"

"And sucks to Cindy!" said Nomusa. "She has no chance of getting the scholarship for herself, now."

"And Nomusa Gule, you might be interested to know," Mrs Grieve continued to address the reporters, "is the daughter of the honourable Mr Justice Gule, a member of the South African parliament."

"And the other one, Delaney?" asked a reporter.

"Jessie Delaney is, er…," Mrs Grieve looked stumped for a moment, then her face cleared. "A very talented artist! This is not the first time that these three girls have been instrumental in efforts to save our environmental heritage, either. Last year they helped bring down a gang of foreign fisherman who were illegally fishing in our coastal reserves and doing great damage to, er, loggerhead turtles."

"Leatherbacks," all three girls corrected automatically.

"Can we have a picture of the heroines?" asked a photographer.

"Yes, I need some footage of them, too," said the cameraman.

"And I'd like to do an interview," said a reporter, waving her notebook in the air.

"Samantha, Nomusa, Jessie – please come up now," said Mrs Grieve, smiling proudly.

There was a much louder round of applause as the trio wound their way through the seats to the top table. Sam heard a couple of girls ululating and from over on the side where the boys sat, they were some loud cheers, an appreciative whistle and, unmistakably, a wolf-howl.

Standing up front, with Jessie on her one side and Nomusa on the other, Sam smiled back at the faces in front of her. Poppy, Uvani, Mercy, Charné, Carol, Skye – all were clapping and cheering. Even whiney Pat Mbalula grinned and held two thumbs up at them. Cindy and Kitty alone sat unsmiling, their arms tightly folded. Julie Clayton started clapping, but faltered when Cindy glared across at her. Then she turned to face the front and clapped louder still.

Over on the boys' side of the room, Sam's gaze found Apples's. He stood up, smiling and still applauding, and all around him, others followed suit. He shouted a few words towards her. Sam saw his lips move, but she could not hear the words over the applause and Dan's chant of, "Jes-sie, Jes-sie, Jes-sie!"

Sam, Jessie and Nomusa linked arms, and Jessie pulled them down into a little bow.

Sam's eyes turned to the open door of the dining room, where a glimpse of the dark night was just visible. Out there, beyond this noise and light and motion, just a walk away through the grass and starlit darkness, was another gathering. A still and silent dance of hunters and shamans, of spirits and elands, leaped across the hushed sandstone cliffs, ceaseless and timeless, rock steady.